Peter Lovesey began his writing career with *Wobble to Death* in 1970, introducing Sergeant Cribb, the Victorian detective, who went on to feature in seven more books and two television series. His recent novels have alternated between two contrasting detectives: Peter Diamond, and the Victorian sleuth, Bertie. Lovesey's mysteries and short stories have won him awards all over the world, including both Gold and Silver Daggers of the Crime Writers' Association, of which he was Chairman in 1991–2.

After a career in further education, Peter Lovesey became a full-time author. He now lives near Chichester.

Do Not Exceed the Stated Dose

Peter Lovesey

WARNER BOOKS

A *Warner* Book

First published in Great Britain in 1998
by Little, Brown and Company

This edition published by Warner Books in 1999

"Because It Was There" was first published in *Whydunit* (Severn House) 1997;
"Bertie and the Boat Race" in *Crime Through Time* (Berkley) 1996; "Bertie and
the Fire Brigade" in *Royal Crimes* (Signet) 1994; "Disposing of Mrs Cronk" in
Perfectly Criminal (Severn House) 1996; "The Case of the Easter Bonnet" in the
Bath Chronicle, 1995; "The Mighty Hunter" in *Midwinter Mysteries 5* (Little,
Brown) 1995; "Murder in Store" in *Woman's Own*, 1985; "Never a Cross Word"
in *You* (*Mail on Sunday*) 1995; "The Odstock Curse" in *Murder for Halloween*
(Mysterious Press) 1994; "A Parrot Is Forever" in *Malice Domestic 5* (Pocket
Books) 1996; "Passion Killers" in *Ellery Queen's Mystery Magazine*, 1994; "The
Proof of the Pudding" in *A Classic Christmas Crime* (Pavilion) 1995; "The
Pushover" in *Ellery Queen's Mystery Magazine*, 1995; "Quiet Please—We're
Rolling" in *No Alibi* (Ringpull) 1995; "Wayzgoose" in *A Dead Giveaway* (Warner
Futura) 1995.

A CIP catalogue record for this book is available from the British Library.

ISBN 0 7515 2318 6

Typeset in Baskerville by M Rules
Printed and bound in Great Britain by Clays Ltd, St Ives plc

Warner Books
A Division of
Little, Brown and Company (UK)
Brettenham House
Lancaster Place
London WC2E 7EN

Contents

Foreword

Are you sitting comfortably?

The appeal of a short story is that it may be read at a sitting, comfortably. In bed, bath, aircraft, cruise ship or train; waiting for one's case to come up in court; under cover of a prayer book in church; propped up against the cornflakes packet over breakfast.

For the writer, also, compactness has attractions. Over the years I have plotted, if not written, short stories in many of the locations mentioned above. Occasionally an idea emerges from a few minutes in one memorable place. In this collection, "The Pushover" was inspired by the sunset celebration at Key West; "Bertie and the Boat Race" by a strange incident at the Henley Regatta; and "The Odstock Curse" by the sight of a gravestone on a dark day in a churchyard in Wiltshire.

To tell it to you straight, your comfort is not high in my priorities. If these stories are comfortable reading I am failing in my job. My hope is that you will find in them crimes that make your heart beat faster and twists that take your breath away. One or two at a sitting ought to be enough—which explains the title I chose.

Peter Lovesey

Because It Was There

They are dead now, all three. Professor Patrick Storm, the last of them, went in August, aged eighty-two, of pneumonia. The obituary writers gave him the send-off he deserved, crediting him with the inspiration and the dynamism that got the new theatre built at Cambridge. The tributes were blessedly free of the snide remarks that are almost obligatory two-thirds of the way into most of the obits you read—"not over-concerned about the state of his dress" or "borrowing from friends was an art he brought to perfection." No such smears for Patrick Storm. He was a decent man, through and through. A murderer, yes, but decent.

The press knew nothing about the murder. I don't think anyone knew of it except me. Patrick amazed me with it over supper in his rooms a couple of years ago. He wanted the facts made public at the proper time, and asked me to take on the task. I promised to wait until six months after he was gone.

This is the story. About January, 1975, when he had turned sixty, he received a phone call. A voice he had not heard in almost forty years, so it was not surprising he was slow to cotton on. The words made a lasting impression; he gave me the conversation verbatim. I have it on tape, and I'll reproduce it here.

"Professor Storm?"

"Yes."

"Patrick Storm?"

"Yes."

"Pat, late of Caius College?"

"'Late' is the operative word," said Patrick. "I was there as an undergraduate in the nineteen-thirties."

"You don't have to tell me, old boy. Remember Simon Brown?"

"To be perfectly frank, no." He didn't care much for that over-familiar "old boy."

"Well, you wouldn't," the voice at the end of the line said in the same confident manner. "I had a nickname in those days. You would have known me as 'Cape'—short for 'Capability.' Does it ring a bell now?"

Patrick Storm had not cast his thoughts so far back in many years. So much had happened since, to the world, and to himself. The thirties were another age. Faintly a bell did chime in his brain. "Cape, you say. Are you a Caius man yourself?"

"The Alpine Club."

"Oh, that." Patrick had done some climbing in his second year at Cambridge. Not much. He hadn't got to the Alps. The Welsh Mountains on various weekends. He didn't remember much else. So "Cape" Brown had been one of the Alpine Club people. "It's coming back to me. Didn't you and I walk the Snowdon Horseshoe together, with another fellow, one Easter?"

"Climbed, old boy. Climbed. We weren't a walking club. The other chap was Ben Tattersall, who is now the Bishop of Westbury, would you believe?"

"Is he, by Jove?"

"You remember Ben, then?"

"Certainly, I remember Ben," said Patrick in a tone suggesting that some people had more right to be remembered than others.

Cape Brown said, "You wouldn't have thought he'd make it to Bishop, not the Ben Tattersall I remember, telling his dirty joke about the parrot."

"I don't remember that."

"The parrot who worked for the bus conductor."

"Oh, yes," said Patrick, pretending he remembered, not wanting to prolong this. "What prompted you to call me?"

"Old time's sake. It's coming up to forty years since we asked some stranger to take that black and white snapshot with Ben's box Brownie on the summit of Snowdon. April 1st, 1936."

"As long ago as that?"

"You, me and Ben, bless him."

"If what you say is right, he can bless us," Patrick heard himself quip.

Cape Brown chuckled. "You haven't lost your sense of humour, Prof. Might have lost all your other faculties—"

"Hold on," said Patrick. "I'm not *that* decrepit."

"That's good, because I was taking a risk, calling you up after so long. You could have had a heart condition, or chronic asthma."

"I've been fortunate."

"Looked after yourself, I'm sure?"

"Tried to stay fit, yes."

"Excellent. And you're not planning a trip to the Antipodes this April? You're game for the climb?"

"The what?"

"The commemorative climb. 'Walk,' if you insist. Don't you remember? Standing on the top of Snowdon, we pledged to come back and do it again in another forty years. The first suggestion was fifty, but we modified it.

Three old blokes of seventy might find it difficult slogging up four mountain peaks."

Patrick had no memory of such a pledge, and said so. He had only the faintest recollection of standing on Snowdon in a thick mist.

"Ben didn't remember either when I phoned him just now, but he doesn't disbelieve me."

"I'm not saying I disbelieve you . . ."

"That's all right, then. Ben has all kinds of duties for the Church, but Easter is late this year, and April 1st happens to fall on a Thursday, so he thinks he can clear his diary that day. He's reasonably fit, he tells me. Does a fair bit of fell walking in the summer. You'll join us on the big day, won't you?"

It would have been churlish to refuse when the bishop was going to so much trouble. Patrick said he would consult his diary, knowing already that the first week in April was clear. "Where are you suggesting we meet—if I can get there?"

A less decent man would have made an excuse.

April 1st, 1976, in the car park at Pen-y-pass. The three sixty-year-olds faced each other, ready for the challenge. "*We* may have deteriorated in forty years, but the equipment has improved, thank God," Cape Brown remarked when the first handshakes were done.

Ben the bishop allowed the Almighty's name to pass without objection. "I think I was wearing army boots from one of those surplus stores," he said. He looked every inch the fell-walker in his bright blue padded jacket and trousers and red climbing boots. Patrick remembered him clearly now, and he hadn't altered much. More hair than any of them, and still more black than silver.

If the weather was favourable, the plan was to walk the entire Horseshoe, exactly as they had in 1936. A demanding route that each of them now felt committed to try. And a sky of Cambridge blue left them no last-minute get-out. There was snow on the heights, but most of the going would be safe enough.

"Just before we start, I'd like you to meet someone," Cape said. "She's waiting in the car."

"She?" said Patrick, surprised. He had no memory of women in the Alpine Club.

"Your wife?" said the bishop.

Patrick could not imagine why a wife should be on the trip. What was she going to do while they walked the Horseshoe? Sit in the car?

"A friend. Come and meet her."

She was introduced as Linda, and she was dressed for climbing, down to the gaiters and boots. However, she was far too young to have been at Cambridge before the war. "You don't mind if Linda films us doing bits of our epic?" Cape said. "She won't get in our way."

"She has a cine-camera with her?" said the bishop.

"You'll see."

Linda, dark-haired and with an air of competence that would have seemed brash in the young women of the nineteen-thirties, opened the boot of the car and took out a professional-looking movie-camera and folding tripod.

"I didn't know you had this in mind," Patrick said confidentially to Cape Brown.

"I thought it was just the three of us," the bishop chimed in. "Three men."

"Don't fret. She'll keep her distance, Ben. Just pretend she isn't there. How do you think they film those climbs on television? Someone is holding a camera, but you never see him. We're the stars, you see. Linda is just recording the event. And she's a bloody good climber, or she wouldn't be here."

In the circumstances it was difficult to object. Nobody wanted to start the walk with an argument. They set off on the first stage, up the Miners' Track towards Bwlch y Moch, with Cape Brown stepping out briskly between the blue-black slate rocks and over the slabs that bridged the streams. Linda, carrying her camera, followed some twenty yards behind, as if under instructions not to distract the threesome on their nostalgic trip.

They paused on Bwlch y Moch, the Pass of the Pigs. Below, Llyn Llydaw had a film of ice that the sun had yet to touch. They hadn't seen a soul until now, but there were two climbers on the coal-black cliff across the lake. "Lliwedd," said the bishop. "I remember scaling that with the Alpine club."

"Me, too," said Cape. "Wouldn't want to try it at my age. Shall we move on, gentlemen?"

The path leading off to the right was the official start of the Horseshoe. Crib Goch, the first of the four peaks, was going to be demanding as they got closer to the snowline. Towards the top it would need some work with the hands, steadying and pulling.

Once or twice Patrick Storm looked back to see how Linda was coping. She had the camera slung on her back and was making light work of the steep ascent.

After twenty minutes, weaving upwards through the first patches of snow, breathing more rapidly, Pat Storm was beginning to wonder if he would complete this adventure. His legs ached, as he would have expected, but his chest ached as well and he felt colder than he should have. He glanced at his companions and drew some comfort from their appearance. The bishop was exhaling white plumes and wheezing a little, and Cape Brown seemed to be moving as if his feet hurt. He had given up making the pace. Patrick realised that he himself had become the leader. Aware of this, he stopped at the next reasonably level point. The others needed no persuading to stop as well. They all found rocks to sit on.

"In the old days, I'd have said this was a cigarette stop," Patrick said. "Time out to admire the view. I'm afraid it's necessity now."

The bishop nodded. He looked too puffed to speak.

Cape said, "We set off too fast. My fault."

They spent a few minutes recovering. Each knew that after they reached the summit of Crib Goch, the most challenging section of the whole walk lay ahead, a razor-edged ridge with a sheer drop either side, leading out to the second peak, Crib-y-Ddysgl.

Presently a cloud passed across and blotted out the sun. The cold began to be more of a problem than the fatigue, so they went on, with Patrick leading, thinking what an idiot he had been to agree to this.

Unexpectedly Cape said, "Tell us a joke, Ben. We need one of your jokes to lift morale."

The bishop managed an indulgent smile and said nothing.

Cape moved shoulder to shoulder with him. "Come on. Don't be coy. Nobody tells a dirty joke better than you."

Patrick called across, "We're not undergraduates, Cape. Ben is a bishop now."

"So what? He's a human being. You and I aren't going to think any the worse of him if he makes us smile. He isn't leading the congregation now. He's on a sentimental walk with his old oppos. Up here, he can say what he bloody well likes."

They toiled up the slope with their private thoughts. Climbing did encourage a feeling of comradeship, a sense that they were insulated from the real world, temporarily freed from the constraints of their jobs.

Cape would not leave it. "The one that always cracked me up was the bus conductor and the parrot. Remember that one, Ben?"

The bishop didn't answer.

Cape persisted, "I can't tell it like you can. I always get the punchline wrong. This bus conductor was on a route through London that took him to Peckham via St Paul's and Turnham Green. He got fed up with calling out to people, 'This one for Peckham, St Paul's and Turnham Green.'"

"No," said Ben unexpectedly. "You're telling it wrong. He was fed up with shouting, 'This one for St Paul's, Turnham Green and Peckham.'"

"Right," said Cape. "I can't tell them like you can. So what happened next? He bought a parrot."

The bishop said in a monotone, as if chanting the liturgy, "He bought a parrot and taught it to speak the words for him. And the parrot said the thing perfectly. Until one day it got in a muddle, and said, 'Bang your balls on St Paul's, Turnham Green and Peckham.'"

Cape Brown made the mountainside echo with laughter and Patrick felt compelled to laugh too, just so that it didn't appear he disapproved. The joke was at the level of a junior school of forty years ago. Odd, really, that a bishop should have retained it all this time, but then not many risqué jokes are told to bishops.

Ben Tattersall's face was already pink from the effort of the climb. Now it had turned puce. He took a quick glance over his shoulder. Fortunately Linda and her camera were well in the rear.

The cloud passed by them, giving a stunning view of the Glyders on their right.

Scrambling up the last steep stretch, they reached the summit of Crib Goch in sunshine. Ahead, the mighty expanse of Snowdon was revealed, much of it gleaming white. Cape Brown unwrapped some chocolate and divided it into three.

"Shouldn't we offer some to your friend Linda?" Patrick asked.

"She's not my friend, old boy. She's just doing a job."

And when Linda caught up, she did her job, circling them slowly with the camera, saying nothing.

"So what's the world of academia like?" Cape asked Patrick, when the filming was done and they were resting, trying not to be intimidated by the prospect of the next half-hour. "At each other's throats most of the time, are you?"

"It is competitive at times," Patrick confirmed.

"And is it still a fact that a pretty woman can get a first if she's willing to go to bed with the prof?"

"In my case, definitely not."

"A clever woman, then."

"A clever woman gets her first by right," Patrick pointed out.

"The clever ones don't always have the confidence in their ability," said Cape. "They can be looking for another guarantee."

"I won't say it hasn't happened."

"We're all ears, aren't we, Ben?" said Cape.

The bishop gave a shrug. He was staring out at the black cliffs of Lliwedd. He'd looked increasingly unhappy since finishing the joke about the parrot.

Patrick sympathised. Out of support for the wretched man, he felt an urge to be indiscreet himself, to share in the impropriety up there on the mountain. "There *was* a student a few years ago," he said. "Quite a few years, I ought to say. She was very ambitious not merely to get a first, which was practically guaranteed because she was so brilliant, but to beat the other high flyers to a research scholarship."

"And she gave you the come-on?" said Cape.

"I knew what she was up to, naturally, but it still surprised me somewhat. This was in the nineteen-fifties, before casual sex became commonplace. One summer afternoon in my rooms in college, I yielded to temptation."

"And she got her scholarship?"

"She did. She went on to get a doctorate, and she is now a Government Minister." He named her.

"That's hot news, Pat," said Cape. "What was she like in bed— playful?"

"All this is in confidence," said Patrick. He looked across at Linda, and she was filming the view, too far away to have heard. "It was terrific. She was incredibly eager."

"You heard that, Ben?" said Cape. "The Minister bangs like the shithouse door in a gale. Don't go spreading it around the clergy."

Ben Tattersall was hunched in embarrassment.

Patrick felt a surge of anger. The whole point of his story had been to take the heat off Ben. "How about you, Cape? Ben and I have been very candid. We haven't heard much from you—about yourself, I mean."

"You want the dirt on me? That's rich."

"Why?"

"Ironic, then. Fine, I can be as frank as you fellows, if it keeps the party going. You may not have seen me in forty years, but I'll bet you've seen my work on television. Have you watched The Disher?"

"The what?"

"The Disher. The series that dishes the dirt on the rich and famous. It's mine. I'm the Disher. As you know if you watch it, my voice isn't used at all. You have to be so careful with the law. No, my subjects condemn themselves out of their own mouths, or the camera does it, or one of their so-called friends."

Patrick was too startled to comment.

The bishop said, "I don't get much time for television."

"Make some time about the end of February. You'll be on my programme telling the one about the parrot."

The bishop twitched and looked appalled.

"I mean it, Ben. That's my job."

Patrick said, "Remember what day it is. He's having us on, Ben. She didn't film us when you were telling the joke. I checked."

Cape said, "But you didn't check the sound equipment in my rucksack. It's all on tape. The parrot joke. And your sexy Minister story, Pat. We don't expect you to talk to camera when you spill the beans. We tape it and use the voice-over. A long shot of us trekking up the mountain, and your voices dishing yourselves. Very effective."

"Let's see this tape-recorder."

Cape shook his head. "At this minute, you don't know if I'm kidding or not. I'd be an idiot to confirm it, specially up here. But I warn you, gentlemen, if you try anything physical, Linda is under instructions to get it on film."

"He's bluffing," Patrick told the bishop. "He probably sells used cars for a living."

Ben Tattersall was on his feet. "There's a way of finding out. I'm going to ask the young woman. Where is she?"

Cape said, "She went ahead, to film us crossing the ridge."

It was becoming misty up there, with another cloud drifting in, and Linda was no longer in view.

"This will soon blow across," Cape said. "We can safely move on. Then you can ask Linda whatever you like." His calm manner was reassuring.

The others followed.

Curiously enough, the snow was not a handicap on this notorious ridge. It was of a soft consistency that provided good footholds and actually gave support. Had the night before been a few degrees colder, the frozen surface would have made the near vertical edges a real hazard.

The mist obscured the view ahead, which was a pity, because the rock pinnacles and buttresses are spectacular, but Patrick was secretly relieved that he was unable to see how exposed this razor edge was. He kept his eyes on the footprints Cape had made, while his thoughts dwelt on his own foolishness. What had induced him to speak out as he had, he could not think. To a degree, certainly, it was out of sympathy for Ben Tattersall after that mortifyingly juvenile joke. There was also, he had to admit, some bravado, the chance to boast that a university professor's life was not without its moments. And there was the daft illusion that this expedition somehow recaptured lost youth, with its lusts and energy and aspirations.

I must be getting senile, he thought. If it really does get out, what I told the other two, the tabloid press will be onto her like jackals.

He had never heard of this television programme Cape claimed to work for. But in truth he didn't watch much television these days. He preferred listening to music. So it might conceivably exist. Some of the things he had seen from time to time were blatant invasions of people's privacy.

No, the balance of probability was that Cape was playing some puerile All Fools' Day joke. The man had a warped sense of humour, no question.

On the other hand, a programme as unpleasant as The Disher—if it existed—must have been devised by someone with a warped sense of humour.

"It goes out late at night on ITV," Ben Tattersall, close behind him, said, as if reading Patrick's thoughts. "I've never seen it, but a Master of Foxhounds I know was on it. He resigned because of it."

"It's real?"

Cape Brown, out ahead, turned and said, "Of course it's real, suckers. You don't think I was shooting a line?"

In turning, he lost balance for a moment and was forced to grab the edge of a rock while his feet flailed across the snow.

"Hold on, man," said Patrick, moving rapidly to give

assistance. He grabbed the shoulder strap of Cape's ruck-sack. Ben Tattersall was at his side and between them they hauled him closer to the rock.

In doing so, they disturbed the flap of his rucksack. Out of the top fell a sponge-covered microphone attached to a lead. It swung against his thigh.

Patrick stared in horror and looked into Ben Tattersall's eyes. Despair was etched in them.

"Look away."

"What?" said the bishop.

"Look away."

Impulse it was not. These things always appear to happen in slow motion. Patrick had ample time to make his decision. He put a boot against Cape Brown's arm-pit and pushed with his leg. The fingers clutching the rock could not hold the grip. Cape let go and plunged down-wards, out of sight, through the mist. He made no sound.

"He lost his grip," Patrick said to Ben Tattersall. "He lost his grip and fell."

Nobody else had witnessed the incident. Linda was far ahead, her view obscured by the mist.

Cape Brown's body was recovered the same afternoon. Multiple injuries had killed him. The sound equipment in his rucksack was smashed to pieces.

Each of them appeared as a witness at the inquest. Each said that Cape lost his grip before they could reach him. After giving evidence, they didn't speak to each other. They never met again. Ben Tattersall died prematurely of cancer two years later, and was given a funeral attended by more than twenty fellow bishops and presided over by an archbishop.

Patrick lived on until this year, having, as I explained, confessed to me that he had killed Cape Brown. He need not have spoken about it. How typical of him to want the truth made public.

And there is something else I must make clear. As Patrick explained it to me, his story about the Minister offering to sleep with him to earn her scholarship was pure fabrication. Nothing of the sort happened. "I made it up," he said. "You see, I had to think of something worse than a bishop telling a dirty joke, just to spare him all that embarrassment. After I'd concocted the story, I knew if it went on television everyone would believe it was true. People *want* to believe in scandals. Her career would have been ruined, quite unjustifiably. So you can imagine how I felt when I saw that microphone fall out of the rucksack."

You must agree he was a decent man.

Bertie and the Boat Race

People close to me sometimes pluck up courage and ask how I first became an amateur detective. I generally tell them it began in 1886 through my desire to discover the truth about the suspicious death of Fred Archer, the Tinman, the greatest jockey who ever wore my colours, or anyone else's. However, it dawned on me the other day that my talent for deduction must have been with me from my youth, for I was instrumental in solving a mystery as far back as the year 1860. I had quite forgotten until some ill-advised person wrote to my secretary to ask if HRH The Prince of Wales would care to patronise the Henley Regatta this year.

Henley!

You'd think people would know by now that my preferred aquatic sport is yachting, not standing on a towpath watching boats of preposterous shape being manoeuvred along a reach of the Thames by fellows in their undergarments.

The mystery. It has a connection with Henley, but the strongest connection is with a young lady. Ah, the fragrant memory of one I shall call Echo, out of respect for her modesty, for she is a lady of irreproachable reputation now. Why Echo? Because she was the water nymph who loved the youth Narcissus. The real Echo is supposed to have pined away after her love was not returned, leaving only her voice behind, but this part of the legend you can ignore.

She was the only daughter of a tutor at Christ Church College, Oxford, and I met her during my sojourn at the University. I was eighteen, a mere stripling, and a virtual prisoner in a house off the Cornmarket known as Frewin Hall, with my Equerry and Governor as jailers. My father, Prince Albert, had rigid views on education and wanted me to benefit from the tuition at Oxford. Sad to relate, he deemed it unthinkable for the future King to live in college with boisterous young men of similar age. Six docile under-graduates of good family were accordingly enlisted to be my fellow students. They attended Frewin Hall and sat beside me listening to private lectures from selected pro-fessors. I don't know who suffered the greatest ordeal, my fellow-students, the tutors, or myself. I was not academi-cally inclined. The only inclination I had was towards the stunningly pretty Echo.

I met her first across the dinner table, Papa having insisted that dinner parties should feature in my curricu-lum. I was to learn how to conduct myself at table, use the cutlery, hold a conversation and so forth. Most of my guests were stuffed-shirts, the same studious fellows who shared my lectures, together with various professors and clergy-men, but, thank heavens, it was deemed desirable for members of the fair sex to be of the party. Some of the tutors brought their wives. One—I shall call him Dr Stubbs—was a widower and was accompanied by his daugh-ter.

Echo Stubbs. My pulse races now at the memory of her stepping into the anteroom, standing timidly so close to her father that her crinoline tilted and revealed quite six inches of silk-stocking—I think the first sighting I had of a mature female ankle in the whole of my life. When I finally forced my eyes higher I was treated to a deep blush from a radiantly lovely face. Her black hair was parted at the centre in swathes that covered her ears like a scarf. She curtsied. Dr Stubbs bowed. And while his head was lowered I winked at Echo and she turned the colour of a guardsman's jacket.

I shall not dwell on the subtle process of glances and signals that sealed our attachment. She didn't say much, and neither did I. It was all in the eyes, and the barely perceptible movements of the lips. She enslaved me. I resolved to see her again, if possible in less constricting company. I lost all interest in my studies. Every waking moment was filled with thoughts of her.

My difficulty was that she and I were chaperoned with a rigour hard to imagine in these more indulgent times. If my beautiful Echo ventured out of Christ Church, you may be sure her po-faced Papa was at her side. The only opportunities we had of meeting were after Morning Service at the Cathedral on a Sunday, when every word between us was overheard by General Bruce, my Governor, and Dr Stubbs. So we spoke of the weather and the sermon while our eyes held a more intimate discourse altogether.

During lectures I would plot strategies for meeting her alone. I seriously considered ways of gaining admittance to the family's rooms in Christ Church by posing as a College servant. If I had known for certain which room my fair Echo slept in, I would have visited the College by night and flung gravel at her window. But in retrospect it was a good thing I didn't indulge in such heroics because we had lately been troubled by a series of burglaries and I might have suffered the embarrassment of being arrested. My amorous nature has more than once been the undoing of me and it would have got me into hot water even at that tender age were it not for a piece of intelligence that reached me.

The worthy Dr Stubbs, I learned, was a rowing man. He had been a "wet bob" at Eton and a Blue at the University. For the past two years he had acted as umpire at the Henley Royal Regatta.

I've already made clear my views on rowing, but I happened to be in possession of two useful facts about Henley. The first: that it was *de rigueur* that the fair sex patronised the Regatta in all their finery, congregating on the lawns of the Red Lion, near the finish. And the second: that the umpire followed all the races from the water, rowed by a crew of the finest Thames watermen. Do you see? I had the prospect of Dr Stubbs being aboard a boat giving undivided attention to the races whilst his winsome daughter was at liberty on the river bank.

I devised a plan. I would go to Henley for the Regatta and hire a small craft, preferably a punt, without revealing my identity to anyone. I would furnish it with a hamper containing champagne and find a mooring close to the Red Lion. As soon as Echo appeared, I would invite her aboard my punt for a better view of the rowing. Need I go into the rest of the plan?

Now one of the unfortunates who sat with me through those dreary lectures in Frewin Hall was a runt of a fellow called Henry Bilbo, about five feet in stature, and he happened to be the coxswain to the College First Eight. I'd noticed Bilbo being treated with undue civility by Dr Stubbs long before I learned of his connection with the Boat Club. If anyone else, myself excepted, arrived late for a lecture, he would be severely rebuked. Not Bilbo. He was an arrogant little tyke, too.

"You would appear to lead a charmed life, Henry," I remarked to him one morning after lectures.

"Oh, I have the measure of old Stubbsy, Your Royal Highness," he told me. "We rowing men stick together. He's relying on us to win the Ladies' Plate at Henley this year."

"Henley, when is that?" I affected to ask. I didn't want Bilbo to know how eager I was.

"The Monday and Tuesday after we go down. Don't you know, Bertie? It is the Royal Regatta."

"Only because my father condescended to be the Patron," I said. "Because it's Royal by name, it doesn't mean Royal persons are obliged to attend. Rowing bores me silly."

"Won't you be supporting us?"

"I have other calls upon my time," I said to throw him off the scent. "Do you have a better-than-average chance of winning?"

"Only if we can match the Black Prince," he told me.

"Who the devil is that?"

"First Trinity. The Cambridge lot. They've won it more times than anyone else. They're defending the Plate. But with me at the tiller-ropes, we should give them a damned good race. Dr Stubbs has stated as much."

"He takes an interest, then?"

"He's our trainer. It matters so much to him that he's passing up the chance to be umpire this year. It wouldn't be sporting, you see, for Stubbsy to show partiality."

This was devastating news, but I tried to remain composed. "So he won't be on the umpire's boat?"

"Didn't I make that clear? He'll be on the bank, supervising our preparation. You really should be there to see us." As a lure, he added, "The adorable Echo has promised to come."

Trying to sound uninterested, I commented, "I suppose she would."

"She'll watch us carry the boat down to the water and

launch it. She'll be all of a flutter at the sight of so many beefy fellows stripped for action." He grinned lasciviously. "Her pretty chest will be pumping nineteen to the dozen. Wouldn't you care for a sight of that?"

"Sir, you exceed yourself," I rebuked him.

He apologized for the ungentlemanly remark. I'd always thought Bilbo ill-bred, even though his father was a Canon of the Church of England.

After he left, I spent a long time considering my options. If Dr Stubbs was to be on the bank, he would expect his daughter to be beside him. My punting plan had to be abandoned.

On the same afternoon, I announced my intention of calling on Dr Stubbs at Christ Church. I sent my Equerry to inform him how I liked my afternoon tea: quite simple, with poached eggs, rolls, cakes, scones, shortcake and a plate of preserved ginger. Anything else spoils dinner, in my experience.

The beautiful Echo was not at home, more was the pity. She had left early to visit a maternal aunt, her father explained. I came to the point at once. "I understand, Dr Stubbs, that you are taking a personal interest in the College Eight."

"That is true, sir. We have entered for the Ladies' Plate at Henley."

"I should like to be of the party."

"You wish to pull an oar, sir?" he said in some surprise, for I had never evinced the slightest interest in rowing.

"Heaven forbid," said I. "My intention is merely to accompany you and any other members of your family who may be with you."

"There's only Echo, my daughter. She likes to watch the rowing. We'll be honoured to have you with us, Your Royal Highness. I think I should mention, however, that I will be occupied to some degree with the College Eight."

"You needn't feel responsible for me," I assured him. "I'm capable of amusing myself."

He said, "I'm sure the stewards would be honoured if you would present the trophies, sir."

There was only one trophy that interested me. "No," I told him firmly. "I prefer to attend *incognito*. Once in a while I like to behave like one of the human race." I helped myself to another cake.

I could see that his mind was working over the consequences of this arrangement. He said, "I wouldn't wish you to feel encumbered by my daughter. It could be embarrassing—you, sir, in the company of a young lady. I could easily arrange for her to join another party."

Encumbered? "On the contrary, Dr Stubbs," I said, "if anyone is to join another party, it is I. Your charming daughter's place is at your side, encouraging the crew. After all, they have entered for the Ladies' Plate. To have a lady in attendance is a good omen."

He said, as he was bound to say, that my presence was equally indispensable. "I just hope there's a Ladies' Plate to win on the day," he added. "At the rate the silver is disappearing from the colleges, I wouldn't bet on it. There was another burglary last night."

"Oh?"

"Yes, at Merton. A fine pair of candlesticks was taken. The fellow got in through a pantry window, apparently. He's deucedly good at squeezing into small spaces."

"Is it a youth, do you suppose?" I suggested.

I could see he was impressed by my acuity.

On my way out, by the porter's lodge, I met Bilbo. He'd seen which door I came from, so I was forced to admit the reason for my visit—the ostensible reason, at any rate.

"You want to cheer us on?" he piped in disbelief. "I thought you regarded rowing as a silly sport."

"I wouldn't even call it a sport," I confirmed, "but one

likes to support one's *Alma Mater*. Who knows? Perhaps I'll be so captivated by the sight of you fellows that I join the Boat Club myself."

He said, "It's back-breaking for the oarsmen, Bertie."

"But a sure way to impress the ladies."

"Indeed," he enthused. "Echo Stubbs treats me like one of the gods since I got into the First Eight."

"But you're only the cox," I commented with disdain.

"With respect, Bertie, that shows how little you know about it," he had the neck to tell me. "The coxswain is the brains of the boat. The rest of them rely on me to steer the best course, and that's no little achievement at Henley."

I could hardly wait for the regatta. Not for one moment did I believe Bilbo's boast that Echo held a torch for him. It was unthinkable. Apart from everything else, she was several inches taller than he.

The Ladies' Plate was decided on the Tuesday, and it started cloudy, but by lunchtime the sun condescended to appear and we had a perfect afternoon for the Aquatic Derby. Glorious Henley. That dimpled span of water with its wooded heights and enamelled banks was occupied by hundreds of floating picnic parties, whilst others promenaded along the river bank. There is no question that rowing brings out the most gaudy attire, and not only among the fair sex. If an invasion of crinoline had transformed the scene, it was matched by the effrontery of the coloured blazers and boaters on view. The scene was exhilarating, even for one without a jot of interest in the contests on the water. I will admit to having a *conquest* in mind.

Amid such gaiety I was able to move inconspicuously, scarcely recognized (for in those carefree days my likeness was not in every illustrated newspaper one opened). At leisure, I strolled the length of the course, sniffing the new-mown hay and rehearsing my overtures.

My thoughts were sharply interrupted at three o'clock, when a gun was fired in the meadows to warn those afloat to clear the course. A few minutes later the celebrated crew of London Watermen came dashing through the bridge, transporting the umpire ceremoniously to the start. What a pity it wasn't Stubbs.

The Ladies' Challenge Plate was the fourth race on the card. No preliminary heat had been necessary. It was to be a straight race between First Trinity and Christ Church, a distance of a mile and a quarter from the starting point above the Temple Island to the winning post opposite the Red Lion, below the town bridge.

The Oxford boats were sheltered under a large tent erected beside the river on the far side of the bridge. The scene here was in stark contrast to the merriment along Regatta Reach. An air of serious endeavour prevailed, the oarsmen preparing for the ordeal to come, nervously pacing the turf, saying little. The observers here seemed also to be infected with the sense of what was at stake. They stood at a respectful distance. I spotted Echo at once, looking ravishing in the Christ Church colours, standing with her father.

I doffed my boater and Echo gave a sweet curtsey.

"Please," I said. "No ceremony. Let's all be family today." Turning to Dr Stubbs, I asked, "Are the crew in fine fettle?"

"The best I've seen, sir," he told me. "They've been here for a week, staying at the Red Lion, getting in hours of practice."

"Not at the bar, I trust," said I, evincing a delightful laugh from Echo. "Shall we offer them our good wishes?"

"Oh, yes!" said Echo, with a shade more passion than seemed appropriate. She made a beeline for a diminutive figure in blazer and flannels whom I recognized as Bilbo.

"He's our cox," said Dr Stubbs, as if I didn't know. "He steers a canny course."

"Is there some skill involved?" I said.

"Good Lord, yes. The steering is paramount. He'll be steering for the church."

I didn't understand. I hadn't heard that Bilbo had religious affinities. "Do you mean Christ Church?"

"No, sir. You misunderstand me. Henley Church is the object to have in one's sights until Poplar Point is cleared. We've drawn the Berkshire station and that should be to our advantage. He'll make it tell. You'll see."

Not choosing to add to the adulation, I passed a few words with several of our oarsmen, who would, after all, be putting their bodies on the rack to win the race. But I kept an eye on what was happening and I saw Echo blush deeply more than once. I hoped nothing indiscreet had been said. Finally, Dr Stubbs himself went across to remind Bilbo that it was time to lift the boat off its trestles and take to the water.

Even I will admit that I was stirred by the sight of eight blades cutting the water in concert as they moved into the stream to row down to the start. But we couldn't linger. Stubbs had decided to watch the race from Poplar Point, a quarter of a mile from where we stood.

As we threaded a route through the crowd, with Dr Stubbs leading, I turned to Echo and enquired if she was feeling nervous.

"Terribly," she admitted.

I leaned closer and confided, "If you'd care to hold my hand and give it a squeeze, I wouldn't object in the least."

She blushed and murmured her thanks.

I said, "Speaking for myself, the main excitement will be standing close to you."

She lowered her eyes. I have that effect on the fair sex.

Stubbs was right: Poplar Point was a fine vantage place, even if we had to stand shoulder to shoulder with others. I took out my binoculars. There were signs of activity from the Umpire. The crews were poised for the off. I saw Bilbo take a hip-flask from his pocket and knock back a swig of whisky to calm his nerves. Dr Stubbs enquired if I had a good view. I put down the glasses, eyed his daughter and said I could see everything I wanted.

At length the word was given, and the oars dipped in. The Black Prince had the better of the start and for two hundred yards kept a narrow lead. The Christ Church men remained calm, pulling splendidly, their blades scarcely creating a ripple. Bilbo put his megaphone to his mouth to raise the rate.

"If they can stay in contention, the Berkshire station will be in their favour towards the finish," I told Echo, exhibiting the expertise I had picked up from her father.

Some know-it-all turned and said, "They'll need it with this wind blowing. The Bucks station will be sheltered by the bushes. Christ Church are going to struggle."

Beside me, Echo was taking quick, nervous breaths. I felt for her right hand and held it. My own pulse quickened.

Christ Church came up level as they approached the first real landmark, at Remenham. I thought I heard Echo say, "He can do it!" She was so involved in the race, poor child, that she ascribed a personality to our boat.

Steadily, with never more than a canvas between them, the crews approached Poplar Point. Echo was pressing so close to me that I could feel the steel hoops of her dress making ridges in my flesh. It was peculiarly stimulating.

Then a strange thing happened. Something fell into the water from the Christ Church boat: Bilbo's megaphone. It floated a moment before disappearing. Bilbo half-turned, and evidently decided he could do nothing about it. They had reached the critical stage of the course and they were definitely in the lead, but he was steering dangerously close to First Trinity's water.

The umpire picked up his own megaphone and his voice travelled over the water. "Move over, Christ Church."

"What's wrong?" I asked.

"He's in danger of fouling," said Dr Stubbs in a strangled tone. "Move over, man!"

As if he could hear, Bilbo tugged on the rudder, but too powerfully, for our boat lurched to port, and was now in danger of running aground.

"What's his game?" cried Dr Stubbs. "He'll lose it for us."

The Black Prince had drawn level. In fact, it was slipping by whilst our erratic steering was causing uncertainty in the boat. The crew were losing their form, bucketing their strokes, uncertain whether to reduce their effort as the boat veered off course.

"For God's sake, pull to starboard, man!" Dr Stubbs bawled. Bilbo couldn't possibly hear.

Echo let go of my hand and covered her eyes. I put a protective arm around her shoulders. Her Papa was far too occupied to notice.

The Christ Church boat was out of control. It glided inexorably towards the bank. People in punts screamed in alarm. Parasols fell into the water. The bows hit one of the punts with such force that the front of the eight rode straight over it. A man tumbled into the water. The stern dipped below water level. It started to sink. Several of the crew freed themselves and leapt clear. I looked to see what Bilbo was doing, for his inept steering had caused this catastrophe, but he remained at his post, head lowered, as the water crept up his chest.

Meanwhile, the Black Prince rounded Poplar Point in fine style and cruised towards the finish, past the band of the Oxford Rifles on their raft and the cheering thousands along the banks and in the stewards' grandstand. The drama at Poplar Point had been unseen by those at the finish and they must have waited vainly for Christ Church to come into view.

My pretty companion was in distress. "Oh, Bertie, we must see if he's all right! We must go at once!"

We made the best speed we could down to the towing path. But movement was difficult in the throng of people anxious to observe the accident. We couldn't get close. Someone was being lifted from the water. There were shouts for a doctor.

"Who is it?" I asked. "What's happened?"

"The coxswain. He went down with the boat and almost drowned."

"Henry?" cried Echo. She fainted in my arms—some consolation for the lamentable end to my romantic afternoon.

"Hold on, sir," said Dr Stubbs. "I've got some whisky here." He felt into his hip pocket. Then tried his other pockets. "Where the devil is my flask? Hell's teeth, I must have dropped it in all the excitement."

They took Henry Bilbo to the local cottage hospital. We visited him there and found him in a more serious state than any of us expected, in a coma, in fact. He would not respond to anything that was said. Some of the crew volunteered to remain at the bedside, but I deemed it wise to escort Echo and her father out of that place as soon as possible. I didn't care for the look of Bilbo, and I was right. He never recovered consciousness. He died the same night.

It was widely assumed that the wretched fellow had been too overcome with shame over his mistake to free himself from the sinking boat. In college circles, he was being spoken of as a martyr.

This was the point in the story when the detective in me first began to stir. I couldn't for the life of me understand why Bilbo had behaved so oddly. The more I thought about it, reviewing the events of that afternoon, the more suspicious I became that there was something rum about his death. I recalled watching him drink from that flask of whisky at the start, beginning the race competently in charge, but later dropping the megaphone over the side and, shortly after, losing control of the steering. Had he imbibed too much?

Without reference to anyone except my Equerry, I returned to Henley a day or so later and spoke to the doctor who had conducted the post-mortem examination. He appeared satisfied that drowning had been the cause of death. He insisted that the classical signs (whatever they may be) had been present. I asked if further tests would be carried out and he thought this unlikely.

"What caused him to drown?" I asked.

"The inability to swim, sir."

"But this was in shallow water."

"Then perhaps he was trapped in the boat. These matters are for the coroner to investigate."

"Trapped?"

"Conceivably he was exhausted."

"He was the cox," I shrilled in disbelief. "He hadn't even lifted an oar."

Far from satisfied, I asked if Bilbo's clothes had been retained. The doctor said they had been destroyed, as was usual in such cases. The only item not disposed of was a silver hip-flask. It would be returned to the family.

I asked to see it.

"Returned to the family, you say?" I queried, turning the flask over in my hand. "To Bilbo's family?"

"That is my understanding. Is there something amiss, sir?"

"Only that the initials on the outside are not Bilbo's," said I. "'A.C.S.' doesn't stand for Henry Bilbo. These are the initials of Dr Arthur Stubbs, of Christ Church College."

I was in no doubt that I had recovered the lost hip-flask.

Better still, it had been well corked and some of the liquor remained inside.

"If this does, indeed, belong to Bilbo, I shall see that his family receives it," I told the doctor. "If not, I shall return it discreetly to Dr Stubbs. We don't want poor Bilbo's reputation being muddied for any reason." With that, I took possession of the flask.

On the train back to Oxford, I was sorely tempted to take a nip of the contents of that flask. What a good thing I didn't, because when I turned matters over in my mind, it seemed wise to discover some more about the liquor Bilbo had swigged prior to the race. Without speaking to anyone else, I took it the next morning to be analysed by Sir Giles Peterson, the leading toxicologist of the day, who was resident in Oxford.

Eventually he told me, "Your Royal Highness, I examined the contents of the flask and I found a rather fine malt whisky."

"Only whisky?"

"No. There was something else. The mixture also contained chloral hydrate."

"Chloral?" said I. "Isn't that what people take to send them to sleep?"

"Yes, indeed, sir. Many a nursemaid uses it diluted to subdue a troublesome child. It's harmless enough in small quantities, but I wouldn't recommend it like this. The whisky masks the high concentration."

"Could it be fatal?"

"Quite possibly, if one took about 120 grains. Death would occur six to ten hours later." He hesitated, frowning. "I hope no one offered this to you, sir."

I laughed. "Certainly not. Whisky isn't allowed at my tender age."

The laughter vanished later, when I considered the implications. Somebody had laced Dr Stubbs's whisky with a lethal dose of chloral. By some dubious set of circumstances it had come into Henry Bilbo's possession. He had imbibed and rapidly succumbed during the boat race.

Who would have plotted such a dangerous trick, and why? One's first thought was that one of the opposing crew had sabotaged our boat, but I could think of no way it could have been done, and even Cambridge men are not so unsporting as that.

After pondering the matter profoundly, I arrived at the only possible explanation. I decided to share my thoughts with Dr Stubbs. I made an appointment and called at his rooms at six in the evening.

But I was in for a surprise. Instead of the manservant, or Stubbs himself, I was admitted by Echo—the first I had seen of her since the fatal afternoon. She looked *distrait*. Beautiful, but *distrait*. And dressed in black.

"By George, I didn't expect to be so fortunate," I told her.

She pressed a finger to my lips. "Papa is asleep. He hasn't been feeling well since the regatta. It upset him dreadfully."

"But I made an appointment."

She nodded. "And I took the liberty of confirming it. I wanted a few minutes alone with you, Bertie." She ushered me into their drawing room.

I could scarcely believe my luck.

"What did you want to discuss with Papa?" she asked.

"Oh, it can wait," I told her, seating myself at one end of a settee.

She remained standing. "Was it about the flask?"

I confirmed that it was. I told her about the lethal mixture.

"Lethal?" said she in horror. "But chloral is a sedative, not a poison."

From the look in her eyes I knew for certain that she—my innocent-seeming Echo—had spiked her father's whisky, and I knew exactly why.

"Whoever was responsible simply intended to make your father sleepy," I suggested.

"Yes!" said Echo.

"You—the person responsible, I mean—that person planned that your father should feel so tired that he would lie somewhere on the river-bank and take a very long nap. You would be free—free to dance the night away at the Regatta Ball."

She nodded, her brown eyes shining.

"Only the plan misfired," I pressed on. "Henry Bilbo picked your father's pocket."

"Henry?" she piped, shocked to the core. "You're implying that Henry was a thief? Oh, no, Bertie!"

"Oh, yes," I disabused her. "I don't like to speak ill of the dead, but he was a bad lot, a burglar, responsible for that spate of thefts we had. He was just a titch, after all. Quite easy for him to get through small windows. I've no doubt that he was the one. And when your father came over to speak to him before the race, Bilbo couldn't resist the temptation. He saw the flask in your Papa's back pocket and slipped it out."

She put her hand to her throat. "Not Henry!" She swayed ominously.

I stood up and supported her in case she swooned again. "Come and sit on the settee. Your secret is safe with me, my dear."

She stared at me, aghast that I had worked it out.

"After all, my pretty one, your motives were unimpeachable."

"Were they?" she whispered, wide-eyed.

I embraced her gently. "All that you wanted was some precious time alone with me whilst your father was out to the world. That *was* your reason for tampering with the flask, was it not?" I gently probed.

"You won't tell anyone, Bertie? Not even my Papa?"

"You can count on me."

Her response, like the Echo in the myth, was to present her adorable mouth for a kiss.

And in spite of the myth, Narcissus did not disappoint her.

Bertie and the
Fire Brigade

One of the favourite pastimes of the British while reclining in a hammock is to think up worthwhile jobs for the Prince of Wales. Everyone from the Sovereign downwards has his two-pennyworth, regardless of the fact that most of the occupations suggested are utterly unsuitable for me. I can't imagine how the idea got abroad that time hangs heavy on my hands. Between laying foundation-stones and receiving visiting Heads of State, I have precious little time for my social obligations, let alone earning "an honest crust," as one newspaper impertinently proposed.

However, since the rest of the nation indulges in this sport, why shouldn't I? I'll tell you how I could have earned a handsome living if circumstances allowed. As a detective. Given the opportunity, I would certainly have risen to high rank in the police, for my deductive skills as an amateur sleuth-hound are well attested, if not well known. And I could also have made a decent show as a fireman.

Yes, a fireman.

The great British public is largely ignorant of my pyro-exploits, as I call them, my adventures with the gallant officers of the London Fire Brigade. I don't mind confiding in these memoirs that I have attended fires all over London for the past twenty years. Frequently—when not attending to affairs of state—I can be found enjoying a game of billiards at the fire station in Chandos Street with my old chum, the Duke of Sutherland, another gentleman fire-fighter, while we wait for the alarm to be sounded. We both have the kit, you know: full uniform, with helmet, boots and axe. Oh, how I relish the ride on the engine, bell jangling, horses at the gallop!

Are you intrigued? Then I shall tell you more. I once triumphantly combined my skills as detective and fireman. It happened in the summer of 1870 when I was twenty-nine and "under fire" myself, so to speak. There had been some deplorable publicity in February of that year when I was called as a witness in a divorce case, to emerge, I may add, with my character unsullied, utterly unsullied. The husband who had been so misguided as to name me and several other gentlemen had his petition dismissed on the grounds that his wife was insane and could not be a party to the suit. The wretched newspapers, not content with the result, mischievously set out to stoke up republican sentiments. I remember shortly after being hissed in the theatre and booed at Ascot. *At the races.* Mind, when a horse of mine won the last race, the same fickle crowd cheered me to the echo. I remember raising my hat to them and calling out, "You seem to be in a better temper now than you were this morning, damn you!"

A few days later, on the Friday, I was at my club, the Marlborough, enjoying a short respite from affairs of state in a foursome of skittles, when a message came for Captain Shaw, my partner for the evening. A fire had taken hold in Villiers Street, a mere quarter of a mile away. You must have heard of Shaw, the intrepid Chief of the London Fire Brigade, immortalized by W. S. Gilbert in *Iolanthe* and stigmatized by Lord Colin Campbell in the most notorious of all divorce cases. Personally, I always had a high regard for Eyre Shaw, whatever may or may not have happened with Lady Colin on the dining-room carpet of the Campbell abode in Cadogan Place. The man is a dedicated fire-fighter, so dedicated, in fact, that he chooses to live beside the fire station in Southwark Bridge Road, a particularly unsalubrious area. His house, which I have visited, is most ingeniously fitted with speaking-tubes in every room so that Shaw can be promptly informed of fires breaking out.

Immediately news of the Villiers Street fire was conveyed, Shaw apologized for interrupting our game and called for the helmet which he keeps at the club for just such an emergency.

"Sir, would you care—"

"I should take it as a personal affront not to be included," I informed him.

Ideally, I like to ride to a fire in full kit on the running-board of the engine, but on this occasion we had no time to call at Chandos Street to dress the part, so we hailed a cab and made the best speed we could down Pall Mall to Trafalgar Square and into Villiers Street by way of the Strand.

An awesome scene confronted us. Villiers Street is a narrow, dingy thoroughfare beside Charing Cross Station, sloping quite steeply down to the Thames. It is always cluttered with coffee-stalls, whelk counters, hot potato-cans and wood-and-canvas structures festooned with gimcrack rubbish, and this evening the news of the fire had brought hundreds of sight-seers off the Strand, the station and adjacent streets. The naphtha flares mounted on the stalls showed us a daunting spectacle from our elevated view in the four-wheeler, wave upon wave of toppers, bowlers and greasy caps.

The cabman confided his doubt whether he would succeed in moving the vehicle through such a throng. The feat would not have been impossible, but it would have been deucedly slow in execution, so we elected to climb out and make our own way. Fortunately, the Chief Fire Officer is instantly recognizable when he dons his helmet and to repeated cries of "Make way for Captain Shaw!" we progressed down Villiers Street like Moses through the Dead Sea. As for me, I held on to my hat and followed close with eyes down and collar up, or we should never have got through.

Bright orange flames were leaping merrily at the windows of a large building almost at the bottom of the street and the Chandos Street lads were already at work with two engines. The proximity of the Thames meant that a floating engine had also been deployed. Shaw at once sought out the man directing operations, Superintendent Flanagan, and established what was happening. I knew Flanagan passably well as a competent officer who could handle a hose more expertly than a billiard cue. Like Shaw himself, he was Irish, more than a touch pleased with himself (a weakness of the shamrock fraternity), but conscientious and a respected leader of men. I'd once met his wife at Chandos Street, and a prettier, more beguiling creature than Dymphna Flanagan never crossed the Irish Sea. She had that combination of raven hair and lily-white skin that is unique to Irish women. You can tell the impression she made on me because I seriously thought afterwards of suggesting to some London hostess that she added the Flanagans to the guest-list on an evening I was coming for supper. Finally I abandoned this intention. I was willing to put up with Flanagan's brash manners for an evening with his winsome wife, but I felt that I couldn't inflict him on my fellow-guests.

"Is anyone inside?" was Shaw's first question.

"No, it's empty," Flanagan told him as confidently as if the house were his own.

"You're sure?"

"Sure as the Creed, Captain. The owner died last Friday. There was a manservant and he was dismissed the next day."

"Who told you this?" I asked.

"One of the stall-holders, sir. They miss nothing."

"You say the owner died. The corpse . . . ?"

". . . was moved to the mortuary the same evening, sir."

"Who was he?"

"A retired bookbinder, name of Millichip. It's a pity he was moved from the house."

"Why on earth do you say that?"

"Curious to relate, Mr Millichip was Chairman of the London Cremation League."

"The what?"

He repeated it for me. "They advocate disposal of the dead by burning."

"What a heathenish idea!" I commented. "The Church would never sanction it."

"Ashes to ashes, sir."

Damned impertinence. I wish you could have heard the uppish way he said it, for the tone would have told you volumes about his bumptiousness. Captain Shaw quite properly put a stop to this morbid exchange. "If you'll pardon me, sir, you'd better redirect your hoses, Mr Flanagan. The fire is starting to take hold on the top floor."

Shaw's assessment was correct. It never ceases to amaze me how swiftly a fire can spread. In spite of the best efforts of the crews, huge forks of flame ripped through the upper storey in minutes, sending showers of sparks into the night sky.

"What the deuce burns as fiercely as that?" I asked, but

Shaw had left my side to assist in the work of raising a fire-escape ladder, the better to direct jets of water onto the roof, where slates were already cascading off the rafters. I should have realized that a bookbinder might possess samples of his work, for it later transpired that the top floor was practically lined with books.

But I wasn't there, as most bystanders were, merely to goggle. I set to, and organized a human chain to convey buckets of water from the river as an auxiliary to the pumps. I doubt whether any of my shabby helpers recognized me, but they deferred at once to the authority represented by my silk hat and cane.

For upwards of an hour, we struggled to gain ascendancy. The falling slates became a considerable hazard, and I was obliged to borrow a helmet from a fireman who readily conceded that my skull was more precious than his own. As so often happens, just as we were getting control of the fire, reinforcements arrived from Holborn and Fleet Street. The stop, to employ a term we fire-fighters use, came twenty minutes before midnight. The house was a mere shell by that time.

Wearily, we senior fire-fighters gathered by the nearest coffee-stall and slaked our thirst while the firemen were winding up the hoses. Flanagan looked ready to drop and I told him so.

"I'm feeling better than I look, sir," he said.

Firemen work longer hours than the police or the army. Even a Superintendent takes only one day off each fortnight as a matter of right. Of course he slips away when things are quiet, but he is constantly on call.

"What exercises me about this fire," I remarked to Eyre Shaw, "is how it started. If no one was inside, what could have set it off?"

He nodded, taking my point. The wily Captain Shaw hasn't much faith in the theory of spontaneous combustion.

He said an investigation would be set in train first thing next morning. I offered to take part, if not first thing, then as soon as my other engagements allowed.

My dear wife, the Princess of Wales, had retired by the time I returned to Marlborough House, or she would certainly have passed a comment on my appearance. As it happens, we have separate bedrooms, so it was not until breakfast that she tackled me. By then, of course, I'd bathed and changed my clothes and really believed she would have no clue how I'd spent the previous evening. She doesn't altogether approve of my pyro-exploits. Such is my optimism that I'd forgotten that Alix has a keener sense of smell than your average bloodhound. More than once it has been my undoing over breakfast, and not always due to smoke fumes.

"You really ought not to spend so much time with the Fire Brigade, Bertie. I can smell it in your hair."

"Oh?"

"If your Mama had any idea, she would be deeply shocked."

"Mama is shocked if I cross the road," said I.

"Where was the fire this time?"

I gave Alix an account of my evening and told her about the advocate of cremation who had unluckily been removed to the mortuary before his house burnt down. "If his timing had been better, he'd have had his wish. I wonder if one of his supporters put a match to the place in the belief that the body was still inside."

Alix commented, "It would be rather extreme, burning down an entire house and putting Charing Cross Station at risk."

"True, but someone must have started the fire. The servant wasn't there. He was dismissed the day after Millichip died."

"Who by?"

"One of the family, I gather."

"Well, the servant must have been unhappy about losing his job so suddenly," Alix mused aloud, and then added emphatically, "He came back with a match to deprive the family of their inheritance."

It's often said and often demonstrated that women are illogical. Obviously I married a notable exception. I wouldn't have thought of the servant as an arsonist, but Alix was onto him already.

I'm in the habit of taking a constitutional at 12.15, and that morning I directed my steps to the site of the fire, where I discovered Superintendent Flanagan and his deputy, First Class Engineer Henry Locke, in earnest conversation with a tall young man dressed in mourning.

"Your Highness, may I present Mr Guy Millichip, the son of the late owner of this house?"

The young man's grip was clammy to the touch. You can tell a lot from a handshake. I should know; I've shaken more hands than you ever will, I'll warrant, gentle reader. A clammy hand goes with a doubtful character.

"My condolences," I said. "All this must be a fearful shock, coming so soon after your father's passing. Was he a sick man?"

"No, Your Royal Highness. It came out of the blue."

"A sudden death?" My detective brain was already working on possibilities.

"Yes, sir. His heart stopped."

"Isn't that always the case?" said Flanagan in his irritating Irish lilt.

Millichip glared. "I meant to say that the doctor diagnosed a sudden heart attack. The post-mortem has since confirmed it."

"I see. And was anyone with your father when he died?"

"Only Rudkin, the manservant."

"Where were you at the time?"

"Of Father's death? In Reigate, where I live. I hadn't

seen him for over a year. When I noticed the announcement in *The Times*, I came to London directly."

"And dismissed Rudkin directly?"

"He'll find other work. I gave him an excellent character, sir."

"Where is he to be found?"

"Rudkin? I have no idea. He resided here."

"Until he was dismissed?"

"Yes, sir."

"And now he has no address? You consigned him to the streets?"

"I had no use for his services and no certainty of being able to pay his wages, sir."

Here, Flanagan's deputy, Engineer Locke, observed, "You'll inherit something, surely? Aren't you the only son?"

Young Millichip shook his head. "I don't expect to get a brass farthing. Father made it abundantly clear that the entire proceeds of his estate would go to the London Cremation League." He spoke without rancour, as if remarking on the weather. Then he showed himself to be human by adding with a slight smile, "Their windfall has been somewhat reduced by the fire."

"Has the will been read?"

"Not yet, sir. The family solicitor will reveal the contents after the funeral, but I know what's in it. Father told me months ago, when he drew it up. That's why we fell out. I was incensed. It was the last conversation I had with him. Those cremation people will blue it all on beer. They're Bohemians for the most part. Writers and artists. Trollope, Millais, Tenniel. People like that. They meet once a month in some plush hotel in the West End with no prospect of achieving their aims."

"If it isn't impertinent to ask, how much was your father worth?"

"A cool three hundred pounds, sir."

"That's a lot of beer."

When the young man had left us, Flanagan pre-empted me by commenting, "I recommend that we look for signs of arson."

"I should have thought that goes without saying," said I in a bored voice. "Clearly the servant must be found and questioned at once."

"The servant?" said he, as if I'd named the Archbishop of Canterbury. "I was about to suggest that Millichip must have set the place alight."

"Millichip? But why?"

"To deprive the Cremation League of its legacy. He's a very embittered young man, sir."

I wasn't persuaded. However, we had much to do. I proceeded to examine the building with Flanagan and Locke. The ash was thick on the ground, but so are shoeblacks at Charing Cross, so I didn't hesitate. It's fascinating to look at a gutted building with a man of Flanagan's experience. He had no difficulty in finding the seat of the fire, which was in the basement, close to the street, and he rapidly concluded that arson was the most likely cause. By picking at fragments of ash and sniffing his finger and thumb he was able to inform us that a paraffin-soaked rag had been used as tinder, probably set alight and pushed through a broken window by the arsonist.

"So simple, if a person is really bent on destroying a house," he said. "We had a similar case two weeks ago, didn't we, Henry?"

"That is correct, sir," Locke confirmed without much animation, for it presently emerged that the Friday in question had been his day off duty and he had missed a spectacular blaze. As he'd also missed the Villiers Street fire for the same reason, Henry Locke had every right to feel deprived. Most of the calls the fire service deal with are chimney fires, which can be very tedious.

"An empty house in Tavistock Street went up like a beacon," Flanagan explained for my benefit. "We fought it for three and a half hours. It belonged to the eminent zoologist, Professor Carson. He left on a trip to the Amazon a couple of days before. The police are investigating."

"How could I have missed it?" I mused aloud, then remembered that a supper engagement had taken me to Gatti's restaurant on the night in question and to a private address thereafter. I was bending my efforts to *raise* a fire that night, so to speak, not to dowse one. "Well, the police have a straightforward task in this case. I shall instruct them to detain Rudkin, the servant."

I spoke confidently, showing my contempt for Flanagan's theory that Millichip was the arsonist and incidentally omitting to mention my reservations about the efficiency of the Metropolitan Police. Straightforward their task may have been, but in the event the raw lobsters required five days to find Rudkin, in cheap lodgings in the shabby district of Notting Hill. I had him brought to Chandos Street Fire Station for questioning on the following Thursday.

James Rudkin may have looked the worse for wear from his new way of life, but in deportment and speech he was still the gentleman's gentleman, with airs of refinement. I suppose he was forty-five years of age, dark-haired, with mutton-chop whiskers going grey. He claimed to know nothing whatsoever about the fire. "This is calamitous. When did you say it occurred, Your Royal Highness? Last Friday? Was there serious damage?"

"Never mind that," I told him, eager to catch him out, for Flanagan and Shaw were sitting beside me, and I wanted to prove a point or two. "Where were you last Friday evening?"

"Me?" He piped the word as if to imply that anything

connected with himself was unworthy of consideration. "You wish to know where *I* was, Your Royal Highness?"

Indifferent to the wretched fellow's play-acting, I tapped the ash from my cigar and waited.

Rudkin hesitated, apparently collecting his thoughts. "Last Friday evening. Let me see. Oh, yes. I was at South Kensington, at the Art Training School."

"The Art School?" I said in total disbelief. "You're an artist? I can't believe that. How could you afford the fees?"

"Oh, I wasn't required to pay a fee, sir. They paid me. I was, em, sitting."

"*Sitting?*"

"Well, reclining, in point of fact, sir. The School advertised for models and I applied. It was force of necessity. I needed the money to pay for a night's lodging."

"I follow you now. What time was this?"

"The class lasted from 7 to 9 p.m., sir, but I had to report early to remove my clothes."

"Good Lord! You were posing in the buff?"

"It was the life class, sir."

I turned to Eyre Shaw. "At what hour did the fire break out?"

He coughed nervously. "Approximately 8.30, sir. Certainly no later."

That evening, I told the Princess of Wales that her theory about the servant had been confounded and in a manner acutely embarrassing to me personally. "Rashly I asked the fellow if he could prove this extraordinary alibi of his and he said there must be twenty drawings of his anatomy from every possible angle. He couldn't swear that every one would be a good likeness, but I was welcome to enquire at the school. Imagine me—asking to examine drawings of a naked man."

"It wouldn't be advisable, Bertie."

"Don't worry, my dear. I may have been a trouble to you

on occasions, but I'll not be caught looking at drawings of a butler in his birthday suit. I'm just relating the facts so that you can see how mistaken you were. Rudkin cannot possibly be the arsonist. It was such a persuasive theory when you mentioned it."

"I'm not infallible, Bertie."

I sniffed. "Regrettably, it seems that Flanagan—that bombastic Irishman from Chandos Street—is the one who is infallible. Young Millichip put a match to the house to prevent it from passing to the London Cremation League. I shall suggest to the police that they arrest him in the morning. Frankly, I'm not interested in questioning him a second time."

Alix continued with her sewing.

"It's a great pity," I maundered on, more to myself than Alix. "I should have liked to have solved a case of arson. I shall have to bide my time, I suppose. My chance will come. It's becoming a common crime—every other Friday, in fact."

"Speak up, Bertie."

Alix is somewhat deaf.

"I said arson happens every other Friday. A slight exaggeration. A house in Tavistock Street three weeks ago, and the Villiers Street fire last week."

She stopped her sewing and gave me a penetrating look. "You didn't mention two cases of arson when we discussed the case."

"At that time, my dear, I hadn't heard about the Tavistock Street fire. I missed it. I was, em, otherwise engaged that evening . . . putting the world to rights with the Dean of St Paul's, if I remember correctly."

"Two houses set alight?" said Alix.

"Two."

"On Fridays?"

"Yes."

"Both started maliciously?"

"Apparently, yes."

"Was anyone hurt?"

"No, no. Both houses were uninhabited."

"Then let us suppose both fires were started by one individual. How would he—or she—have known that no one was inside?"

I said, "I'm damned if I know. One individual? What makes you say that?"

She ignored my question. "Presumably, the late Mr Millichip's death was reported in the newspapers."

"That is true," said I. "His son read it in *The Times*."

"And do you know the identity of the owner of the Tavistock Street house?"

"That was Carson, the explorer. He left for the Amazon three weeks ago."

"Was his expedition reported in *The Times*?"

"It may well have been. He's a famous man. I'll speak to the editor and find out, if you think it's important."

She gave a slight shrug and lowered her eyes to the needlework. Poor Alix. She never knows whether to encourage me in my investigations. But she'd said enough to stoke up my analytical processes again. I asked myself whether it was conceivable that some wicked arsonist was lighting fires at random. No, not at random, but by reference to *The Times*. If so, it would be devilish difficult to identify him. What facts did we have? He was a reader of *The Times*, presumably a Londoner. He selected houses that were empty and he favoured Friday evenings for his fire-raising. Would there be another fire this week, or next? If so, where?

There was a panic below stairs when I asked the head butler for the entire week's issues of *The Times*. Normally I never see a copy that has not been freshly ironed and then they tend to get creased and sprinkled with cigar-ash in the course of my perusal. Lord knows what happens after I've finished with them. One thing was certain: the prospect of retrieving six copies and getting them fit for inspection caused my head butler's eyes to resemble coach-lamps, even after I assured him that ironing would not be necessary. In the end, six immaculate newspapers were supplied from heaven knows where and I set to work compiling a list of recently vacated properties. Within a short time I realized the scale of the task I'd set myself. The deaths column alone ran to fifty or sixty names each day. I therefore confined myself to names in the vicinity of Chandos Street Fire Station, where the two previous fires had taken place. At the end of two hours, I had a list of twelve residences that I considered prime candidates for arson.

I was so pleased with my detective work that I showed Alix the list. Somewhat to my surprise, she laughed. "Oh, Bertie, what will you do now—travel the district on a bicycle keeping watch on all these houses?"

"That isn't the object," I explained. "If one of them goes up in flames tomorrow night, I shall know for certain that my theory is correct. The arsonist selects the houses from *The Times*."

"And then you can make another list next week," said Alix with a lamentable lack of sensitivity.

"What else do you propose?" said I chillingly.

"I make no claim to be a detective, but I would look for a motive, my dear."

"It's all very fine to talk in such terms," I protested, "but why would anyone put a match to a house? To see a damned good fire. Believe it or not, there are people who derive a morbid pleasure from watching a property go up in flames."

"Oh, I believe it, Bertie."

"They are known as pyromaniacs."

She regarded me steadily. "Yes."

"Then what is the use of looking for a motive?"

"There may be a more practical motive."

"I doubt it," said I.

But later, in bed—my own bed—I paid Alix's last observation the compliment of considering it at more length. Suppose there was a practical motive. Why set light to a building if it isn't for the undoubted satisfaction of seeing it ablaze? It wasn't as if some insurance swindle was involved in either incident, so far as I was aware. And there was no attempt to put anyone in personal danger; in fact, the reverse was true. The arsonist appeared to have gone to some trouble to select an empty house and so avoid an accident.

In the small hours of the morning, a theory began to form in my brain, a brilliant theory that I was perfectly capable of putting to the test. It encompassed both motive and opportunity. I could hardly wait for Friday evening to learn whether the arsonist would strike again.

He did not.

I had to wait another full week and compile another list of properties from *The Times* before this drama came to its conclusion.

Two weeks to the day since the Villiers Street fire, I took high tea instead of supper and arrived at Chandos Street Fire Station sharp at 7. Captain Shaw had not yet appeared and nor had the Duke of Sutherland, so after changing into my fireman's uniform I had a game of billiards with Superintendent Flanagan and beat him soundly. Then I put my proposition to him.

"If there's a fire this evening, I'd like to have command of one of the escapes—with your consent, of course."

He pricked up his eyebrows. Generally, I'm content to take a subordinate role in fire-fighting. "Is there a reason for this, sir?"

Damned impertinence. I ignored the remark. "You have no shortage of escapes?"

"Oh, we have more than we ever use."

"Mine can be surplus to requirements, then." I added cuttingly, "I wouldn't want to hamper the work of the London Fire Brigade through inexperience."

He had the grace to mumble, "That's unthinkable, Your Royal Highness."

"Very good, then. And Flanagan . . ."

"Sir?"

"We won't mention it to the others."

"As you wish, sir."

George Sutherland arrived soon after, and restored my *joie de vivre* in no time. He's an old friend and a marvellous eccentric who happens to own more land than any other man in the kingdom. The Shah of Persia (another notable eccentric) once advised me that Sutherland was too grand a subject and I'd be well advised to have his head off when I come to the throne. I never miss an opportunity to remind George of this.

The alarm came at twenty minutes past eight. A house at the Leicester Square end of Coventry Street was well alight. Marvellous! It was on my list. The owner had died ten days ago, according to *The Times*.

I told nobody the significance of the address at this juncture. I was playing a cautious hand, by Jove. I made sure that I was last in the rush to the fire-fighting vehicles. I watched two engines and an escape being whipped out, bells jangling. Flanagan and George Sutherland were aboard the first to leave.

My team of two firemen waited deferentially for me to step up to the driver's box, and I took my time, making certain that everyone else was out of the yard and would be clear of Chandos Street before we followed.

"All ready, Your Highness?" the driver asked.

I nodded. "Except that we shall not be going to the fire. Kindly drive to Eagle Street."

"*Eagle* Street, sir."

"Eagle Street, the other side of Holborn."

"I know it, sir, but I didn't know there was a fire there."

"Wait and see," I said cryptically.

We set off northwards up St Martin's Lane. People are pretty considerate when they see a fire appliance coming and we rattled through to High Holborn at a good trot.

"Has the engine gone ahead, sir?" the driver enquired.

"An engine won't be required," I told him. Perhaps I should explain that an escape, such as the vehicle I had commandeered, is simply a cart with extending ladders. The fire engine is the vehicle that provides the steam for the pumps. It is unusual, to say the least, for an escape to attend a fire in the absence of an engine. You can imagine the look on the face of my driver. The look became a study in disbelief when we turned into Eagle Street and there was no engine and no fire. Not even a puff of smoke.

"Shall I turn about, sir?" he asked.

"No," I told him. "Draw up outside number 39."

"That's Mr Flanagan's address," he informed me. "Our Superintendent."

"I'm aware of that. Just do as I say."

We trundled to a stop. There was no sign of a fire at 39, Eagle Street. Nobody was at the windows shrieking, or on the roof.

"Raise the main ladder," I ordered. "And make as little sound as possible."

The firemen exchanged mystified glances. Fortunately, they didn't dare defy me. They cranked the ladder upwards.

"That will do," I presently said. "Now can you swing it closer to that large window at the top?"

I made sure that the top of the ladder didn't touch the window-sill, but it was pretty close. "Is it stable?" I asked. "In that case, I'm going up."

Watched by an interested collection of bystanders, I mounted the ladder briskly, as firemen do. I have an excellent head for heights and this was only three storeys high, so I went up almost without pause. I drew level with the window and looked in. This being a September evening, there was still a good light and the curtains had not been drawn. What I saw may offend some readers; it would have offended me, had I not been prepared. Indeed, I might well have fallen off the ladder.

This was the Flanagans' bedroom. There was a large double bed, occupied by the personable Dymphna Flanagan and a man who couldn't possibly have been Flanagan, because Flanagan was fighting a fire in Coventry Street. Without wishing to be indelicate, I have to say that Dymphna and her visitor clearly weren't discussing Irish politics. They were naked as cuckoos. I should state here that I'm no prude, and I'm no Peeping Tom either. The reason I remained staring into the room for two more minutes is that I needed to be certain of the man's identity. I was waiting for him to turn his head. When he did, our eyes met. He saw me on my ladder and I saw Engineer Locke, Flanagan's deputy.

I had fully anticipated this, of course. Friday—every other Friday—was Henry Locke's day off. He had been setting unoccupied houses alight once a fortnight in order to make sure that Flanagan was usefully occupied for the evening. And I had deduced it.

One cannot defend an arsonist, yet I must admit to some sympathy for Henry Locke. It's a frightful shock to be caught *in flagrante* by anyone, let alone the Heir Apparent in a fireman's helmet poised atop a ladder.

I descended, stepped to the front door and knocked. Dymphna herself answered, having flung a garment over her head in the short time it took me to dismount from the ladder. She even managed a curtsey. Perhaps she hoped that I hadn't recognized her lover, for when I asked to speak to Engineer Locke she clapped her hand to her mouth. To his credit, Locke then stepped forward. There was a distinct whiff of paraffin coming from his clothes— more confirmation, if needed, that he was the arsonist.

It was not needed, for he confessed to the crimes. Manfully he refused to implicate Dymphna in the fire-raising, though I'm privately certain she was an accessory.

In November, 1870, Henry Locke pleaded guilty and was sentenced to penal servitude for life. You may think it a harsh sentence—as I do—for a *crime passionnel*, but that's the penalty for arson, and it *was* a dangerous way to court a lady.

Dymphna Flanagan parted from her husband soon after and took off to France with an onion-seller. Flanagan lost all his bounce and retired prematurely from the London Fire Brigade in 1873.

To end on a rising note, Captain Shaw kindly offered the unemployed servant Rudkin a job as a fireman third class, which he accepted. When I last enquired, he was performing ably. All things considered, I would recommend the fire service as a satisfying career for any man with a sense of public duty and a wife he can trust.

The Case of the
Easter Bonnet

Good Friday, 1995. In their usual box at the Theatre Royal, John and Olga Hitchman were enjoying the new production of *The Seagull* unaware that a thief had just forced his way into their mansion on Lyncombe Hill. There would be rich pickings. The Hitchman family had made millions out of Bath stone and expanded into mineral extraction world wide. John had succeeded his father as company chairman.

The thief was a high earner in his own line, a top professional, identified only by the name the press had given him: Macavity. '*For when they reach the scene of crime—Macavity's not there!*' runs the line in T. S. Eliot's poem. Burglar alarms and security lights didn't inhibit this cat burglar one bit. In the previous six months he had neutralised four expensive systems in the Bath area and profited by upwards of fifty thousand pounds. He picked his victims shrewdly, studied their routine and struck when they were not at home. He knew what he was after this time: Olga Hitchman was from a Russian emigré family. She owned a Fabergé egg her great-grandmother had been given by the Tsarina as an Easter gift in 1911. Gold, of course, intricately crafted, enamelled and inset with emeralds and rubies, it was insured for a six figure sum.

It was to be Macavity's present to his partner Jenny. Her Easter Egg.

Eventually he found the correct combination and removed the prize from the safe. The job had taken under two hours. He had left no prints and he took nothing else. He was out and into his black Alfa Romeo and away along the drive. Another coup for Macavity. Except that on his way downstairs he passed through a sensor he hadn't been aware of. It triggered an alarm at Manvers Street Police Station and a response vehicle passing down Wellsway was diverted to the house.

With screeching tyres the police car turned into the long drive leading up to the Hitchman residence. Macavity met them almost head on. His reaction was swift. He veered left onto the turf to bypass them. His powerful engine roared, he swung onto the road, and accelerated. The police had to turn to give chase, and he got away.

Bath's outsize detective, Superintendent Peter Diamond, ambled up the drive next morning and looked at the tracks the car had made. "Our mystery cat made a mess on your lawn, I see," he remarked light-heartedly to John Hitchman, who was unamused.

Those tracks were useful. The police were able to get a clear tread pattern and establish which tyres had been fitted to the car. Moreover, the driver of the patrol car was convinced that the thief had been driving an Alfa Romeo sports model. The Police National Computer carries records of all registered cars. The Alfa Romeos of that type in the Bath area can be counted on one hand.

Towards noon, Diamond drove over the cobbles in front of the Royal Crescent and found a space two cars away from a black Alfa Romeo. All other enquiries had proved negative.

This Easter weekend had turned out fine, but chilly, particularly on the exposed slope where the Crescent is sited. Diamond stood rubbing his arms by the sports car while the sergeant compared the tread pattern on the tyres. "No chance, I'm afraid," the sergeant said finally.

"You're certain?"

"These are another make altogether, sir. Mind you, they're new. They've still got some shreds of rubber where they were taken from the mould. It's worth asking when these were fitted."

A man in a blue sweatshirt and black jeans answered the door and before Diamond had opened his mouth said, "Piss off, will you? Out of it. Get some fresh air."

It was only when Diamond felt some pressure against his leg that he realized the remarks were meant for a cat, a large ginger tom that was trying to return indoors. The man put a foot against its rump and steered it away from the door. "You've got to be firm with them," he said. "I don't want it cluttering up the flat all day."

Diamond explained who he was.

The young man, whose name was Mark Bonney, invited him in. He introduced Diamond to his partner, a dark-haired woman in a denim suit. She offered to make coffee.

In the next twenty minutes, Bonney insisted that he had not been out at all the previous evening. He had watched a video with his partner and they had retired early. He had not used his Alfa Romeo since Thursday, two days before.

"I was looking at the tyres," said Diamond. "They're brand new. Changed them recently, did you?"

"Thursday afternoon," said Bonney. "Want to look at the receipt? It's right here."

It was from Tyrefast in Weston and the date was clearly written as 13/4/95. Thursday. The robbery had been on Friday evening.

"That seems to settle it," Diamond had to concede. "I've no further questions, Mr Bonney. Thanks for the coffee."

After the door was closed, Bonney and his partner watched discreetly from the window as the portly detective walked across to his colleague, shaking his head.

"You're brilliant," Jenny said. She had taken out the Fabergé egg and was holding it to her chest. "Brilliant! How did you manage it?"

"Manage what?"

"The receipt. You had the new tyres fitted only half an hour ago, for God's sake."

"No problem," said Bonney, putting an arm around her. "I changed the date myself, as soon as I was given the receipt. The lad wrote his 5 like a letter S. All it wanted was an extra stroke across the top. Now they're convinced I haven't used the car since Thursday."

They watched Diamond return to the police car, still shaking his head. Before getting in, he hesitated.

"What's he staring at?" said Jenny.

"My car," said Bonney. "Oh, Jesus! That bloody cat!"

The ginger tom was sitting forlornly on the Alfa Romeo, pressing itself against the still faintly warm bonnet.

Diamond strolled across and put his hand flat to the bonnet. Then he gestured to the sergeant and they approached the house and knocked again.

Macavity was about to be nicked.

Disposing of
Mrs Cronk

"Foolproof."

Gary shook his head. "Too simple."

"The simple ideas are the best."

"What if he susses us?"

And now Jason shook his cropped head. He made you believe in his wild ideas, did Jason. Those pale blue eyes of his, as still as the stones in a mosaic, watching you. The mouth like a crack in the earth.

"What's my action, then?" asked Gary, weakening.

"Collect the readies."

"Five grand?"

"More if we like. We set the fee."

"Five is enough," said Gary with the measured calculation of a young man behind with his rent and trying to subsist on unemployment benefit of forty-two pounds a week. "And all I do is collect?"

"And look the part."

"How?"

"Suit. Tie. Shades."

"What do I say?"

"Not much. You just collect, I said."

"Alone?"

"I can't hold your bleeding hand, Gary. I'm doing all the heavy stuff, aren't I?"

There was a pause for thought.

"All right, Jay. You're on."

"How's it going, Mr Cronk?" Jason asked, grasping the crowbar he used to strip the casing from the frames of the wrecks that were brought in.

"Same as usual."

"Mrs Cronk still giving you grief?"

"Don't ask, Jason."

Jason hauled on the crowbar and exposed the burnt-out interior of a Vauxhall Cavalier. "Not much here worth keeping."

"Pity. Try the engine, son."

With two or three expert stabs at the front of the car, Jason forced up the bonnet. "Battery looks all right. I'll have that out."

His employer prepared to watch the swift dissection of the mangled vehicle. In other parts of the yard, other beefy youths were dismantling derelict pieces of machinery, fridges, cookers, lawn-mowers, for scrap metal. It was not a bad living in these grim times. There was money in scrap. Call it waste disposal, recycling, totting, what you like, it paid. Not many overheads. Low wages. These were young lads straight from the dole queue, glad of anything. With the basic tools, a breakdown lorry, a second vehicle to cart the good stuff down to the dealer and fly-tip the rest, you were set up. Cash for trash.

If only his domestic life worked as neatly as his business.

Jason leaned over the bonnet, peering at the way the hoses were fixed. Then he ripped them out with his large hands. He was the pick of the bunch, in spite of his aggressive looks, the nearest thing to a foreman on the site.

"I knew a bloke had grief from his old lady," Jason said, turning to pick up another tool. "Funny business. She couldn't get enough of it. Know what I mean, Mr Cronk? Big, healthy woman. Soon as he got into his pit, she was on him, regular, and when I say regular I mean three, four, five times a night and coming from all directions. Too many hormones, I reckon. No bloke could have stood it. Knackered, he was. His work suffered. His pecker was in permanent shock. He gave up going out with his mates. Got the shakes. Anyway, he faced facts in the end. It couldn't go on. So he went to the Fixer, paid the fee, and slept soundly ever after."

Mr Cronk reflected on the matter while Jason lifted out the battery.

"What do you mean by the Fixer?"

"I thought you'd know about the Fixer, Mr Cronk."

"I don't mix in your circles, Jason."

Jason applied himself to the heavy work, his biceps rippling.

"He takes care of problems. This geezer's problem was his old lady, so the Fixer fixed her."

"How?"

"Disposal." Jason ripped out the radiator and slung it onto a heap of rusted metal. Unlike the others, Jason never confused ferrous and non-ferrous.

"You mean he . . . ?"

"Yup. It wasn't crude, mind. The Fixer's a pro. No come-back. This bloke is free now. Free to marry again if he wants, but I don't think he will. Once bitten . . ." Jason gave a coarse laugh and picked up the bolt-cutter.

"What happened to the woman?"

"Accident, they said. She didn't know nothing about it, that's for sure. Drove her car off the road. The thing was, this road was next to a two-hundred foot drop. The coroner reckoned she fell asleep at the wheel."

"Accidental death?"

Jason grinned.

Mr Cronk gaped.

"The insurance paid up, easily covered the Fixer's fee."

He severed a bunch of cables and wrenched them out. There wasn't much left of that engine.

"What sort of fee does he charge?" Mr Cronk eventually asked.

"Ten grand."

"As much as that?"

"It sounds a lot, but it's like cars. You pay for a decent motor and you get value. Believe me, he's the Roller of his profession. He don't let people down."

Towards the end of the afternoon, Mr Cronk passed Jason again. The parts worth keeping had been stripped from the car, sorted and stacked neatly nearby. He was already sledgehammering another vehicle. He was a lad you could depend on.

"Er, Jason."

"Mr Cronk?" He rested the sledgehammer on his shoulder.

"You're feeling hot, I expect."

"What do you expect? I ain't picking daffodils."

"How would you like a cool swim? I've watched you working. You deserve it. Come home with me. I've got a thirty-foot pool."

"What, now?"

"Now's the right time."

"I'm covered in muck."

"You can take a shower at my place. We do have soap, you know."

Mr Cronk's house and garden were so palatial that Jason wished he had put the Fixer's price higher than ten grand. The pool had a glass roof that retracted at the push of a button like the sun-roof on a posh car. The bottom of the pool was lined with blue, green and gold tiles. There was money in recycling, more money than Jason had dreamed was possible.

He took a slow shower, soaping himself thoroughly in the shower-gel Mr Cronk had provided. He watched the grime go down the chromium plughole. Then he dried himself with the huge, pink, fluffy bath-towel and put on the boxer shorts Mr Cronk had lent him.

"So there you are, clean as a vicar," Mr Cronk shouted from across the water. "Come and meet my good lady."

Mrs Cronk.

She was reclining on one of those long, padded swing-seats suspended in a large frame. She must have been twenty years younger than Mr Cronk because she looked terrific in a black two-piece. Blonde, bronzed and superbly groomed, she was the biggest surprise yet.

Friendly, too. "Hi, Jason. Check those tattoos."

She didn't budge from the recliner, so he had to move in, crouch down and show her his biceps. She smelt expensive.

"Pure art. And on such an expansive canvas. Do you pump iron?"

"No, I break up cars for your old man."

She laughed. "So do I, but it doesn't give me muscle tone like that."

"You don't want it."

Mr Cronk said, more to himself than the others, "Many a true word." Then he turned to Jason. "Why don't you try the water?"

"Cheers. I will."

He wasted no time. He took a header, needing to get submerged fast, and not just because he was coming out in a sweat again. The water was deliciously cool. He was not a bad swimmer and he showed off a bit with his powerful crawl, doing a racing turn at the deep end.

After six lengths he stopped and stood up in the shallow end.

The swing-chair was no longer occupied.

"She's getting changed," her husband said. "She's got to get to her flamenco class." Mr Cronk had changed too, into a T-shirt, shorts and sandals.

"Is she learning flamenco?"

"She teaches it, four nights a week."

Jason swam another four lengths, lazily, on his back, thinking about Mrs Cronk dancing the flamenco. After a bit, he turned over and swam on his front.

When he got out, there was a fresh towel ready. Mr Cronk handed it to him. Jason sat on the edge of the pool with the towel draped around his shoulders, dangling his feet in the pool.

Mr Cronk handed him a can of lager, ice-cold. He said, "You look so cool, I think I'll join you, Jason." He stepped out of his sandals and sat beside Jason. The light on the water shimmered over the coloured tiles, distorting the shapes.

"That chap you mentioned today. The, em, Fixer."

"Yeah?"

"You said he was reliable."

"Hundred per cent."

"Ten thousand pounds, the man paid, for his services?"

"Ten grand, yes."

"Tell me, Jason. How does the money work?"

"Come again, Mr Cronk?"

"Well, is he paid by results? Does he get the money after performing the, em . . .?"

"I'm with you. No, there's got to be trust on both sides. Standard terms for that kind of job are half on agreement, half on completion. Five grand down, five at the death, so to speak."

After some reflection, Mr Cronk said, "It seems fair enough."

"Cash, of course. No point in cheques in a business like his."

"Or writing them, if you hire him," said Mr Cronk, churning the water with his feet, he was so amused by his own remark. "Do you know this fellow personally?"

"I've met him, yeah."

"Any chance I could meet him, just out of interest, so to speak?"

"No chance," said Jason.

"Oh."

"He doesn't meet no one on spec. Too risky."

"How did he ever meet the man you were telling me about?"

"It was set up by a third party. The bloke made it known he wanted to hire the Fixer. There was a meeting on neutral ground, the bloke and the Fixer. Five grand was handed over. Nothing spoken. When the job was done, the other five grand had to be left in a case in a left luggage box. The key was handed to the third party, who gave it to the Fixer."

"Neat."

"That's the way it's done the world over, Mr Cronk." Jason stood up. "I'd better get changed and toddle off. I'm sure you've got things to do."

"I'll drive you back. No problem," said Mr Cronk.

Towards the end of the drive back to the flat Jason shared with Gary, Mr Cronk said, "I suppose you couldn't act as third party."

"In what way?" Jason tried to sound puzzled.

"As a contact with the Fixer. You said you met him."

"Just the once, a while ago." He paused. "I suppose I could sniff around, see if he's about."

"I'd make it worth your while—later."

"Five hundred?" said Jason.

"All right. When it's all over."

They drove on for a while in silence.

"This'll be all right. Drop me here."

Mr Cronk stopped the car. "Don't think too badly of me, Jason. I'm a deeply wounded man. Mine is nothing like the case you mentioned. Almost the reverse."

"I don't judge no one, Mr Cronk."

"You'll let me know?"

"Get a grip, Gary. He's the one wearing brown trousers, right?"

"Right."

"You look great. Wear the shades, and your rings. Walk tall. And don't forget to check the money."

"Where will you be, Jay?"

"Where I said—down the tube with the cases and the tickets. Piccadilly Line to Heathrow, the night flight to Athens and six weeks bumming around the Greek Islands. Any problem with that?"

"No problem, Jay."

"There's nothing he can do. I lose my job, and you get the golden handshake, eh, Gary?"

"Yes, sure."

"Try and look the part, then."

Mr Cronk emerged from a taxi and entered the ticket hall of the tube station at precisely 4 p.m. He was carrying a sportsbag containing five thousand pounds in twenty-pound notes. As instructed, he waited to the left of the news kiosk. He was trembling uncontrollably.

At 4.03, a tall young man in dark glasses and a black suit and bootlace tie walked right up to Mr Cronk and said, "Is it all there?"

Mr Cronk fumbled and almost dropped the bag as he handed it over to the Fixer.

The young man unzipped the bag and made a quick assessment of the contents.

Mr Cronk said, "When will you . . .?"

"You'll get a phone call," the Fixer promised. He zipped the bag up again. Then he turned and walked quickly through the barrier and down the escalator.

Gary was all smiles on the platform. "Dead simple."

"Give us the bag," said Jason. He took it and looked inside. "Sorted."

The Heathrow train came in. They picked up the cases. On the journey, they opened one of the cases and stuffed the bag inside.

"It was a dream," said Gary, his confidence fully restored. "He was dead scared. You know what? If we played it right, we could roll him for the other five grand as well. Have a nice holiday, go back and screw him for the bloody lot. He wouldn't know it was a con till he got back and found his old lady still breathing."

Jason fixed him with those stone eyes and said, "You're a laugh a minute, Gary."

"Am I?"

"She's already dead."

"What?" Gary went white. "No! Jay, you never?"

"Couldn't let my old boss down, could I?" said Jason, enjoying this.

"For Christ's sake, mate, are you crazy?"

"Went for a swim with her this afternoon, didn't I? Pushed her face under the water and kept it there." He glanced at his watch. "He'll be finding her about now. He'll be saying, 'Jesus, that Fixer didn't waste time.' And when we get back to England, he'll pay up like a lamb."

Gary practically gibbered, "It was a scam, Jay, it was only meant to be a scam. We never agreed no violence."

Jason took pity. He'd had his fun, and other people in the train were starting to look at Gary. "I bet you still believe in the bloody tooth fairy and all. I never touched her."

Gary's breathing subsided. "Honest?"

"Honest. How could I? I was humping these cases to the station."

"Bastard."

"Get real, pal. We're on our way."

Their flight was due to take off at 23.10 from Terminal Four. They had plenty of time in hand. After checking in their cases and going through the passport control, they had a leisurely meal and a few drinks and started to get into the holiday mood.

"How long do you reckon it's going to take before old Cronk finds out he's been ripped off?" said Gary.

"Week. Longer," said Jason. "He might smell a rat when I don't come into work, but he'll think I'm ill, or something."

"And he can't do sweet f.a. about it. It's neat, Jay. Real neat."

"I'll drink to that."

Their flight was called. They walked to the departure lounge and showed their tickets and passports. One of the officials in suits said, "Would you come with me, gentlemen?"

"What for?" said Jason.

"This *is* your passport?"

"Yes."

"You are Jason Richardson and you, sir, are Gary Morton? You won't be boarding this flight. We're police officers with orders to arrest you."

After a scuffle, the pair were handcuffed and led away to the airport police office. They were cautioned and then questioned about their movements.

"You've got nothing on us," Jason said.

"We opened your luggage," the inspector said. "Almost five grand in twenties?"

"It's a long holiday," said Jason cleverly.

"Don't waste your breath, lad. We heard about you from Mr Cronk, getting yourself invited to his place and sussing it out for a robbery, knowing how scrap metal merchants have to handle large amounts of cash. That's naughty enough, but beating an innocent woman to death is evil."

Mrs Cronk dead?

Jason went cold. Suckered. He couldn't believe Mr Cronk had it in him.

Gary whimpered.

"Take their prints. See if they match up to the prints on the sledgehammer found at the scene. I'm confident they will. Armed robbery, murder and conspiracy to murder. Yes, it will be a long holiday, gentlemen."

The Mighty Hunter

George Blackitt sniffed the bottle suspiciously, poured some of the stuff on his finger-tips and sniffed again. This would be the first time in a life of seventy years that he had used aftershave.

He took another look at the label. *Surfaroma for Roughriders*. It certainly smelt rough, he thought, wondering how he had allowed himself to be conned into buying a product so overpriced. Embarrassment, really, he admitted. He wouldn't easily live down the giggles of the two young girls in the village shop when he'd given them his prepared speech. "I want it for my nephew in London actually. He's a bit of a ladies' man, wears the latest clothes and drives a sports car. Do you get the idea?"

Having sold him the bottle of Surfaroma, the pert little miss had caused a fresh eruption of mirth from her workmate by asking pointedly if his nephew required anything else from the shop. George had reddened deeply and fled.

In his day, it would have been unmanly to have used aftershave. Or the other things. He dabbed Surfaroma on his face and winced. It stung.

A large black tomcat stirred in his favourite armchair

across the room, opened his eyes and changed position. Catching a whiff of the aftershave, he raised his head just enough for a more informative sniff, then buried his nose under his tail.

"I don't blame you, Nimmy," George confided to his cat. "However, needs must, old friend. Can't expect a lady like Edith Plumley to entertain a gentleman smelling of soap, oh no. She's used to certain standards from her admirers. A sophisticated lady, Chairperson of the Darby and Joan Club, Queen of the formation dancing, Treasurer of the village fete committee. Quite a good catch, if she's willing to be caught, as I believe she is."

Nimrod had fallen asleep.

George gave up talking to the cat and talked to himself instead. He picked up his clip-on bow tie and stood in front of the mirror to adjust it. "You haven't seen action in a while, George Blackitt, but things are about to change." His reflection looked silently back, smart but strained, not totally impressed by this bravado. He turned away and reached for the jacket of his dark suit. "Well, you haven't worn this since Ivy's funeral." He sighed as he put it on. "Three years last month. Ivy, old girl, you wouldn't have wanted me to stay lonely for the rest of my life, would you?"

If a response had come from across the great divide, George wouldn't have heard it because he immediately started talking to the cat again. "Nimmy, old pal," he said, "it's time for another funeral. My own." He leaned over the chair and stroked the glossy, warm fur. "This is goodbye and R.I.P. to George Blackitt, the wretched widower. And welcome to George Blackitt, debonair, superbly groomed and shortly to cause a flutter in the heart of one Edith Plumley. Stand by for an announcement." He scratched Nimrod's head. "Come on, old fellow, I'd better get you fed. Who knows, it could be a long night. I'm not saying what time I'll be back. Come on, Nimmy. Nimrod."

Nimrod stood, arched his back and stretched. His name had been called in the proper tone, though the time was earlier than usual. At ten years old, the big, black tom had one companion he would never leave: the blue ceramic feed bowl just behind the door.

"Here we go, old chum," George said whilst filling the bowl with brawn. "This ought to keep you going till I get back." A fleck of meat jelly landed on one of his highly polished black brogues. The cat pounced on it in an instant. George looked down fondly. "I named you well, didn't I? '*Nimrod, the mighty hunter before the Lord.*'" No small mammal was safe within range of the cottage. In the summer Nimrod would be gone for hours, checking the hedgerows and the little wood across the meadow. Sometimes he went without processed catmeat for a week. He brought back what he couldn't consume and left it by the front door, birds, mice, voles and sometimes baby rabbits, hopeful always that when he went back and prodded one of the small corpses it would revive and test the reaction of his right forepaw.

George sang a line from an old song from years past. "Wish me luck as I go on my way."

Nimrod had his head in the feed bowl.

Two hours later, George was sitting uncomfortably in a rocking chair in Edith Plumley's cottage, regretting having agreed to a second helping of the steak and kidney pie. The meat had been tough and the pastry only semicooked. He sipped the tea she had given him and tried to wash away the after-taste.

"Biscuit, Mr Blackitt?"

"Well—"

"Do have one. I like a man who can eat."

George took a digestive. He bit with concentration lest the damned thing disintegrate into a pile of crumbs on his lap. "It was a meal to remember, Mrs Plumley."

"I'm so pleased you enjoyed it, Mr Blackitt." Mrs Plumley looked radiant and George noticed that she, too, had made an extra effort. She'd had her hair done and she was wearing a lace blouse. She had some kind of slip underneath, so it was perfectly decent.

He said, not untruthfully, "First class cooks are hard to find."

"I've had plenty of practice. You like steak and kidney?"

"You couldn't have made a better choice."

She smiled. "Most men seem to like it."

There was a pause in the conversation. The grandfather clock in the corner was ticking audibly.

"Nice weather for the time of year," said George.

A twinkle came to Edith Plumley's eye. "Next thing you'll be asking if I come here often. Please, just relax. I suggest it would help if we used first names."

He felt himself blush. "If you like." He still found her attractive, even if she couldn't cook. She was young in her manner. He guessed she was about sixty-three, but she could have passed for less.

"George."

"Yes . . . Edith?"

"I want to tell you something now, and I want to be sure I'm understood. I'm not in the habit of entertaining gentlemen in my home. In fact you are the first since . . . since I parted from Gregory. If I seem a little eager to be friends it's just that at our time of life I believe we have earned the right to dispense with—for want of a better word—the foreplay."

"Oh," said George, and accidentally set the chair rocking and slurped tea into his saucer.

Edith continued, "There isn't time for all that pussyfooting. Let's dispense with it, George. Let's admit that we're human beings with needs and impulses."

The digestive snapped. His crotch was covered in

crumbs. He moved his hand there to cover his incompe-
tence. He managed to say, "I wouldn't argue with that,
Edith."

"Good." She gave him a long, expectant look.

George swallowed hard. Why had she stopped talking?
Why did her eyes beg his for a response? Why was a little
drop of sweat rolling down his spine? Why hadn't he met
her forty years ago?

"If you'd like to know," said George, "I really fancy you,
Edith." He jerked his leg and set the chair going again. He
was horrified. The statement sounded so crude. Where
had it come from?

Edith laughed heartily. "You're a smooth talker, George,
and an old rogue, too. I suspect you're making fun of me."

"No, Edith. Absolutely not. I didn't mean it. I mean I did
mean it, in a way, but not in another way, if you know what
I mean." He was no better than a tongue-tied schoolboy on
his first date.

Like a lifebelt, Edith's command rescued George from
his sea of embarrassment. "Come with me. You've been
frank with me, and I don't mind admitting that you took me
by surprise. And now it's my turn. After what you said, we
should definitely hold nothing back. Put down your cup."

Without a word he got up and followed her ample form
through the door beside the stone hearth. They entered
her bedroom.

It was all so sudden. George felt a confusing mixture of
guilt, elation and panic. Up to now he had always believed
in the afterlife. As he stepped onto Edith Plumley's pink
carpet and saw her double bed with its muslin canopy ele-
gantly draped above the pillows, he told himself that
atheism might, after all, be more appealing as a philoso-
phy. He didn't want dear Ivy's immortal soul watching the
witless ease of his seduction—on one glass of Australian
sherry and a half-cooked pie.

And he wasn't entirely confident of satisfying Edith Plumley's expectations.

She turned and said, "This is the only way to get to it."

He said manfully, "I'm game for anything."

She crossed the room and opened another door. The *en suite* shower-room, he guessed. Fair enough. He, too, would be happier undressing in private.

She paused with her hand on the doorknob. "Come on, then."

He hesitated. "Both at once?"

She said, "There's room. Come on in." She giggled and disappeared inside.

George took a deep breath like a diver and followed her into the darkened room. It had a curious smell for a shower-room, a dry, musty aroma, vaguely familiar. George couldn't place it, but he didn't care much for it.

Edith felt for his hand and gripped it. Then she turned on the light. "Meet my little ones," she said. "Now everyone say hello to my friend George."

This wasn't a bathroom after all. It was a small dressing room, but instead of a wardrobe there were two shelves stacked with glass cages.

"You keep *mice?*" said George, too obviously in the circumstances. He knew the smell now. It was that of the local petshop where he bought Nimrod his supply of brawn.

"That's my secret," said Edith proudly. "Thirty-nine at the last count. All selectively bred over the last two years."

"Pedigree mice?"

"Well, of course! Look." She pointed to the back wall, a mosaic of rosettes and certificates. "One more win and I'll be a lifetime member of the National Fancy Mouse Society. That's my ambition, George."

George discreetly put a handkerchief to his nose and tried breathing through his mouth.

"I may have given you the wrong impression just now,"

said Edith, "bringing you through my bedroom, but that's the only way in, you see. I just loved the expression on your face."

"I wasn't expecting this," he admitted.

"You wondered what the invitation amounted to, didn't you, and I dare say you're heartily relieved," she said. "Heavens, we're too old to get up to things we shouldn't. I think I'd die if anyone saw me in bed."

"I can't think why," George gallantly said.

"Well, someone I hardly know."

"We could remedy that," said George.

"Given time, perhaps," said she.

"Not too much time," he said, feeling bolder now that the immediate challenge had been deferred.

"Any friend of mine would have to get used to the mice," said Edith. "And the smell. It all comes with me, I'm afraid. I keep them as clean as I can. Come and look at these." She indicated a cage set apart from the rest.

George peered politely at the two mice inside.

"Long-haired black and white hooded. The classic breeding pair," whispered Edith, her eyes rooted on the feeding mice. "The final show of the year is in Warminster in September. Only a short-haired silver-hood could possibly beat them. And there haven't been any shown at Warminster since 1985."

"You can see they're special," said George. He'd told white lies about the steak and kidney pie, so why not about these pesky mice?

Edith turned from the tank to look at George, her eyes shining. "You probably think I'm dotty, but these are my life. Would you really like to be part of it? Would you come with me to the Warminster show? I want someone to share my proudest moment with me. Then, who knows?"

"Edith, I can't think of anything I'd rather do," said George. Confident at last, he took her in his arms and kissed her. Their worlds collided gently amongst the sunflower seeds and sawdust.

He was home before eleven. Nimrod was out, enjoying his night life.

Ten days later, new neighbours moved into the empty cottage next door. George watched from his window in a fatalistic way as an immaculate Land Rover drew up. The place had changed hands several times in the past few years and he'd never got to know the people properly. They had been young couples from suburbia with unreal dreams of living in the country. One winter was usually enough; the familiar red and white 'For Sale' board would go up again and the garden would get overgrown until the new owners came in. Mind, the long grass made a happy hunting ground for Nimrod.

This time the young lady seemed friendly, knocking on George's door to introduce herself before the removal van arrived. In her middle twenties, with what used to be called a 'county' accent, but vivacious and attractive, she said she was Hannah from Dorking and her 'man' was Keith— which George took to mean that they were not married. He didn't object. The world had changed, and his own views on morality were changing too. He offered Hannah tea. They worked in television, he learned. She was a freelance researcher (whatever that meant) and Keith was a floor manager, which Hannah seemed to imply was something more exalted than keeping the floor clean, which was George's first assumption. Hannah said she had travelled on ahead of Keith who was with the removal gang to supervise the handling of some of the more precious items.

The van arrived and Hannah ran out to unlock for them. George settled down to watch the activity from the window. He was rather less obvious about it than Nimrod, who was sitting in the road gazing steadily into the back of the removal van. The Sutton boys from two doors up were out there as well, gaping. George had nothing but contempt for parents who allowed their children to be so blatantly nosy.

Keith, it appeared, was one of the four hefty fellows in T-shirt and jeans unloading the van. George had difficulty guessing which of them was the most likely to be the live-in lover of the elegant Hannah. She looked far too classy for any of them. But in mid-afternoon the van left, taking three in the cab and leaving one sitting on the drystone wall smoking a cigarette. He had cropped hair and a silver ear-ring.

George remarked to Nimrod, who had come in to be fed, "She's all right, but I'm not so happy about having him next door." He put on the kettle again, preparing do the neighbourly thing and take them both some fresh tea and biscuits.

"Into the fray, Nimmy, old friend," he said as he ventured out of the door, tray in hand.

Keith didn't even get off the wall. "For us? Nice timing, squire," he said without removing his cigarette. "Go right in, mate."

"George Blackitt, from next door," said George still holding the tray and therefore unable to offer his hand as he would have wished.

Keith shouted in a voice the whole village must have heard, "Han, are you there? Guy here with some Rosy Lea."

George stepped gingerly into the cluttered living room. Furniture and boxes stood in disorder everywhere.

"Mr Blackitt, what a marvellous thought!" said Hannah, appearing from the kitchen. "This is so generous."

"I'll leave it on the piano, shall I?" said George. "There's no hurry for the things. Tomorrow will do."

"Please don't rush off," she said. "Stay and have some with us. Don't worry, I've got a spare mug somewhere. That's one thing we have unpacked."

"Moving is a pain in the arse, ain't it, George?" Keith's voice said from the doorway. "Park yours on the chair, mate. Han and I don't mind squatting on the floor."

George took the mug Hannah handed him and sat like a throned king with slaves at his feet. Hannah offered some carrot cake that they'd brought with them. George politely declined.

"Don't blame you," said Keith. "Hippie food. We'll feed it to the mice."

"Mice?" said George.

Hannah laughed. "Don't worry. The cottage hasn't got mice, so far as I know. Keith has just bought this pair for breeding."

"Caged mice?"

"I'll show you." Keith was on his feet and searching among the packing cases. "Here we are." He brought out a glass tank and held it under George's nose. "Ollie and Freda, my latest investment. Still kipping from the journey."

George glanced into the tank with trepidation. The mice weren't visible. They were hiding under a shelter of sawdust and shredded newspaper in one corner. It moved in tiny spasms as Keith tapped the glass.

"Here, put the tank on your knees a sec," said Keith. Immediately he plunged his hand into the sawdust and hauled a mouse out by its tail. "It's either Ollie or Freda. Not easy to tell."

"Put it down, Keith," said Hannah.

"That's how you handle them," said Keith with nonchalance, but he then allowed the mouse to rest in his free hand. It crouched shivering. "I've never been without a pet, but fancy mice are something new."

"It looks a very fine specimen," said George, who was also beginning to know a little about mice.

"Short-haired silver-hood."

George felt his blood run cold. From all his conversations with Edith, short-haired silver-hoods were the only variety capable of outclassing her long-haired black and white hooded mice. And these people possessed a pair. "These . . . these are really rare, I believe."

"Yeah." Keith released the mouse into the tank. "They cost me a bomb. Well, if you're breeding, you don't want to use rubbish."

"Are you interested in mice, George?" asked Hannah.

"Well, em," George said guardedly. "A friend of mine keeps some and she and I . . . well, we take a passing interest."

"So you'll be going to the Fancy Mouse Show at Warminster, will you?" exclaimed Hannah, bringing her hands together in delight.

"Well, possibly. It's a long time off."

"Oh, do! It should be a hoot. We read about it in the local paper. Imagine, giving rosettes to mice." She giggled. "If Keith wins one, he says he's going to pin it up in the little room."

"Yeah," said Keith. "And if Ollie and Freda get on with it, we'll have a totally red silk bog this time next year."

"Cool," said Hannah.

"Yes, cool," said George dismally.

Two weekends later he was horrified to see Keith unloading ten glass cages from the Land Rover. They went straight into the shed at the bottom of their garden.

George slept fitfully that night. He hadn't slept so badly since the summer of 1940, only this time it wasn't the threat of German air-raids that kept him awake; it was the prospect of umpteen short-haired silver hooded mice in the garden shed next door. September was fast approaching and with it the culmination of Edith's breeding programme to secure her election to the National Fancy Mouse Society. He hadn't said a word to her about the newly-arrived competition. He knew it would break her heart.

"George, you look so downcast. I suspect that you aren't looking after yourself properly," she remarked in the men's outfitters when they were buying George a new linen jacket for the occasion. "Chin up, now. Is anything the matter?"

"Nothing, Edith," he lied.

"Come over on Saturday and I'll cook you a pie."

George had spent many hours watching the activity in the garden shed. Sacks of feed had gone in. And an electric cable, presumably to supply heating next winter. The shed was built on the far side of Keith and Hannah's garden, but if George weeded his verge by the dividing fence he could just see the darkened outlines of the mouse tanks inside. And often he saw Keith in there, handling his mice.

One August morning he called out, "How's it going, then?"

"What's that?" said Keith.

"The breeding."

Keith laughed. "They breed like mice, mate."

"Could I see them?"

"Love to show you, George, but I'm on location this week. Got to fly."

"You don't appear to have any lids on the tanks that I can see . . . Not that I've been prying, of course."

"George," said Keith smugly, "they're mice, not salamanders. They can't climb sheer glass walls, mate. Don't worry, none of the little beggars will get out. If they did, your old cat would have them, and who could blame him? But I keep the shed locked, so don't lose any sleep over it."

On the Thursday before the show, George had a stroke of luck. He had just been running Saturday's ghastly scenario through his head when Hannah called.

"Oh, Mr Blackitt," she said. "I hardly like to ask, but you

were so kind when we moved in. I wonder if you could do us a favour. Keith is doing a night shoot at the Tower of London on Friday. With it being open for visitors, that's the only time the cameras can get in there. I've never been and it's a wonderful chance. Would you mind keeping an eye on the cottage for us? It's just one night, but you never know."

A spark of hope glimmered in the ashes of George's sunken aspirations. "I'll be only too pleased. But what about the mice? Would you like me to feed them?"

"No, they'll be perfectly all right. Keith will feed them before we go and we'll be back first thing on Saturday."

"My dear, there's no need to rush back."

"Oh, but there is. We've entered for the Mouse Show, just for a laugh, as Keith says. We'll see you there, I hope."

Just as she turned to leave, Nimrod came in through the cat-flap. "Aren't you beautiful?" Hannah said, stooping to stroke him. "What's his name, Mr Blackitt?"

"Nimrod." Usually George explained the origin of the name. This time he chose not to.

Hannah tickled Nimrod under his chin. The cat purred, arched his back luxuriously and boxed her hair with his paw. "You're quick and powerful, aren't you, Nimrod," she cooed softly, "but you'll promise to keep away from my Keith's shed, won't you?"

George slept better that night. By Friday evening he had worked out every detail of his masterplan.

Nimrod hadn't been fed since the morning and the cat-flap was wedged shut. He was prowling about the cottage like a caged lion.

George poured himself a large scotch. "You won't have much longer to wait, old friend," he said. "Fresh food for you tonight. Living food, none of that prepacked slop. How about mouse mousse for supper? Short-haired silver hooded mouse mousse. Patience, old friend, patience."

Nimrod's mewing was becoming positively feral in tone. He kept running to the table leg that he used as a scratching-post and clawing it agitatedly.

The plan was deliciously simple. At about nine o'clock, when it was dark, George would go out. Under one arm would be the football he kept for his grandchildren to play with when they visited the cottage. With the other, he would be carrying a travelling bag containing Nimrod, by now ravenous. George would let himself into next door's garden and go to the far side of the shed, the side nearest the Suttons' cottage. The Suttons had the three boys under twelve, the local tearaways. He would smash the window with the football and push it through. Then he would unzip the bag containing Nimrod and help him through the broken window. Nimrod would embark on an orgy of rodent-killing.

As soon as Keith returned to collect his prize specimens for the Fancy Mouse Show, Nimrod would make his dash for freedom, leaving the brash young punk to discover the mass murder and the football, and draw his conclusions. The next time George saw Keith and Hannah and heard the gruesome story, he would say that he thought he'd overheard some sounds in the garden about nine last night and guessed it was cats. He knew the shed was kept locked, so he hadn't gone out to check. Then he would apologize profusely for Nimrod's blood-letting spree and Hannah would say that you couldn't blame the cat—or George. And if Keith said that the Suttons disclaimed ownership of the football, George would give a shrug and say, "What else do you expect of modern kids?"

After two more scotches, George looked outside to check how dark it was and fetched the plastic travelling bag from his wardrobe. Nimrod actually came running to investigate, so it was simple to sweep him up and bundle him inside. He fought savagely to escape. "Save your energy, old fellow. You're going to need it presently," said George, zipping up the bag. "Okay, dinner should be ready."

He collected the football, picked up the bag, let himself out and moved stealthily past the unlit cottage next door and into Keith and Hannah's back garden. He rested the bag on the ground and took a precautionary look around him before pressing the football hard against the window. The glass shattered easily and he thrust the football through so hard that he heard it break another pane of glass in one of the tanks. He lifted the bag to the level of the window and unzipped it. Nimrod's head popped out, his fang-teeth bared. George helped his old friend safely through the hole and felt the strength in the struggling shoulders. The Mighty Hunter had got the whiff of the mice. The energy coming from the black fur was awesome.

George whispered, "*Bon appetit!*" Having released Nimrod, he picked up the bag and walked back to the house feeling twenty years younger.

The Fancy Mouse Show next day was a revelation. George wandered up and down the rows of tanks and cages in the municipal hall marvelling at the doting owners as much as the mice competing for the titles. They groomed and stroked their tiny charges in an attempt to catch the judge's eye. First there were the competitions to decide the best in each class. Later would come the accolade everyone coveted, for supreme champion.

Edith clutched George's arm. "See, George," she said. "See how exciting it all is? I'm not an eccentric old fool, am I?"

"I never said you were," George answered.

The judging of the long-haired black and white hooded class took place at noon. Edith's pair took first place. George and Edith embraced.

"I love you, Edith Plumley," George declared. "There isn't anything I wouldn't do for you."

"Just keep your fingers and toes crossed for me," she said tremulously. "They go forward to the supreme championship, on the stage at four o'clock. George, we're virtually certain to win. Only the late arrival of a truly rare breed would deprive my little beauties of the title."

"So what happens now?" said George.

"I just told you. We wait for the judging."

"No, what happens to us now, Edith. What about our future?"

A rough hand grabbed his shoulder.

"So here you are," said Keith.

George felt the hairs rise on the back of his neck. Fear gripped him. He was certain his neighbour was about to punch him.

But he did not. "George, old pal," he said, "I'd like to buy you a drink."

"That isn't necessary," said George, suspicious that this was only the prelude to violence.

"To celebrate, man," Keith said in the same friendly tone. "We just won first prize in our class. In fact, we're the only entry in our class. The silver-hoods. Extremely rare, the judge said. They created quite a stir. And they're going to win the supreme champion rosette. No problem."

George heard a whimper of distress from Edith. He'd almost forgotten her in his anxiety. "Edith, this is Keith, my neighbour," he said quickly.

He was about to add for Keith's benefit that Edith was a friend, but Edith said in a horrified voice, "Your *neighbour*?" Then she covered her face and fled. There was no point in going after her. He'd never explain it to her satisfaction.

"What's wrong with her?" said Keith. "Wasn't me, was it?"

George couldn't find words for some time. "I could do with that drink," he whispered finally.

After they had been standing at the bar some time while Keith held forth about the idiocy of Fancy Mouse Shows,

George managed to say, "Those prize-winning mice of yours—where do they come from?"

"What do you mean—where do they come from?" said Keith. "Other mice, of course." He laughed.

"No, where did you keep them? The shed?"

"Not the shed. They're valuable mice, mate. I wouldn't keep my silver-hoods in the shed. No, they live in luxury, on top of the piano. I just had time to get home and grab them and get them here for the judging."

"What about the mice in the shed?"

"They're nothing special. They're feeders."

"Feeders?" repeated George.

"Oh, Christ, Han didn't want me to tell you this. People living next door can get nervous, but there's no need. The mice are for Percy. You must have seen him on TV commercials. He pays for his keep. He stays coiled up in his tank at the bottom of our shed. It's got a glass top, mate, so Percy won't get out. He gets through hundreds of mice. Well, he would. In the wild, a fourteen-foot python would be swallowing live pigs and all sorts. They're terrific hunters. So quick. They have these dislocating jaws that . . . What's up, George? Hey, George, you look terrible."

Murder in Store

"Hey, miss."

"What is it now?"

"Something's up with Santa."

"That's quite enough from you, young lady," Pauline said sharply—unseasonably sharply for Christmas week in an Oxford Street department store. The Toy Fair was a bedlam of electric trains, robots, talking dolls and whining infants, but the counter staff— however hard-pressed— weren't expected to threaten the kids. The day had got off to a trying start when a boy with mischief in mind had pulled a panda off a shelf and started an avalanche of soft toys. Pauline had found herself knee-deep in teddies, rabbits and hippos. Now she was trying to reassemble the display, between attending to customers and coping with little nuisances like this one, dumped in the department while their parents shopped elsewhere in the store.

"Take a butcher's in the grotto, miss."

Pauline glared at the girl, a six-year-old by the size of her, with gaps between her teeth and a dark fringe like a helmet. A green anorak, white corduroy trousers and red wellies. She'd been a regular visitor ever since the school

term ended. Her quick, sticky hands were a threat to every
toy within reach. But she had shining brown eyes and a way
with words that could be amusing at times less stressful
than this.

"I think Santa's stiffed it, miss."

"For the last time . . ."

A man held out a green felt crocodile, and Pauline rolled
her eyes upwards and exchanged a smile. She rang up the
sale, locked her till and stepped around the counter to look
for Mark Daventry, the head of the toy department. The
child had a point. It was 10.05 and Santa's Grotto should
have opened at 10.00. A queue had started to form. There
was no sign of Zena, the "gnome" who sold the tickets.

It was shamefully unfair. Mark hadn't been near the
department this morning. No doubt he was treating Zena
to coffee in the staff canteen. When blonde Zena had first
appeared three weeks ago in her pointed hat, short tunic
and red tights, Mark had lingered around the grotto
entrance like a six-foot kid lining up for his Christmas present. Soon he'd persuaded her to join him for
coffee-breaks: the Mark Daventry routine familiar to
Pauline and sundry other ex-girlfriends in the store.
However, Zena wasn't merely the latest temp in the toy
department. She wasn't merely an attractive blonde. She
happened to be the wife of Santa Claus.

Big Ben, as he was known outside the grotto, was a
ready-made Santa, a mountainous man who needed no
padding under the crimson suit, and whose beard was his
own, requiring only a dusting of talc. On Saturday nights,
he could be seen in a pair of silver trunks, in the wrestling-
ring at Streatham. This time, Mark was flirting dangerously.

"Coming, miss?"

Pauline felt her fingers clutched by a small, warm hand.
She allowed herself to be led to the far end of the grotto,
the curtain that covered the exit.

"Have you been sneaking round the back, you little menace?"

The child dived through the curtain and Pauline followed. Surprisingly, the interior was unlit. The winking lights hadn't been switched on and the mechanical figures of Santa's helpers were immobile. There was no sign of Ben and Zena. They generally came up by the service lift that was cunningly enclosed in the grotto, behind Santa's workshop. They used the workshop as a changing-room.

"See what I mean, miss?"

Pauline saw where the child was pointing, and caught her breath. In the gloom, the motionless figure of Santa Claus was slumped on the throne where he usually sat to receive the children. The head and shoulders hung ominously over one side.

It was difficult not to scream. Only the presence of the child kept Pauline from panicking.

"Stay here. Don't come any closer."

She knew what she had to do: check whether his pulse was beating. He might have suffered a heart attack. Ben was not much over thirty, but anyone so obviously overweight was at risk. She took a deep breath and stepped forward.

She discovered that he wasn't actually wearing the costume. It was draped over him. Somehow, she had to find the courage to look. She reached out for the furry trim of the hood, took it between finger and thumb and lifted it. She gave a start. She was looking into a pair of eyes without a flicker of life. But it wasn't Ben.

It was Mark Daventry. And there was something embedded in his chest—a bolt from a crossbow.

Pauline rushed the child out of the grotto and dashed to the phone.

She called Mr Beckington, the store manager, but got through to Sylvia, his secretary. Even suave Sylvia, supposed to be equal to every emergency, gave a cry of horror at the news. "Mark? Oh my God! Are you sure?"

"Is Mr Beckington there?"

"Mr Beckington? Yes."

"Ask him to come down at once. I'll make sure no one goes in."

When she came off the phone, Pauline looked around for the small girl. She'd wandered off, probably to spread the news. Soon the whole store would know that Santa was dead in his grotto. Pauline shook her head and went to stand guard.

She told the queue that Santa was going to be late, and someone made a joke about reindeer in the rush-hour. This is totally bizarre, Pauline thought, standing here under the glitter with these smiling people and their children, and "Jingle Bells" belting out from the public address, while a man lies murdered a few yards away. Her nerves were stretched to snapping-point.

Fully ten minutes went by before Mr Beckington appeared, smoking his usual cigar, giving a convincing impression of the unflappable executive in a crisis. He liked customers to be aware that he managed the store, so he always wore a rosebud on his pinstripe lapel. He nodded sociably to the queue and murmured to Pauline, "What's all this, Miss Fothergill?" as if she were the cause of it.

She took him into the grotto.

They stopped and stared.

The winking lights were on. The model figures were in motion, wielding their little hammers. Santa was alive and on his throne, dressed for work. Zena the gnome was powdering his beard.

"Ho-ho," Ben greeted them in his jocular voice, "and what do you want in your Christmas stockings?"

Mr Beckington turned to Pauline, his eyes blazing

behind his glasses. "If this is some kind of joke, it's in lamentably bad taste."

She reddened and repeated what she'd seen. Ben and Zena insisted that everything had been in its usual place when they'd arrived in the lift a few minutes late. They certainly hadn't seen a dead body. The Santa costume had been on its hanger in the workshop.

She gaped at them in disbelief.

Mr Beckington said, "We're all under stress at this time of the year, Miss Fothergill. The best construction I can put upon this incident is that you had some kind of hallucination brought on by overwork. You'd better go home and rest."

She said, trying to stay calm, "I'm perfectly well, thank you. I don't need to go home."

Ben said in the voice he used to his infant visitors when they burst into tears, "Now, now, be a sensible girl."

"If it's all my imagination, where's Mark Daventry?" Pauline demanded.

Mr Beckington told her, "He's down with 'flu. We had a message."

"Darling, I think some meany played a trick on you," Zena suggested. "That kid with the teeth missing is a right little scamp. Some practical joker must have put her up to it."

Pauline shook her head and frowned, unwilling to accept the explanation, but trying to fathom how it could have been done.

"If you're not going home, you'd better get back to your position," Mr Beckington told her. "And let's get this blasted grotto open."

She spent the rest of the morning in a stunned state, going through the motions of selling toys and answering enquiries while her mind tried to account for what had happened. If only the small girl had returned, she'd have got the truth from her by some means, but, just when the kid was wanted, she'd vanished.

About 12.30, there was a quiet period. Pauline asked Zena to keep an eye on her counter for five minutes. "I want to check the stock-lists in the sports department."

"Whatever for?"

"To see if a crossbow is missing."

"You still believe this happened?"

"I'm certain."

The sports department was located next to the toys on the same floor. Disappointingly, Pauline found that every crossbow was accounted for. She told herself that if the murderer was on the staff, he could easily have borrowed the weapon and replaced it later. But what about the bolt?

She examined the crossbow kits. Six bolts were supplied with each. She checked the boxes and found one with only five. She *hadn't* been hallucinating.

"What are you going to do about it?" Zena asked, when Pauline told her.

"I've got some more checking to do."

"Proper Miss Marple, aren't you? You're wasting your time, darling."

"Coming from you, that's good."

Zena said without a hint of embarrassment, "Jealous of my coffee-breaks, are you? That's all water under the bridge. Look, I still say this is someone playing silly games. It could even be Mark himself."

Pauline shook her head. "Zena, he's dead, and I'm going to find out why. Tell me, did you and Ben arrive together this morning?"

Zena smiled. "You bet we did."

"What's funny?"

"He guards me like a harem-girl since he found out Mark was chatting me up. We had a monumental row last week, and I told Ben straight out that he shouldn't take me for granted. Now he watches me all the time." She adjusted her pointed hat. "I find it rather a turn-on."

"But you definitely finished with Mark last week?"

"Absolutely. I wouldn't say he was heartbroken. You know how he is. Adaptable."

"That isn't the word I'd use," said Pauline, thinking of all the women Mark had "chatted up."

In her lunch-hour, she went downstairs and talked to the security man on the staff entrance, a solemn Scot who'd made himself unpopular with everyone but the management by noting daily who was in, and at what time. Pauline asked if by any chance Mr Mark Daventry was in.

"Yes, he's here. He arrived early this morning, just after 8.15."

She said, "Are you sure?"

"Positive."

"Someone told me he was down with 'flu."

To prove his point, the security man showed her Mark's overcoat in the staff locker-room. She knew Mark's camel-hair coat with the leather buttons and the shoulder-flaps. There was no question now that what she had seen was true.

She asked the security man about Ben and Zena. They'd arrived together at their usual time, 9.50—which was odd, not to say suspicious, considering how late the grotto had opened.

She decided to have it out with them. The grotto closed between 1.00 and 2.00, so she found them out of costume in the staff canteen. They'd finished lunch and Ben had his arm protectively around Zena's chair. They looked up like two choirboys on a Christmas card, innocence per-sonified.

She warned them that she'd been checking downstairs. "I want a straight answer. Why weren't you ready to open the grotto at ten this morning?"

"There's no mystery, darling," answered Zena. "We had to wait ages for the lift."

A reasonable explanation. The lift was their only means of access to the grotto. Pauline had to accept it for the moment. She said, "I'm going to make a search of the grotto."

Ben said affably, "Fine. Let's all make a search."

They had twenty minutes. Pauline had hoped to find bloodstains on Santa's throne, but it was painted red. She went behind the scenery, where it was supported on wood and chicken-wire. "There's something under here."

It was a wooden packing-case. Ben dragged it out and pulled off the lid. There was a layer of the small white chips of polystyrene used in packing. Ben dug into them with his large hands.

Zena screamed as a tuft of dark hair was revealed. It didn't take much more digging to confirm that Mark's body had been crammed into the packing-case.

"I suppose all three of us are imagining this!" Pauline said pointedly.

"We'd better report it," said Ben in a shocked voice. Reassuringly, he and Zena gave every sign of being genuinely surprised at the discovery.

"Before we do," said Pauline, "would you mind looking in his pockets?"

"Why?" asked Zena, but Ben was already starting a search. In one of the inside pockets was the note that Pauline hoped to find. *Something* must have lured Mark to his death in the grotto early that morning.

It was a short, typed message: *See what Santa has for you, darling. Tuesday morning, 8.45.*

"I've seen that typestyle recently," said Ben.

"On our letter of appointment," said Zena.

"Sylvia?" said Ben, frowning. "Mr Beckington's secretary?"

Pauline and Zena exchanged a long, uncomprehending look.

They covered the body and took the lift to the management floor above. On the way up, Pauline said, "I've thought of something terribly important. Did you find out why you had to wait so long for the lift this morning?"

"Not for certain," Ben answered. "The usual cause is a storeman delivering goods."

Pauline said, "I believe it was the murderer, jamming the lift-door open at our floor so that no one would interrupt the killing. When it finally arrived, did you see a storeman?"

"No," said Zena, "it was empty." She hesitated. "But we smelt cigar smoke."

There wasn't time to reflect on that, because the lift-doors opened at the top floor and Mr Beckington was waiting there, a cigar jutting from his mouth. At the sight of the three of them together, his features twisted in alarm. He turned and made a dash for the emergency stairs.

"Ben!" shouted Zena.

Ben set off in chase.

The commotion brought people from their offices, among them Sylvia. Pauline grabbed her arm and drew her into the lift. Zena pressed the button for the ground floor and the three women started downwards.

"Mr Beckington," Zena blurted out. "He murdered Mark."

Sylvia's hand went to her mouth.

"But why?" said Pauline.

Sylvia said in a small, shocked voice, "He was jealous. Silly man. He was forever trying to start something with me, but I wasn't interested. I mean, he's married, with a daughter my age. Then last week Mark started taking an interest in me. I always thought him dishy, and . . . well, on

Friday evening we spent a little time together in the grotto."

"By arrangement?"

Sylvia nodded. "When everyone else was gone."

Pauline showed her the note they'd found in Mark's pocket.

"I didn't type this!" said Sylvia.

"Mr Beckington did," Pauline explained, "on your type-writer, to make sure Mark turned up this morning. He killed Mark in the grotto and he must have still been in there when the child sneaked in. He must have been hiding behind the scenery when I came in. I raised the alarm, and while I was standing outside like a lulu, he hid the body in a packing-case. I just hope Ben catches him."

"My man's strong," said Zena, "but fast he isn't."

The lift gave a shudder as they reached the ground floor. When the doors opened, a police sergeant was waiting. Two constables were nearby, standing at the foot of the stairs.

"All right, girls," said the sergeant. "Just stand over there, well out of the way."

In a moment, there was the clatter of footsteps on the stairs, then Mr Beckington ran straight into the arms of the waiting policemen. He offered no resistance.

Pauline felt a tug on her skirt and looked down at the small girl. "You?" she said. "You called the police?"

The child smiled smugly and nodded.

"And you believed her?" Pauline said to the sergeant.

"She's my daughter, miss. The way I see it, if my little girl tells me Santa's snuffed it, I've got to be very, very concerned."

Never a Cross Word

Poison, perhaps.

Quick-acting, if you choose the right sort. No mess. Simple to administer.

The problem with a poisoning is that science has progressed so far that you can't expect to get away with it any more. The police bring in people who make a whole career out of finding symptoms and traces.

Poison is not practical any more.

"I'm putting on the cocoa, blossom," Rose calls from the kitchen. "Did you switch on the blanket?"

"Twenty minutes ago, my love," answers Albert, easing his old body out of the armchair.

"And I thought you were day-dreaming. I ought to know better. My faithful Albert wouldn't forget after all these years. Is my kettle filled?"

He puts his head around the door. "Yes, dear."

"And the hottie—is it emptied from last night?"

"Emptied, yes, and waiting by the bed."

"You're a treasure, Albert."

"I do my best, sweetpea."

"I sometimes wonder how I ever got through the night before we bought the electric blanket. I've always felt the cold, you know. It isn't just old age."

"We had ways of keeping warm," says Albert.

"You've always had a marvellous circulation," says Rose for the millionth time. "You don't know how lucky you are."

Perhaps suffocation is the way. The pillow held firmly over the face. No traces of poison then. How do they know it isn't a heart attack? Mental note: visit the library tomorrow and find out more about suffocation.

"Nearly ready, honeybunch," says Rose, in the kitchen stirring the milk in the saucepan. "We're a comical pair, when you think about it: I make the cocoa to send us to sleep. You make the tea that wakes us up."

And wash up your sodding saucepan. And the spoon that you always leave by the gas-ring, coated in cocoa. And wipe the surface clean.

"I couldn't bear to get out of bed as early as you do," says Rose. "My dear old Mum used to say . . ."

Six hours sleep for a man, seven for a woman and eight for a fool.

". . . six hours sleep for a man, seven for a woman and eight for a fool. I don't know how true it is. Sometimes I feel as if I could stay in bed for ever."

"It's coming to the boil, love."

"So it is, my pet. Where are the mugs?"

Albert fetches them from the cupboard and Rose spoons in some cocoa, pours in the steaming milk and stirs. She gives Albert a sweet smile. "And now it's up the stairs to Bedfordshire."

"I'll check everything first," he says.

"Lights?"

"Yes."

"Doors?"

"Of course, my darling."

"See you presently, then."

"Careful how you go with those mugs, then."

A fall downstairs? Probably fatal at this age. Maybe that's

the answer—the loose stair-rod near the top. Not entirely reliable, more's the pity.

In bed, sipping her cocoa, Rose says, "Nice and cosy. Pity it can't stay on all night."

"The electric blanket? Dangerous," says Albert. "They don't recommend it."

"Never mind. I've got my hottie and my kettle ready."

"That's right."

The hot-water bottle and the electric kettle are on Rose's bedside table ready for the moment, about two in the morning, when her feet get cold. She will then switch on the light above her head, flick the switch on the kettle and wait for it to heat up. Some nights Albert doesn't notice the light and the kettle being switched on, but he unfailingly hears the slow crescendo of the kettle coming to the boil. Then Rose will fill the hot-water bottle and say, "Have I disturbed you, dear? It's only me filling my hottie."

Depressed, Albert stares at the wrinkled skin on the surface of his cocoa. Separate bedrooms might have been the answer, but he's never suggested it. Rose regards the sharing of the bed as the proof of a successful marriage. "We've never spent a single night apart, except for the time I was in hospital. Not a single night. I look at other couples and I know, I just know, that they don't sleep in the same bed any more." So the guest bedroom is only ever used by guests—her sister from Somerset once a year when the Chelsea Flower Show is on and, once, his friend Harry from army days.

Rose says, "Did you notice the Barnetts this afternoon? Am I mistaken, or were they being just a bit crotchety with each other?"

A night in the guest room would be bliss. Uninterrupted sleep. Just to be spared the inevitable "Have I disturbed you, dear?" at two in the morning.

"Albert, dear."

"Mm?"

"I don't think you were listening. I was asking if you noticed anything about John and Marcia this afternoon."

"John and Marcia?"

"The Barnetts. At bridge."

"Something wrong with their game?"

"No. I'm talking about the way they behaved towards each other. It may have been just my imagination, but I thought Marcia was more prickly with him than usual—as if they'd had words before we arrived. Didn't you notice it?"

"Not that I can recall," says Albert.

"When he had to re-deal because of the card that turned face up?"

"Really?"

"And when he reached for the chocolate biscuit. She was really sharp with him then, lecturing him about his calories. He looked so silly with his hand stuck in the air over the plate of biscuits. You *must* remember that."

"The chocolate biscuit. I do."

"Unnecessary, I thought."

"True."

"Humiliating the poor man."

"Yes."

"I mean, it isn't as if John is grossly enormous. He's got a bit of a paunch, but he's over seventy, for pity's sake. You expect a man to have a paunch by then."

"Goes without saying," says Albert, who actually has no paunch at all.

Rose drains the last of her cocoa. "You know what would do those two a power of good?"

"What's that?"

"If they spent some time apart from each other. Since he's retired, she sees him all day long. They're not adjusted to it."

"What would he do on his own?"

"I don't know. What do men do with themselves? Golf, or bowls. Fishing."

"When I go fishing, you always come with me and sit on the riverbank talking."

"That's different, isn't it? We're inseparable. We don't need to get away from each other. We haven't the slightest desire to be alone."

There is an interval of silence.

Rose resumes. "They won't catch you and me saying unkind things to each other in public, will they?"

"Or in private," says Albert.

She turns and smiles. "You're right, my love. Never a cross word in forty-seven years."

"Forty-eight."

Rose frowns. "No dear, forty-seven. This is 1995. We were married in 1948. The difference is forty-seven."

"Yes, but we met in 1947."

"I wasn't counting that," Rose says.

"It's another year."

"Of course, looked at like that . . ."

"No arguments when we were courting. Lovers' tiffs, they would have been."

"But there weren't any. Ah, well." She puts her mug on the bedside table and switches out the light on her side. "It's far too late for mental arithmetic. Time to get my beauty sleep. Nighty-night, darling." She turns for the goodnight kiss. They've never gone to sleep without the goodnight kiss, in forty-seven years, or is it forty-eight?

Their lips meet briefly.

"Sweet dreams."

Albert gets rid of his mug and reaches for the light switch. He yawns, wriggles down and turns away from her, wondering what time the library opens.

He's in an aircraft about to take off for Australia. Off for a long holiday, time to adjust, to get over the grief, he has been telling everyone. The engines of the Jumbo are roaring, louder by the second, building to the immense power needed for take-off.

A voice says, "Have I disturbed you, dear?"

"What?"

"It's only me filling my hottie."

He emerges from the dream and looks at the clock. Five past two.

"I couldn't survive without my hottie," Rose says. "I don't know how you manage, really I don't."

"Marvellous circulation," Albert says silently, moving his lips unseen.

Rose says, "It must be your marvellous circulation. Well, there it is: a nice hot bottle for my poor cold feet. Now I'll be off to sleep again in two shakes of a lamb's tail."

Forty minutes later, Albert is still awake, thinking about ways of faking a suicide.

He is up as usual on the dot of six, groping for his slippers. He feels as if he could sleep three more hours, given the opportunity, but the habit of rising at six is too deeply rooted ever to change. He knows he'll feel better after the first cup of tea.

He edges around the bed to her side and unplugs the electric kettle.

Picking it up, he shuffles towards the bathroom.

Down in the kitchen, he cleans the saucepan and the spoon from the night before and wipes the surface clean. The kettle boils.

The tea is a life-saver.

In the library, while Rose is looking at the Romance section, Albert covertly inspects a volume entitled *Essentials of Forensic Medicine.* The chapter on Suffocation and Asphyxia runs to several pages. The list of post-mortem appearances, external and internal, is so daunting that he abandons the whole idea. But another chapter, Electrocution, catches his eye and captures his imagination.

"Do you want to borrow it?"

He snaps the book shut and looks to his right. Rose is at his side. He pushes it back into the first space he can see and says, "No, I was just browsing really."

"This is the medical section, isn't it?"

"Yes, I was only whiling away the time, checking up on my rheumatism. Have you picked yours, my love?"

"I'm going to borrow three, just in case I find I've read one of them before."

"Good thinking."

That afternoon, when Rose is deep in her romantic novel, Albert tries to slip away unnoticed to the bedroom.

"Where are you off to, honeybunch?"

"I think some air must have got into one of the radiators. I'd like to check."

Rose says admiringly, "My handyman."

"I shouldn't be more than twenty minutes."

"I think I *may* have read this. I'm not sure."

"If you have, you could always try one of the others."

He goes upstairs, straight to the bed and lifts up the undersheet on Rose's side. The electric blanket lies there, the single size, only on her side—because his marvellous circulation keeps him warm without artificial help. This blanket been doing its job for at least ten years and has lost most of its original colour. The fabric at the edges is getting frayed, and where her feet go, it has worn thin. He stares at it thoughtfully. He looks at the flex leading to the twin point where it is kept plugged in.

"Will it take long, dear?" Rose calls up. She must be standing at the foot of the stairs.

Hastily, Albert tugs the undersheet over the electric blanket again.

"Not long, my dear," he answers, adding in a whisper, "It should be very quick."

"Shall I put the kettle on? I wouldn't mind a cup."

"Good idea."

A few precious minutes. He folds the sheet back again, takes a penknife from his pocket, opens it, and begins scraping at the thin covering where her feet go. Cutting would be too obvious. It must look as if it has worn away naturally. He scrapes at several places and finally the threads begin to part and the copper element beneath is laid bare. He continues to work, exposing more of it, until he gets the call that the tea is ready downstairs. He scoops the loose threads into his hand, pockets the penknife and straightens the undersheet and tucks it in.

"Is that job done, my love?" Rose calls up.

"I hope so, my dear," answers Albert, planning the next part of the operation. It can wait until the evening.

"Have some tea, then. You deserve it."

About nine-thirty, after watching the news on television, he gets up as usual to take the kettle upstairs and switch on the electric blanket. Rose remains in her chair, knitting. Albert has done this so many times that he doesn't even have to tell her where he is going.

He collects the kettle, fills it with water in the kitchen, and carries it upstairs, placing it on Rose's bedside table. He switches on the electric blanket.

The hot water bottle is in the bathroom as usual, and has to be emptied. He unscrews it and stands it upside down in the wash basin to drain. Then he gets to work on the stopper. He pulls the rubber washer away from the base. This should ensure that the bottle leaks. To be quite certain, he makes a test, half-filling it, screwing in the stopper and holding it upside down. Sure enough, it drips steadily.

The preparations completed, he goes downstairs and joins Rose for the last hour before retiring.

When the milk is simmering in the saucepan, Rose asks, "Did you remember to switch on the blanket, Albert darling?"

"An hour ago, my love."

"So thoughtful."

"I think the milk—"

"Quick! The mugs."

Rose lifts the saucepan from the hob. Albert places the mugs beside the cocoa tin and Rose does the rest.

Everything is in place, as the politicians like to say. There is little else for Albert to do. At two in the morning, he will be wakened as usual while Rose fills the hot water bottle. She will push it down by her cold feet. In two shakes of a lamb's tail, as she will tell him, she will be asleep. For the next hour it will seep, seep over the undersheet, slowly saturating the electric blanket. While it remains warm, she won't notice. And when he judges the moment right, Albert will get out of bed, move around in the dark and switch on the blanket.

An unfortunate accident, they will decide at the inquest. Faulty equipment.

"Is it up the stairs to Bedfordshire?" says Rose.

"I think it is, dear."

"Will you lock the doors and turn out the lights?"

"Depend upon it," says Albert.

In bed, they drink their last cup of cocoa together, sitting up.

"People are so stupid," says Rose.

"What do you mean, dear?" says Albert.

"When you hear about so many marriages breaking up. So much unhappiness. If they'd only have a little more consideration for each other."

"True," says Albert.

You bloody old hypocrite, thinks Rose. Driving me to the brink of insanity with your sanctimonious smile and your "Yes, my darling," while you pursue your own selfish ways, waking me every blasted morning at six. Heaving yourself up with a groan and a yawn, to put on your slippers, regardless that it all causes a minor earthquake in the bed. Groping around the edge of the mattress to collect the damned kettle. Switching on the bathroom light. Flushing the toilet. Clumping downstairs and turning on the radio. Forty-seven years of it, I've endured. His farting, his fishing and his football on television.

And never a cross word between us. I wouldn't give you that satisfaction. I've held out all this time.

"Oh, dear."

"What's the matter, love?" says Albert.

"I've forgotten to go to the bathroom—and just when I was getting nice and cosy." She sighs. "I suppose I shall have to get out."

"That's one thing I can't do for you," says Albert.

"Snuggle down, dear. I shan't be long."

From the bathroom Rose collects a chair and takes it to the landing, stands on it and removes the bulb from the landing light. She returns the chair to the bathroom and collects the length of Albert's fishing twine she has earlier concealed under the mat. She takes it to the top of the stairs and attaches it firmly to a nail in the skirting board. Then she ties the other end to one of the banisters to form a tripwire over the top stair. In the dark at six in the morning he will never see it.

Rose returns to bed and gets in.

"Nighty-night, my darling."

"Sleep well, sweetpea."

They exchange the goodnight kiss and turn out their lights.

The Odstock Curse

"**F**inally, ladies and gentlemen, finally I want to come close to home, to your home, that is to say, to Odstock and the bizarre events that happened in your village almost two hundred years ago, events that I venture to suggest still have the capacity to chill your spines."

Dr Tom Staniforth peered over half-glasses at his awestruck audience. Truth to tell, he felt uneasy himself, not at his spine- chilling material so much as the fact that he had consented to give this talk to an open meeting in a village hall on—of all evenings—October 31st. The timing had not been his suggestion and neither had the title, *Horrors for Halloween*. He dreaded the possibility that some university colleague had seen the posters or otherwise got wind that a senior member of the Social Anthropology Department was sensation-mongering in the wilds of Wiltshire. He had come simply because Mother had insisted upon it. Pearl Staniforth had arranged the whole thing as a personal tribute to a former colleague of her late husband. And now, wearing one of her appalling red velvet hats, Mother was seated beside this old gentleman in the second row giving a sub-commentary and beaming maternally at regular intervals.

He was almost through, thank God.

"Forgive me if what I have to say about the Odstock curse is familiar to most of you, but I suggest it can still bear telling. I thought it would be instructive in the first place to relate the legend and afterwards to pick out the truth as far as one can verify it from reliable sources—by which I mean parish records, legal documents and, perhaps less reliable, the memoir of a contemporary witness, the village blacksmith. In the anthropological scale of things, it is all very recent." He paused, widening his eyes. Having abandoned his academic scruples, he might as well milk the subject for melodrama. Spacing his words, he went on, "In the churchyard is an old gravestone partially covered by a briar rose. The stone has an intriguing inscription: '*In memory of Joshua Scamp who died April 1st, 1801. May his brave deed be remembered here and hereafter.*'"

With strange timing came a distant rumble of thunder that cued an uneasy murmur in the audience. The storm had been threatening for hours.

"Thank you, Josh, we heard the commercial," Tom Staniforth adroitly remarked, giving the opportunity for everyone to laugh aloud and ease the tension. "The brave deed is a matter of record. The unfortunate Mr Scamp allowed himself to be hanged for a crime he did not commit. He was a gypsy accused of stealing a horse, which was a capital offence in those Draconian times. The real thief and villain of the piece was his feckless son-in-law, Noah Lee, who not only stole the horse but planted a coat belonging to Joshua at the scene of the crime. Joshua was arrested. He refused to plead and maintained a stoic silence throughout his interrogation and trial. He went to the gallows—a public execution in Salisbury—without naming the true culprit. You see, his daughter Mary was expecting a child and he could not bear to see her bereft of a husband, facing a life of misery and destitution.

"Joshua's heroic act might have gone unremarked were it not for the gypsy community, who protested his innocence. They recovered the corpse of the hanged man from the prison authorities, brought him home to Odstock and gave him a Christian burial. Hundreds attended. And later the same year the real horse-thief, Noah Lee, was arrested at Winchester for stealing a hunter. He was duly hanged, which you may think made a mockery of Scamp's noble sacrifice. But the truth emerged because Joshua's daughter Mary no longer felt constrained to remain silent. Great sympathy was extended to her and she was well cared for. And Joshua Scamp became a gypsy martyr. The briar rose was planted at the head of his grave and a yew sapling at the foot. Each year on the anniversary of his execution they would make a pilgrimage here, large numbers from all the surrounding counties.

"Now it seems that after some years the annual visit of the gypsies became a nuisance." Another clap of thunder tested Staniforth's powers of improvisation.

"Have it your way, Josh," he quipped, and earned more laughter, "but there must have been some justification for the rector of Odstock to have sworn in twenty-five special constables to keep the peace. Well, the blacksmith's memoir claims that the yew tree by the grave had become unsightly and the rector insisted that it was pulled up by the roots—a job that the sexton duly carried out. Unfortunately this measure deeply upset the gypsies and a mob of them descended on the church. There were scuffles as attempts were made to keep them off the sacred ground. The crowning insult was when Mother Lee, the Gypsy Queen, was evicted from the church, where she had come to pray, and the door locked behind her. The lady in question was venerated by the gypsies. She was the elderly mother of Noah Lee, the horse-thief, and she had earned enormous respect for disowning her son and praising the bravery of Joshua Scamp.

"Whatever the rights and wrongs of it—and I imagine there was cause for grievance on both sides—the gypsies were deeply angered. They took their revenge by breaking into the church and attacking everything inside. The pews, the windows, the communion plate, the vestments, the bell-ropes: nothing was spared. The constables were vastly outnumbered and powerless to prevent the desecration. This is all on record.

"Late in the evening, Mother Lee, having allegedly spent some hours in the Yew Tree Inn, returned to the church-yard where her people were still at work uprooting trees. Perched on the church gate, she called them to order and addressed a crowd that included most of the villagers as well as her own flock. Gypsies, as you know, have always claimed powers of divination. Speaking in a voice of doom Mother Lee pointed to the rector and told him that he would not be preaching in Odstock at that time next year. She told the church-warden who had engaged the special constables, a farmer by the name of Hodding, 'For two years bad luck shall tread upon thy heels. No son of thine shall ever farm thy land.' The sexton was informed that by next April he would be in his own grave. Two half-gypsy brothers unwise enough to have been employed as special constables were told, 'Bob and Jack Bachelor, you will die together, sudden and quick.' And finally she dealt with the door that had been slammed in her face: 'I put a curse on this church door. From this time whoever shall lock 'un shall die within a year.' And legend has it that all the curses came true."

Tom Staniforth let the drama of the story hold sway for a moment. He looked out at his audience and made brief eye contact with several. How gullible people are, he thought. They patently believe this codswallop.

"However, I promised to deal in facts, not legend," he resumed in a businesslike tone. "Let us see what survives of the Odstock curse when we test it against reliable sources.

The parish records are helpful. They tell us that the rector retired within a year, so that part is true, though we have no contemporaneous evidence for the throat cancer which was said to have robbed him of his power of speech. Nothing is known of bad luck afflicting Farmer Hodding except that his wife had a series of stillborn infants, which was not unusual in those days. I was unable to verify the story that his crops failed and his herd had to be slaughtered after contracting anthrax. The sexton, it is true, appears in the records of burials a few months after he was cursed. As for the Bachelor brothers, they are not mentioned in the register again, but superstition has it that a pair of skeletons found in 1929 in a shallow grave on Odstock Down belonged to them." Staniforth raised his hands to the audience. "So what? Even if they *were* the brothers, a supernatural explanation is unlikely. The possibility is high that the gypsies took revenge and disposed of the bodies. The so-called power of the gypsy's curse is undermined if they had to resort to murder to make it come true. To sum up, ladies and gentlemen, I have to say that I find the Odstock curse a beguiling story that, sadly for believers in the occult, falls well within the bounds of coincidence and manipulation."

He stepped from behind the table. "That concludes my talk. I hope you are reassured and will sleep peacefully tonight. I certainly intend to, and I have spent more time on these legends than most."

The reception he was given was gratifying. Pearl Staniforth, smiling this way and that as she clapped, prolonged it by at least ten seconds.

And there was a curious effect when the clapping died, because the storm outside had just broken over Odstock and the beating of rain on the roof appeared to sustain the applause. While the downpour continued no one was eager to leave, so the speaker invited questions.

A man at the back of the hall got up. He was one of the committee; earlier he had taken the money at the door. "What a wonderful talk, sir—a fitting subject for the occasion, and so eloquently delivered. I can't remember applause like that. Just one question, sir. I don't know if it was deliberate, only when you were discussing the evidence for the curse, you omitted to mention the gypsy's warning about the church door. What are your views on that?"

"I apologize," said Staniforth at once. "An oversight. I didn't mean to ignore it. The story goes that in the years since the curse was made, two people locked the door and suffered the promised fate within a year. But one is bound to ask how many hundreds, or thousands, must have turned the key and survived. You are up against statistical probability, you see." He smiled, a shade too complacently.

"No, sir," said the questioner in his broad south Wiltshire tones. "With respect, you're misinformed. The door has been locked twice since the curse, and only twice in almost two hundred years. The first time was in 1900, in defiance of the curse, when a carpenter was employed to make new gates. He was given the story, but he mocked it, turned the key and paid the price within the twelvemonth. They buried him under the path, between the gates he made and the door he locked. The second time was in the 1930s, when a locum was appointed while the rector was away. This locum dismissed the story as blasphemous and locked the door to uphold the power of the Lord, as he saw it. He was gathered shortly after. When the rector returned, he threw the key into the River Ebble just across the road and the church has never been locked since."

Deflated, Staniforth said, "I'm obliged to you. I stand corrected then, but I'd still like to see paper evidence of the two alleged deaths."

"If it didn't happen, why would the rector throw the key away?"

"Oh, the church rejects superstition as much as modern science does. No doubt he thought it the best way to put an end to such foolishness."

Happily for Staniforth the questioner was too polite to pursue the matter. The questions turned to the safer topic of witchcraft and after ten minutes a vote of thanks was proposed, coupled with the suggestion that as the rain had eased slightly it might be timely to call the evening to a halt.

For Tom Staniforth it had scarcely begun.

Old Walter Fremantle had invited the Staniforths back to his cottage for supper, not a prospect Tom relished, although he felt some obligation for the sake of his late father. Piers Staniforth and Walter Fremantle had gone through Cambridge together as history students and remained close friends even after their careers had diverged. Walter had become a museum curator and Piers a nationally known television archaeologist until his death abroad in the 1960s. From things Pearl had let slip occasionally it seemed that Walter had helped them financially after Piers died.

"Your father would have been so proud tonight," Pearl enthused while Tom cringed with embarrassment. "You had that audience in the palm of your hand—didn't he, Walter?"

"Oh, emphatically," said Walter, as he tried to pour brandy with a tremulous hand.

Tom offered to help. It was a case of all hands to the pump. Already his mother had supervised the microwave cooking and he had served the soup and the quiche. And it tasted good. Convenience food—but less of a risk than home cooking by a seventy-five-year-old bachelor.

They had not been settled long in deep armchairs in front of the fire when Walter launched into a confession. Frail as he appeared, he was still articulate and there could be no doubt that what he told Tom and his mother was profoundly important to him. "Your talk tonight has stirred me to raise a matter that has troubled me for many years. I didn't know you were an expert on the curse—didn't even realize you would mention it. Up to now I have hesitated to bring up the subject, mainly, I think, because I am a coward by nature."

"Far from it, Walter!" Pearl strove to reassure him.

Mother, will you shut up? thought Tom.

"It concerns Piers, your father. It was, I think, in 1962, towards the end of his life, that he came to see me for lunch one day. He was between expeditions, as I recall, just back from Nigeria and about to leave for South America in two or three weeks."

"Our life was like that," Pearl now chose to reminisce. "I scarcely saw him unless I went on the digs. I could have gone. The television people would have paid for me, but it was the travel, the packing and the unpacking. I was weary of it."

"Mother, Walter is trying to tell us something."

"Does that mean the rest of us have to be silent? It was never like that in the old days, was it, Walter?"

Walter gave a nod and a faint smile. "We were back from lunch and unpacking some of the objects Piers had generously brought back from Africa to present to the museum when I was phoned from downstairs and told that a woman had come into the museum and wished to donate an item to the local history collection. I'm afraid one gets all sorts of rubbish brought in and I was sceptical. This lady was apparently unwilling to return at some more convenient moment. However, Piers, ever the gentleman, insisted that I speak to her, so I invited her up to my office. The woman who presently came in was a gypsy, dressed like Carmen herself in a black skirt, white blouse and red shawl, which was most unsuitable because she was sixty at least, and large. I've nothing personal against such people, but she struck me immediately as someone I didn't care to deal with. My guess was that she wished to sell me something."

"They always do," said Pearl, "and if you don't buy they spit on your doorstep and give you the evil eye."

"Is that so? In fact, this person, who wouldn't give her name, incidentally, made herself a nuisance in another way, by relating the legend of the Odstock curse, at interminable length."

"How tedious," said Pearl, without much tact.

"I was familiar with the story," said Walter, "and I tried to tell her as much, but she would insist on giving us her version, which she claimed was gypsy lore. At another time I might have been more inclined to listen, because there is a lot of interest in preserving oral folklore, but my time with Piers was precious and she was invading it. Piers was extremely patient and good-mannered about the whole thing. I think it interested him."

"What was behind it?" Pearl asked.

"Mother, Walter is coming to that."

"Well, I've no need to keep you in suspense," said Walter. "She produced an iron key, heavily coated with rust, from under her shawl and placed it on my desk. Her son, she said, had found it on the river bank during the summer when the water level went down several feet. As a true Romany she knew it to be the cursed key of Odstock Church."

"Good Lord! And she expected you to buy it?"

"She was making a gift of it to the museum. She said she wouldn't offer it to the church in case someone tried to defy the curse. She said it would be safer in a display cabinet in a museum. I asked her if she seriously believed that the so-called curse was still potent. She gave me a look fit to shatter my skull and said that Joshua Scamp himself would deal with anyone so foolish as to lock the church door."

"The hanged man?"

"Yes. The curse is everlasting."

"Are you saying she actually believed that Scamp had some influence in the world of the living?"

"My dear boy, it's the gypsy version of the tale. I thought it poppycock myself."

"Exactly the point I was about to make," said Tom. "You were being asked to believe in a malevolent spirit, as well as the curse. There are limits."

Walter nodded. "That was my view when she presented me with the key. After she had finally been persuaded to leave, Piers asked me how much of the story I believed and I told him it was no doubt founded on a real incident that had been much embroidered over the years. Piers asked whether I proposed to display the key in the museum and I said certainly not. It seemed to me unlikely in the extreme that a key recovered from the river would be the very one that the rector had thrown in thirty years ago. Piers was more cautious in delivering a verdict."

"That's Piers all over," Pearl commented with a smile.

"My point was that we had nothing with which to authenticate the key except the gypsy woman's assertion. I said the only way to test it was to take the damned thing to the church and see if it fitted the lock. Piers advised me most adamantly not to take such a risk. He said the woman had impressed him and the power of the gypsies should never be under-estimated. We had an amiable dispute. I remember accusing him of superstition and he said he'd rather be superstitious and safe than sceptical and dead." Walter hesitated and stared into the fire. Some of the rain was penetrating the chimney and hissing as the droplets touched the embers.

Tom asked, "Did you ever try the key in the door?"

Walter turned and Tom noticed that his eyes were suddenly moist and red at the edges. "Yes, I did. It was from vanity, really. I wanted the satisfaction of telling my old friend that I had been right. I rose early the very next day, determined to prove my point. I was ninety per cent sure the key wouldn't fit, but if it did, I'd display it in my local collection with a note about the execution of Joshua Scamp and its aftermath. I remember it was a glorious morning and the rooks in the tall trees outside seemed to be chorusing me as I walked up the path to the door of St Mary's."

Pearl said impatiently, "Did it fit?"

"Oh, yes. It turned the mechanism inside. The bolt engaged. Only briefly, because I turned it back in the same movement. I was shaking at the discovery."

"Remarkable."

"And you lived to tell the tale," Tom said robustly to the old man. "Well done, Walter! You struck a blow for rational thought. What happened to the key? Did you put it on display?"

"It's in front of you, hanging on that nail over the fireplace."

Tom looked up at the notorious key, a rusty, corroded thing with a shank no longer than his smallest finger. It appeared innocuous enough. "May I handle it?"

"Please don't."

"It doesn't frighten me in the least."

"No. For God's sake hear me out."

"I thought you'd finished."

Walter shook his head. "Bear with me. This is painful. A month or so after trying the key in the door, I was afflicted with physical symptoms I couldn't account for. I became weary after no exertion at all and I lost weight steadily. My doctor put me through no end of tests. I had a full body scan. Everything. There was nothing they could diagnose, yet anyone could see I was wasting away. It was obvious to me that I wouldn't see the year out unless some miracle reversed the process. I kept remembering how I had defied the curse and locked the church door."

"It wouldn't have been that," said Tom. "Whatever was amiss with you, it wouldn't have been that."

"May I continue?" said Walter quietly. "One morning I was shopping in Salisbury and a woman approached me and asked if I would buy a sprig of heather for good luck. She was the gypsy who had presented me with the key. I said I needed all the good luck that was going and told her what I had done. She hadn't recognized me, I had lost so much weight. She was visibly shocked by what I told her. I'm afraid I was feeling so wretched that I begged for her help. I offered her any money if she would help me to lift the curse. She could name the sum. She would accept nothing, not even a silver coin for the heather. She said my only chance was to wait for All Soul's Night—Halloween— and then to invoke the spirit of Joshua Scamp by chanting his name three times. I was so desperate about my health that I was perfectly willing to try, but the rest of her advice was more difficult. I had to find a believer in the curse and speak that person's name aloud." His voice was faltering. "The curse would then be lifted from me and transferred."

Pearl's hand went to her throat. "Oh, my God!"

Tom felt his muscles tighten.

The old man said, "Yes, I thought of Piers. I remembered how he had almost pleaded with me not to try the key in the church door. He was a believer. In the few days left before Halloween, I wrestled with my conscience, telling myself it was all hocus-pocus anyway and Piers was an ocean away in South America. How could the shade of a dead gypsy who had never travelled out of England trouble a modern man in Peru? Yet I still hesitated. If I had not felt so wretchedly ill I would not have taken the risk. When you are reduced to shaking skin and bones, you will try anything. So on the night of Halloween, thirty years ago this night, I did as the gypsy advised. When I had three times invoked the spirit of Joshua Scamp, I spoke the name of my oldest friend." Walter bent forward and covered his eyes.

"What happened?"

His answer came in sobs. "Nothing. Nothing that night. For a week . . . no change. Then . . . the second week, my appetite returned . . . I felt stronger, actually recovering." He looked up, weeping uncontrollably. "In three months I was back to my old weight. The only thing I wanted was a postcard from my old friend in Peru." He paused in an effort to control his emotions and added, barely audibly, "It never came. I heard one evening on the television news about the mud-slip, the fatal accident to Piers. Devastating. What can I say to you both? Through my selfishness you lost a husband and a father."

Before Pearl could respond, Tom said gently but firmly, "Walter, it's typical of your generosity to tell us this, and I'm sure it seemed to make sense to you at the time, but really it's a misconstruction of events. It doesn't bear analysis. I'm sure I speak for Mother when I say you can sleep easy in the knowledge that you had nothing whatsoever to do with Dad's death. It was an accident."

"No."

"Your health improved because you threw off the effects of the virus, or whatever it was. We've all had mysterious illnesses that come and go. Yours was more severe than most."

"I know what happened, my son. Believe me, I was dying. I know why it went away. I don't deserve to be here. Your father should have been at that lecture tonight, not me."

Tom leaned closer to him and said earnestly, "The whole tenor of my talk was that superstitions are founded on coincidence and false reasoning and this is a classic example. You were too close to events to judge them analytically.

You accepted the supernatural explanation. Come on, Walter, you're an intelligent man of good education."

Pearl chimed in with, "I forgive you, Walter."

Tom swung around in his chair. He was incensed. "For God's sake, Mother—there's nothing to forgive! He had nothing to do with Father's death. This whole thing about the curse is mumbo-jumbo—and I'm about to prove it." He got up and snatched the key from its place over the hearth.

"Don't!" cried Walter.

Tom's mother shrieked his name, but he had already crossed the room, grabbed his coat off the hook and stepped outside.

Pearl screamed.

Tom strode along the road towards the church, regardless of the driving rain.

Odstock Church stands alone, a few hundred yards from the rest of the village. Distant lightning gave Tom Staniforth intermittent glimpses of the agitated trees along each side of the road. The castellated tower and steep tiled roof of St Mary's came into view, silvering dramatically each time a flash came. He refused to be intimidated.

Too far behind Tom to influence events, his mother and Walter Fremantle had started in pursuit. Neither was in any condition to move fast, yet they were trying to run.

Tom reached the church gates. Without pause, he stepped under the archway formed by two pollarded trees and up to the timber-framed porch. A lantern mounted on the highest beam lighted the path. The church doors were of faded oak fitted into a stone arch, with iron strap-hinges and a turning latch with a ring handle. A brighter flash of lightning turned the whole thing white. Tom found the rusted key-escutcheon, thrust in the key and turned it. The mechanism was a devil to shift. He was afraid that the key would snap under the strain. Finally it turned through a full arc and he heard the movement of the bolt sliding home.

Done.

He didn't withdraw the key. He wanted others to know that someone with a mind free of superstition had defied the gypsy's curse.

Hearing the footsteps of his mother and old Walter Fremantle, Tom stepped aside, away from the door. They would see the key in the lock. He was triumphant.

The glory was brief. Lightning struck the church roof. The thunder—an immense clap—was instantaneous. The ground itself vibrated. Scores of tiles loosened, slid down the pitched roof and fell. Two, at least, razor-sharp, cracked against Tom's skull and felled him like a pin in an alley.

Neither Walter nor Pearl saw the body when they first came through the gate. The porch-light had blown when the lightning struck. They groped at the door, feeling for the key in the lock.

Walter located it and gasped, "He did it. I tried to stop him. I tried!"

Pearl found her son lying insensible against a gravestone, with blood oozing from a head wound. Whimpering, she got to her knees and cradled his damaged head. He made no sound.

Pearl rocked her son.

"Is he . . . ?" Walter could not bring himself to speak the word.

Pearl ignored him anyway. The pride she had felt in the village hall when Tom was speaking with such authority had ended in blood and tears. She sobbed for the limp burden in her arms and the bigotry of rational thinking. She mourned her wise, never-to-be-forgotten husband and her rash, misguided son.

Gently, Pearl let Tom's bloodied head rest in her lap.

She brought her hands together in front of her, fingers tightly intertwined. Then in a clear voice she called the name of Joshua Scamp. She called it three times. She cried out passionately, "Take Walter Fremantle. He knows the power of the curse better than any man, having used it to kill my husband. He is a believer. Take him. For pity's sake, take him instead."

She remembered nothing else. She didn't see old Walter unlock the church door, remove the key and take it across the road to the river and throw it in. She didn't see him collapse as he tried to climb up the bank.

The next morning, in the intensive care ward at Odstock Hospital, Tom Staniforth's eyelids quivered and opened. His mother, in a hospital dressing-gown, watching through a glass screen, turned to the young policeman beside her, gripped his hand and squeezed it. "He's going to live!"

"I'm happy for you, Ma'am," said the constable. "Happy for myself, too. Maybe your son can tell me what happened last night. What with you having passed out as well, and old Mr Fremantle dead of a heart attack, I was afraid we'd have no witnesses. I'm supposed to write a report of the incident, you see. I know it was the lightning that struck the church, but it's difficult working out what happened, with all three of you going down like that."

"However did you find us?" Pearl asked.

"Wasn't me, Ma'am. Now I'd really like to trace the man who alerted us, but I'm not optimistic. No one seems to know him. Right strange chap, he was. Came bursting into a farm cottage soon after midnight, in fancy dress from one of they Halloween parties. Top hat and smock and a piece of rope around his neck. He nearly scared the family out of their wits, ranting on about a dead'un at the church door. Didn't leave his name. Just raced off into the storm. Drunk, I expect. But I reckon you owe him, you and your son."

*

Author's footnote: I should like to pay credit to three sources for the story of Joshua Scamp and the Curse of Odstock. *Wiltshire Folklore,* by Kathleen Wiltshire (Compton Russell, Salisbury, 1975) gives the version told by Canon Bouverie about 1904; *Wiltshire Folklore and Legends,* by Ralph Whitlock (Robert Hale, London, 1992) has Hiram Witt the black-smith's memoir of 1870; and the fictional story of the lecture and its consequences was suggested by my son, Philip, who visited Odstock with me at Easter, 1993.

A Parrot Is Forever

That eye was extraordinary, dominated by the yellow iris and fringed by a ring of spiky black eyelashes. In the short time I had been watching, the pupil had contracted to little more than a microdot.

"It's magnificent, but it's a lot larger than I expected," I told the young woman who was its keeper.

She said, "Macaws are big birds."

At this safe distance from the perch, I said, "I was expecting something smaller. A parrot, I was told."

"Well, a macaw is a member of the parrot family."

This member of the parrot family raised itself higher and stared over my head, excluding me, letting me know that I was unworthy of friendship at this first meeting.

"No doubt we'll learn to get along with each other," I said. "I'm willing to try, if the bird is." I took a tentative step closer.

Too close for the macaw, because it thrust its head at me and gave a screech like a power drill striking steel.

I jerked back. "Wow!"

The keeper said, "It's a pity. Roger was just getting used to us. Now he has to start over again."

First lesson: you address parrots as you would humans.

The impersonal "it" was unacceptable. This was Roger, a personality.

Roger. About right for this rebarbative old bird. Roger is one of those names redolent of wickedness. Jolly Roger, the pirate flag; eighteenth century rakes rogering wenches; Roger the lodger, of so many dirty jokes. The glittering eye and that great, black beak curved over the mouth in a permanent grin would make you believe this Roger had been everywhere and tried everything.

"He's called 'Sir Roger,' according to his papers," said the young woman, wanting to say something in the parrot's favour. "We were taught a dance at school called Sir Roger de Coverley. I expect he's named after that."

Fat chance, I thought. My Uncle George, the parrot's former owner, was never a country dancer. He was a diamond robber. A long time ago, in May, 1954, Uncle George and two others held up a Hatton Garden merchant and stole twenty-seven uncut diamonds valued at half a million pounds. Half a million was a fortune in 1954. The advantage of uncut stones—if you steal them—is that they are difficult to identify, so it was also a clever heist. The only blemish on this brilliant crime was that the three robbers were rounded up within a week and given long prison sentences. But the diamonds were never recovered. Two of the robbers died inside. Uncle George served twenty-six years. After his release, he seemed mysteriously to come into money. He emigrated to Spain, the Costa del Sol. It was a wise move. He lived another fifteen years, without ostentation, but comfortably, in a villa, in the company of a *señorita* half his age.

In my ultra-respectable family, Uncle George was a taboo topic. My father rarely mentioned him, and never spoke of the robbery. I only learned of it after Dad died and I was going through his papers. There was a newspaper cutting about the release from jail of the old diamond robber.

Now my uncle was dead. He'd gone peacefully last Christmas, in his own bed, at the age of seventy-nine. It seemed he'd known his time was coming and he had made appropriate arrangements. This Blue and Yellow Macaw was bequeathed to me.

In January I had received a solicitor's letter advising me of my legacy. At first I thought it was a practical joke. I was told I must wait six months while the parrot served the six-month quarantine period that applies to all imported animals—as if I was impatient to meet this creature! I hadn't asked for the parrot. I knew nothing about parrots. I was an actor, for pity's sake. How would I fit a Blue and Yellow Macaw into my life? The solicitor informed me when I phoned him that he understood parrots make fine companions. As for my acting career, he'd heard that the late Sir Ralph Richardson had kept a parrot, and it hadn't held him back.

I was in a spot. Only a complete toe-rag would deny an old man's dying wish. My uncle must have been devoted to the parrot to make arrangements for it to be shipped to England. But oh, Uncle George, why to me?

True, I was the only surviving relative, but I have another theory. Uncle George may have seen me on cable television in the part of a wise-cracking villain in some corny crime series. It ran for some weeks. I think he identified with the part.

The crushing irony of all this was that the rest of the estate, consisting of the Spanish villa and all its contents and enough pesetas to provide many years of comfortable living, all went to the *señorita* Uncle George had shared the last years of his life with. The parrot came to me, I guessed because Isabella said she'd strangle it if Uncle George didn't get rid of it.

So here I was at Bird & Board, the aviary close to London Airport. Roger had completed his quarantine and now I had arrived to claim him.

"This is the box he travels in," the young woman informed me, opening the welded mesh grille that was the door of a sturdy plastic pet-container. It was the sort of box used for cats and dogs, the only concession to Roger's comfort being a wooden perch fitted some three inches off the floor and much chewed by his sharp beak. "He doesn't like it much. Would you like me to put him inside?"

"Please."

Roger had seen the box and was already getting agitated, swaying and ruffling his feathers. The moment the keeper started putting on a pair of leather gauntlets, there was a flexing of wings and a series of blood-curdling screams that started off all the other birds and created bedlam.

"They can be noisy," she said as if she were telling me something. "Hope you're on good terms with your neighbours." Skilfully avoiding the thrusting black beak, she grasped the big macaw by the neck and legs, lifted him off the perch and placed him in the box. "He'll calm down presently," she shouted.

And he did. She draped a cloth over the front and the darkness subdued him.

She asked me, "Have you kept a parrot before?"

"No."

"You've got treats in store, then. If Roger gets unbearable, you can always see if one of the tropical bird gardens will take him."

"Would you?" I asked hopefully.

"Couldn't possibly. We deal only with birds in quarantine."

"So I'm lumbered."

"Try not to think of it that way," she said compassionately, then added, "That will be a hundred and fifty pounds, please."

"What will?"

"Roger's account—for staying here. We can't do it for nothing, you know."

"Some legacy!" I said, getting out my chequebook.

"If you do sell him," she told me, "don't sell him cheap. They're worth a few hundred, you know."

"So I'm finding out," I told her as I wrote the cheque.

I carried the pet-container to the place where I'd left my car. Heaven knows, Roger had given me no grounds for friendship, but I muttered reassuring things though the ventilation slits. I continued to speak to him at intervals all the way along the motorway. At Heston I stopped at a garden centre and bought some heavy-duty leather gloves.

When I got home and opened the pet-container, it was some time before my new house-guest emerged. Having seen the size of his beak, and read a little about the damage one peck can inflict, I didn't reach inside for him. In fact, I was extremely nervous of him. After waiting some time, I left the room to get myself a coffee. When I returned, Roger had stepped out to inspect his new quarters.

If nothing else, he had brought some much-needed colour to my home. His back and wings were vivid sky-blue, his chest and the underside of the wings purest yellow, his crown and forehead dark green. Spectacular—but at what cost?

I'd gone to the trouble of making a perch out of beech wood and installing it in my living room. What I hadn't appreciated was that Roger wasn't capable of getting up there unaided. His wings were clipped. I wasn't ready yet to handle him, even with the leather gauntlets. But I didn't need to bother, because he made his own choice. After a cursory inspection of the room, he decided to occupy the sheet-feed of my printer, which projected at a convenient angle and left just enough room for his long blue tail feathers. He reached it by scaling the waste-paper basket and the top drawer of the desk, using his beak and claws.

Once on his new perch, he established his right of residence by hunching his shoulders, lifting his tail and depositing a green dropping on the script of my next TV part, which I'd left behind the printer. I felt the same way about the script, but I replaced it with an old newspaper.

There was sunflower seed and corn in the feeding bowl attached to the perch. I succumbed and moved the bowl close to the printer. The parrot appeared to have no interest in food. He watched me keenly from my office machinery, I suppose to see if I had plans to eject him. To foster confidence, I removed the pet-container altogether and put it in the spare room.

There is no doubt that parrots are exceptional in their ability to communicate their feelings to humans. They have eloquent eyes that dilate and contract at will. The skin around the face can blush pink. With the angle of the head, the posture of the shoulders and the action of the claws, they can express curiosity, boredom, sorrow, anger, approval, domination and submission. All that, before they let go with their voices. Mercifully, Roger hadn't yet screamed in my home.

That night, I left him perched on the sheet-feed. In the morning, although he still hadn't touched the food, he seemed interested to see me. Genuine trust was slow in developing on both sides, but he began to feed and the day came, about a week later, when he succeeded in manoeuvring his way across the furniture to the back of a chair I was seated in. Neither of us moved for some time. It was a distinct advance.

One morning the following week, perched on the printer as usual, Roger put his head at an angle, dilated his eyes and extended a claw to me. With some misgivings, I extended my arm. He gripped it at the wrist and transferred himself from the sheet-feed to me. Acting as a living perch, I walked slowly around the room. When I made to return him to the printer, he clawed his way higher up my arm until he was on my shoulder. He had decided I was not, after all, the enemy.

I suppose the discovery was mutual.

If all else fails, I thought, I can now audition for a part in *Treasure Island.*

In a couple of months, I learned to handle Roger, and he transferred to the purpose-built perch. He had a small silver ring around one of his legs and I could have chained him to the perch, but there was no need. He behaved reasonably well. True, he used his beak on things, but that is standard parrot behaviour. The worst damage he inflicted was to peck through my telephone cable. Sometimes it's an advantage to be incommunicado. At least a day passed before I realized I was cut off. I discovered the damage only when Roger fooled me with a perfect imitation of the phone's ringing tone. I picked up the receiver and the line was dead. This was the first inkling I had that he was capable of mimicry. In time, when he really settled in, he would greet visitors with "Hello, squire," or "Hello, darling," according to sex. He must have been taught by Uncle George. He had no other vocabulary and I didn't want to coach him. I think it undermines the dignity of animals to make them ape human behaviour.

As you must already have gleaned, Roger was winning me over. I found him amusing and appreciative of all the attention I could give him. There were moments when he would regard me intently, willing me to come forward and admire him, utterly still, yet beaming out such anticipation that I was compelled to stop whatever I was doing. The unblinking eyes would beguile me, seeming to penetrate to the depth of my being. As I went closer, he would make small movements on the perch, finally turning full circles and twitching his elegant tail. If I put my face against his plumage, the scent of the natural oils was exquisite.

One evening I returned late from a rehearsal and had a

horrible shock. Roger was missing. I dashed around the house calling his name before I noticed the broken window where the thief had got in. I was devastated. My poor parrot must have fought hard, because there were several of those spectacular blue tail feathers under his perch.

The police didn't give much comfort. "We've had parrots stolen before," said the constable who came. "It's just another form of crime, like nicking car radios. They know where to get rid of them. A parrot like yours will fetch a couple of hundred, easy. Did they take his cage as well?"

"He doesn't have a cage. He lives on that perch."

"How did you get him here in the first place?"

"In a pet-container. It's in the back room . . . I think." Even as I spoke, I knew it was gone. I'd been through the spare room and the box wasn't there. I should have noticed. Well, I had, in a way, but it hadn't registered in my brain until now. The bastards hadn't just taken Roger; they'd had the brass to take his box as well.

"We'll keep a look-out," said the constable in a tone that gave me no confidence. "Would you know your own bird? That's the problem. These Blue and Yellow Macaws all look the same."

I felt bereft. It was clear to me now how important that parrot had become to me. I was angry and guilty and impotent. I'm a peaceful man, or believed I was. I could have strangled the person who had taken Roger.

Each day, I called the police to see if there was news. They'd heard nothing. Almost a week went by. They advised me to get another bird. I didn't want another bird. I wanted Roger back.

I had to move the empty perch into the spare room because the sight of it was so upsetting. My work was suffering. I messed up an audition. I couldn't learn lines any more.

On the sixth day after Roger was stolen, a Sunday morning, my phone rang.

It was Roger.

Reader, don't give up. I haven't gone completely gaga over this parrot. Roger hadn't picked up the phone and dialled my number. Somebody else had. But I could hear Roger at the other end of the line. He was giving his imitation of the phone ringing.

The person who had dialled my number didn't speak. I said, "Who is this?" several times. Roger, in the background, was still mimicking the phone. It *could* have been a second phone, but I convinced myself it was not.

I guessed what it was about. The thief was checking whether I was home. He was thinking of breaking into my home again, perhaps to steal something else.

The line went dead after only a few seconds. Not a word had been spoken by the caller.

I was frustrated and enraged.

Fortunately, there is a way of tracing calls. I dialled the message system and obtained the caller's number. It's a computerised system and you aren't given the name or address.

I thought about going to the police and asking them to check the number, but I hadn't been impressed by the constable who had come to see me. He didn't regard a missing macaw as a high priority.

Instead, I waited an hour and then tried the number myself. It rang for some time before it was picked up and a woman's voice said, "Marwood Hotel."

Thinking rapidly, I said, "Is that the Marwood Hotel in Notting Hill Gate?"

She said, "I've never heard of one in Notting Hill Gate. We're the Marwood in Fulham. Gracechurch Road."

Fulham was just a ten-minute drive from where I lived. I told her I'd made a mistake. I put down the phone and went straight to the car.

Gracechurch Road was once a good address for the Edwardian middle classes. Now it stands under the shadow of the Hammersmith Fly-Over. The tall, brick villas have become seedy hotels and over-populated flats.

My approach wasn't subtle. I went in and asked the woman at the desk if the hotel welcomed pets.

She said in the voice I'd heard on the phone, "Provided they behave themselves."

"A parrot, for instance?"

"I don't know about parrots," she said dubiously.

"You have one here already, don't you?"

She said, "I wouldn't want another one like that. It makes a horrible sound when it's excited. Fit to burst your eardrums."

"Blue and yellow? Big?" I said, my heart racing.

She nodded.

I asked, "Does it belong to the hotel?"

"No, the foreign gentleman in number twelve. The top floor."

"When did he arrive?"

"About ten days ago."

"With the parrot?"

"No, he brought that in one day last weekend. In a box. He says it's only temporary."

"Is he up there now?"

She checked the board where the keys were hung. "He should be. If you want, I can ring up."

I said that on second thoughts I'd call back later. Simply going upstairs and knocking on the door would not be a wise course of action.

She didn't see me double around the side of the house to the back. These old buildings converted into hotels often have fire-escapes and this was no exception. It was the most basic sort, a vertical iron ladder fixed to the brickwork, with access to the large casement windows on each of the three upper floors. With luck, I wouldn't be visible to anyone inside.

This was a chance I had to take. I climbed about fifty rungs to the top floor. The window was a hinged one and it was open. Easy to open wider. There were extra rungs directly under it. All I needed to do was transfer sideways, put my leg over the sill and let myself in. First, I listened for sounds of movement from the room.

I could hear nothing.

I'm not much of an acrobat, but I succeeded in getting my legs through the window and scrambling into the room.

A voice I knew said, "Hello, squire."

Roger!

For me, that reunion was on a par with H. M. Stanley meeting Dr Livingstone.

Roger was perched on the footboard of a double bed. He recognized me. He lifted his claw—a signal that he wanted to transfer to my arm and so to my shoulder. Elated, I took a step towards him. There was a sound behind me. I was not conscious of anything else, except a crushing blow to the back of my head.

I don't know how long I was out.

When the world started up again for me, I was lying on the bed with my hands tied behind me. The foreign 'gentleman' had his thumb jammed into my eye, forcing it open. He spoke some words I didn't recognize.

My head ached. My vision was blurred, but clearing. He looked evil. His shoulders were huge.

I said, "I don't want trouble. I just want my parrot back."

He said with a strong Spanish inflexion, "You own this parrot?"

I told him who I was.

He spoke again. "This parrot Roger, he is stupid. He tell me nothing. Nothing."

I said, "He's just a parrot. What do you expect?"

"You ask what I expect. I expect you have talked to this parrot, yes? He tell you where diamonds are kept."

I said, "I don't know what the hell you're talking about."

He raised his arm and beat me across the face with the back of his hand. My lip split.

He shouted, "Your uncle had many diamonds, yes? Why he send you this parrot when he die?"

I said, "Just who are you?"

He grabbed my hair and forced my head back. "Now you are here, you will talk to Roger. Then he tell you some number, some number of box inside bank."

Box inside bank: I was beginning to understand. "A safe deposit number?"

"*Si.*"

"He doesn't speak numbers."

"Do it. Speak numbers now." Still grasping my hair, he hauled me off the pillow and towards the foot of the bed where Roger was still perched, looking uneasy, swaying slightly, just as he had when I'd first seen him at Bird & Board.

Feeling incredibly stupid and helpless, I started chanting numbers to my parrot. "One. Two. Three. Four."

Roger watched me in a stupefied silence.

"Five. Six. Seven."

"This no good," said the man. "Try three, four numbers together."

I said, "One two three. One two four." My lip had swollen. I could feel warm blood trickling down my chin.

Roger looked away.

"One two five."

I continued speaking sets of numbers, trying to think how this would end.

I said, "Roger is nervous. You've made him nervous. They don't speak when they're nervous."

This seemed to make some impression. Roger played his part by drawing his wings tight to his body and making a groaning sound deep in his chest.

The man produced a flick-knife and cut whatever it was that pinioned my wrists. I sat on the edge of the bed and wiped some blood away from my face. I needed to think. He was far too big to take on.

He said, "Now you try again."

I said, "I'd like to be clear what this is all about. You want a safe deposit number, and you think the parrot will speak it, right?"

He pondered how much to tell me. Then he said, "George, he had diamonds. Isabella, his woman, she search the villa. No diamonds."

"You were sent by Isabella?"

"*Si.* She think maybe there is one deposit box in his bank in Màlaga. No name. Only number, *comprende?*"

"Yes."

"Isabella say George he was crafty old *gringo.* He teach the parrot this number and send it to you."

"I don't think so," I said. "I hardly knew him at all."

This didn't impress my captor. "Stupid old man, he do this to cheat Isabella."

"You're Isabella's friend?"

"Brother."

I doubted if that was true. I said, "I've had Roger for almost a year now. He's never spoken numbers to me. Basically, all he can say is 'Hello'."

Isabella's "brother" struck me across the face a second time.

Roger screamed and spread his wings.

He took a swipe at Roger and just avoided being pecked.

In extreme situations, the brain works faster. I said, "If you'll listen, I have a suggestion. You see the little silver ring attached to his leg? There's something written on it. Very small. I don't know if it's a number. We can look if you like."

"The ring! *Si!*" His face lit up. He reached towards Roger, who dipped forward and tried to peck his hand.

There was no chance of Roger letting him examine that ring.

He said, "You hold him."

I said, "He's nervous."

He said, "You want me to kill you and the parrot?"

I spoke some encouraging words to Roger and held my wrist close to him. If ever I needed my parrot's co-operation it was now. After some understandable hesitation, he put out a claw and transferred to my wrist. Continuing to speak to Roger as calmly as I was able, I fingered the ring with my free hand.

I told the man, "I need more light. I can't read this."

He said, "You come to the window."

I stroked Roger's back and stood up. The man led me towards the light. He said, "No tricks. You show this number to me. You hold the parrot and show me."

Roger was amazingly compliant. He let me finger the ring again. In the better light, I gazed earnestly at the completely blank ring and started inventing numbers. "It looks to me like a three, a five, a nine. Is that a nine, would you say?"

The Spaniard moved to the only position convenient for viewing the ring. He didn't dare come within range of that vicious black beak. He had his back to the open casement window through which I'd climbed.

It was my opportunity. I was poised to give him an almighty push, but Roger forestalled me. He screeched, opened his wings and reared at the man—who rocked back, lost his balance and pitched backwards out of the window. It was a long drop, three floors to a concrete yard. I didn't look out to see the result.

I don't believe Roger understood the consequence of his action. My theory is that he thought he was being taken to the open window. In the year I had owned him—as I discovered later—his wing feathers had grown and he was perfectly capable of flying. He wanted to test those wings. For him, it was the best escape route. When the man blocked his exit, he acted.

I'm not proud of my actions after that, but I ought to set them on record. I grabbed my parrot and pushed him into his travelling-box, which was just inside the door. I carried the box downstairs and drove off without speaking to anyone.

The inquest on the Spanish guest at the Marwood Hotel resulted in an open verdict. Identification was impossible, because he was found to be using a false passport. It was assumed by most people that this was a sad case of suicide.

Within a week, I, too, changed my identity. I moved away from England, sacrificing my TV career for an early retirement to the tropics. For obvious reasons I am not disclosing the name of this island paradise. The climate is a lot better than I'm used to and it suits Roger well. I have a fine stone house, a large swimming pool, servants and a speedboat.

Maybe you are wondering where I got the funds. Roger discovered the seven large uncut diamonds. They were hidden in the hollow wooden perch fixed in the travelling-box he so disliked. He'd pecked through the wood before I got him home from the Marwood Hotel. So Isabella's "brother" had them in his possession for a short time, and never knew it. Sorry, Isabella—I'm certain they were meant for me. They were my legacy from Uncle George. Along with Roger, who is sitting on my shoulder as I write these words.

He's got life running as he wants it, I think.

Passion Killers

The doorbell chimed.

In the kitchen, Gloria looked at the clock. She had to be out of the house by half-past, or she'd certainly be late for choir practice. The tea was too hot, so she added some extra milk to cool it, took a sip and found it didn't taste like tea any more.

Her mother was letting a few seconds pass before going to the door. She wouldn't want it known that she'd been behind the net curtain in the front room for the past ten minutes.

Presently Gloria heard the caller being greeted in a refined accent her mother never used normally. "Is it actually raining outside? I must tell my daughter. She's about to go to choir practice. She's a soloist with the Surrey Orpheus, you know. Gloria, my dear," the message came, still impeccably spoken, like a headmistress in school assembly, "it appears to be raining."

"I know."

Tonight the choir were rehearsing the Cathedral Christmas Concert. "Sheep May Safely Graze" was open on the kitchen table. Nobody seemed to mind that the piece happened to be secular, from the Hunting Cantata; it was so often played in church. Gloria, who would be singing the part of Diana, supported the League Against Cruel Sports really and hoped people wouldn't say she was abandoning her principles just to get out of the chorus. She got up and tipped the tea down the sink, ran some water over the cup and saucer and reached automatically for the tea-cloth, but the tea-cloth didn't come to hand. Instead, of all things, she found that she was about to dry the cup on her mother's thermal knickers. They had been through the washing machine the day before and Mother must have hung them to dry on the towel rail, long-legged things in a hideous shade of pink described in the mail-order catalogue as peach-coloured. Even her mother laughingly called them her passion killers. Gloria clicked her tongue in annoyance and tossed them over the folding clothes-rack where they should have been.

The visitor was Mr Hibbert, the dapper man from number 31. For the last two Fridays he had called on Gloria's mother, Mrs Palmer, at precisely this time, just as Gloria was leaving for choir. The pretext for the visits wasn't mentioned, and Gloria hadn't asked. Her mother was only forty-one and divorced. She was entitled to invite a male friend to the house if she wished. It wasn't as if she was getting up to anything shameful. No doubt Mr Hibbert had a perfectly proper reason for calling. True, Mother had put on her slinky black dress and sprayed herself with Tabu, but it was just to make herself presentable. It couldn't mean anything else. Mr Hibbert had a wife and lived just four doors up the street.

At seventeen, Gloria viewed her mother's social life with detachment. Sometimes she felt the more mature of the two of them. Gloria worked in a small draper's shop in the High Street that had somehow survived the competition from department stores and mail order catalogues. It stocked a tasteful range of fabrics, haberdashery and wools. There were foundation garments discreetly folded away in wooden drawers under the glass counter. Nobody under forty ever went in there. Since leaving school Gloria hadn't kept up with her so-called friends, who had always seemed far too juvenile, obsessed with pop-singers and boyfriends. Even though she was the youngest in the choir by some years, the others talked of her with approval as old-fashioned. The way she plaited her fine, dark hair and pinned it into the shape of a lyre at the back of her head strengthened the perception.

In the hall, she put on her black fitted coat and checked her hair in the mirror. She called out, "I'm off, then. Bye."

From behind the closed door of the front room, her mother called, "Bye, darling." It was a pity she chose to add something else, a terrible pity as it turned out, but she did. First she called out, "Gloria."

"Yes?"

"If you're not in bed by midnight, you'd better come home."

The remark was meant to be funny and Mr Hibbert showed that he thought it was—or that he ought to react as if it was—by laughing out loud. Then her mother laughed too.

Gloria was deeply shocked. She gasped and shut her eyes. There was a swishing sound in her ears. The humiliation was unendurable. That her own mother should say such a thing in front of a man—a neighbour—was a betrayal.

And the way they had laughed together meant that Gloria must have been mistaken about them. Mr Hibbert's visit wasn't the innocent event she had taken it to be. It couldn't be. Decent people didn't laugh at smutty humour. By mocking her, they were affirming their own promiscuity—or at the very least their desire to be promiscuous.

She was disgusted.

To burst into the room and protest would only aggravate the injury. They'd tell her she had no sense of humour. They'd encourage each other to say worse things about her.

She turned towards the mirror again, as if the sight of the outrage on her own features would confirm the injustice of the offence. In the whole of her life she had never given her mother cause to doubt her moral conduct. She'd avoided drugs and smoking and she'd never allowed a boy to take the liberties most other girls yielded blithely. Keeping her standards high had not been easy. She was as prone to temptation as anyone else. She'd had to be strong-willed—and put up with a fair amount of derision from so-called friends who had been less resolute when temptation beckoned. Having to suffer taunts from her own mother was too much.

Mind, she knew that her mother had a streak of irresponsibility. Ninety-nine per cent of the time Mrs Tina Palmer behaved as a mother should. But Gloria could never depend on her. A certain look came over Mother at these times, as if she'd just tossed back a couple of gins (in fact, she didn't drink). Dimples would appear at the ends of her mouth, her eyes would twinkle, and then she was liable to do anything. Anything. Once, at a school speech day, seated in a privileged place in the front row because Gloria was getting a good conduct prize, Mrs Palmer had winked at Mr Shrubb, the PE teacher, who was up on the stage with all the staff. Most of the teachers had noticed and next day it was mentioned or hinted at in just about every lesson. Another time, bored in a supermarket queue, Mrs Palmer had started juggling with oranges and had swiftly drawn a large crowd. Gloria wasn't among them. Too embarrassed to watch the display, she'd slipped out through an empty checkout.

At this moment she wasn't prepared to accept what had been said as yet another example of Mother being skittish again. She was deeply humiliated and ablaze with anger. Her evening was ruined. She was in no frame of mind now to go to choir practice. How could anyone do justice to Bach feeling as she did? She opened the chest in the hall and dropped her music case into it.

She'd go out anyway. Anywhere. She couldn't bear to remain under the same roof while her feckless mother entertained her fancy-man in the front room.

Her hand was on the door in the act of opening it when she noticed Mr Hibbert's coat hanging on the antique hall-stand that was Mother's pride and joy. It was one of those elegant navy blue coats with black velvet facing on the collar. Gloria had once thought men who wore such coats were the acme of smartness. Now she was willing to believe that they were all playboys. She was tempted to spit on it, or pull off one of the buttons. Then a far more engaging idea crept into her mind, a wicked, horrid, but deliciously appropriate means of revenge.

She would give Mr Hibbert something to take home, an unexpected souvenir—the passion-killers, those unbecoming thermal knickers of her mother's. At some point Mr Hibbert would become conscious of something unfamiliar in his overcoat pocket and take it out. His immediate reaction on discovering such a revolting garment could only be guessed at, but he would surely think back and work out with distaste who the passion killers belonged to and try to interpret the message they were meant to convey, just as her mother would at first be mystified at mislaying her thermals and then mortified by the only possible conclusion—that her new friend Mr Hibbert was a secret collector of women's underwear.

Blushing or glowing, she was not sure which, Gloria tiptoed to the kitchen and lifted the thermals off the rack, this time actually grinning at their unspeakable shape and colour. She folded them neatly so as not to make too obvious a lump. Then she went back to the hall and slipped them into the left pocket of Mr Hibbert's beautiful coat: the left because the right already contained his leather gloves. She pushed them well down. In doing so, her fingertips came into contact with a set of keys. His car keys.

Now an even better idea dawned on Gloria.

How much more suggestive if the knickers were to turn up in Mr Hibbert's car, say in the glove compartment on the passenger side, where his wife would very likely discover them for herself. The prospect was delicious: Mrs Hibbert reaching in for a sweet, or something with which to dust the window, and pulling out another woman's drawers. Her wayward husband would really have some explaining to do.

It wouldn't be difficult. There were no garages in King George Avenue. The cars were parked in the street, and Mr Hibbert's was the only silver BMW.

Gloria fished out the thermals and the keys.

She held the thermals at arm's length. The passion killers. Would anyone believe they belonged to her mother? she wondered. Better leave them in no doubt. There was a way to do it.

One of the drawers in the antique hallstand was full of wrapping paper and padded bags people had sent that might be used again. Mother, being economical, kept everything that might be used a second time. When she needed to send a padded bag, she would carefully tear the stamps off one of her collection and cover the old labels with new sticky labels for readdressing. Gloria selected one of appropriate size, folded the pants and slipped them inside. She removed the stamps, but did nothing about the label, which still had her mother's name and address typed on the front. Just perfect. She didn't seal it, either.

As a precaution, just in case some nosy neighbour might see her in the street, she unpinned and unfastened her plaits. Nobody ever caught her with her hair loose. Like this, she suddenly felt a different person, not the high-minded young lady she liked to be known as usually, but a free agent.

She slammed the front door as she went out. The lovers could relax now, believing she was gone for at least two hours and a half. Sheep may safely graze.

The rain had stopped. Darkness had set in some time ago. The street-lamps in King George Avenue were more decorative than effective, but she spotted Mr Hibbert's BMW parked opposite number 31. There could be no question that it was his car because it was well known that he'd paid for a registration with his initials, HPH—a clear sign of vanity, in Gloria's opinion. Nobody seemed to be about, so she went straight across and tried the key on the passenger's side. It was a central locking system and she heard all the doors unlock. When she pulled open the door an interior light came on, so she got in quickly and shut the door and the light went out.

Simple.

The glove compartment opened at the press of a button. Inside were a couple of maps, a roll of peppermints, a half-eaten bar of chocolate and some petrol tokens. She stuffed the bulky envelope inside and closed it.

Now what? There was a sense of anticlimax. Gloria hadn't thought how she would spend the evening now that she wasn't going to choir practice. To go back to the house was out of the question. She'd be a prime suspect if she did. It was a chilly evening. She'd sit here a moment and think.

She'd never been into a pub unaccompanied and she wasn't going to start tonight. She wouldn't feel very safe walking the streets for long. And there was no one she could visit.

The best plan was to go to a film. She'd walk down to the Cannon and find out what was showing.

She was on the point of leaving the car when she heard footsteps close behind. She glanced into the mirror mounted on the side, but saw nobody on the pavement, so she turned her head.

A figure was walking slowly along the centre of the road between the rows of cars. She couldn't see too well, but she was fairly certain that it was a male wearing some sort of crested headgear, a fireman's helmet, perhaps, or a policeman's.

Panic-stricken, she ducked right down with her head over her knees hoping he'd walk past without looking in.

She could feel her heart thumping against her thigh.

Please, please go by.

The footsteps had the heavy tread of boots. They were agonizingly slow.

They stopped right next to the car.

She nearly died of shock when he opened the door on the driver's side and got in. The light came on in the car.

"Bloody hell!"

She remained quite still.

"Are you ill, or somefink?"

If he was really a policeman, he ought to have sounded more assertive, more in control, but she dared not check.

"You just give *me* a nasty turn, any road."

She was petrified. He took a grip on the hair at the back of her head and pulled her upright.

She had another shock when she turned to face him. The crested helmet was in reality a punk hair-style, a bright green Mohican tuft presently being squashed against the roof of the car. He was a youth of about sixteen. There were three silver rings through his left ear and a glittery stud through his nose.

He asked her, "This motor—is it yours?"

She shook her head.

"Your old man's? What you doing, then? Nicking stuff? You deaf, or somefink?"

She succeeded in saying, "Who are you?"

He said, "I asked you a question."

"You asked about five questions." She was beginning to feel safer with him. She was close enough to see that he was just a boy.

"I don't know you," he said, as if the fault were Gloria's. "I don't know you, do I?"

She said, "If you pulled the door properly shut, this light would go out." Immediately she'd said it, she realized that she might be misinterpreted. She was only anxious that nobody should see her sitting in Mr Hibbert's car, with or without a boy with green hair.

He closed the door and said, in the darkness, "Want a smoke?"

She said, "Look, this is someone else's car."

"He won't come out. He's watching telly in one of them houses, I bet. Long time since I tried a BMW." He put his hands on the wheel and it clicked. The steering column must have locked. "Bleedin' hell."

Gloria said, "Mind your language."

"Sod off."

At least she'd registered disapproval.

"If it ain't yours," he said, "how did you get in?"

"With the key. I, em, nicked it," she added, to forestall the next question.

"Jeez. Where?"

"From his pocket."

"Cool." He didn't ask about the circumstances. Instead, he said with admiration, "You're class."

She liked that. Nobody—certainly no boy—had ever referred to her in quite those terms before.

"What's your name?"

"Gloria."

"Gloria—blimey. I'm Mick. Want to go for a ride, Gloria?"

"What do you mean—in this?"

"What else? You just said you got the key."

"Can you drive?"

"I wouldn't be here, would I? Give us the key and I'll show you. I could start it easy, but the wheel's locked."

He was a joy-rider. He'd walked up King George Avenue trying the doors of all the cars to find one open and it had happened to be Mr Hibbert's.

The keys were in her lap. Mr Hibbert's keys. Mr Hibbert, who had laughed at the idea that she might spend the night in bed with someone. She handed them over. "Just a short ride."

He slotted the key in and turned it to free the steering wheel. The engine started first time.

"Nice motor," said Mick, switching on the headlights and revving the engine. He released the handbrake and they moved out of line and cruised quite quickly to the end of King George Avenue, where it met the High Street. Gloria felt an upsurge of excitement. She was joy-riding—and in Mr Hibbert's car.

"Open your window. Get some breeze through."

It worked electronically. She found the button and pressed. The wind was noisy. She glanced at the instruments and saw that the car was doing sixty in a built-up area.

"We can have a burn-up on the by-pass," said Mick apologetically. "These can do a ton, easy." He switched the radio on. A Mozart piano concerto was being played. "God 'elp us. See if you can get somefink with a beat."

She tried the controls, found some rock music and turned it up loud.

"Ace," said Mick.

They were flashing past parked cars at reckless speed.

Gloria was scared, but enjoying it in the way you can enjoy a roller coaster ride. She wasn't even using the seat-belt. That, to a full-blown punk like Mick, would surely have been chicken.

They succeeded in getting to the by-pass without being stopped by the police. On the triple carriageway, Mick moved out to the fast lane.

"Let's see what this heap can do."

Gloria's skin prickled. To think that this could have been choir practice.

The wind stung her face and stretched her hair in what felt like a comic-strip illustration of speed. Mick was steering one-handed, with his free hand resting on her thigh. She didn't mind.

They overtook everything. When anyone had the temerity to block the fast lane, Mick used the horn and headlights together. They weren't held up long.

Gloria looked at the speedometer and saw the needle hovering near 110. They passed the sign for a roundabout. She drew it to his attention in the most tactful way she could. "Let's go round and come back the other way."

"You go for this?" Mick shouted. "Does it turn you on?"

"It's magic."

The hand on her leg moved higher, exploring, but he had to use both hands to swing the car around the roundabout, the tyres screeching, and by that time Gloria had brought her legs up to her chest with her heels on the edge of the seat and her arms tucked around her shins. The one-handed driving was all very macho, but she felt it required Mick's undivided attention.

They raced back along the stretch they had just travelled. Someone in the fast lane refused to give way, so Mick overtook on the inside and made an obscene gesture as they passed. Gloria did the same. She had never felt so delinquent, or so alive.

"You know what?" shouted Mick.

"What?"

"You're neat."

"You're neat, too."

"I'll get you a present. What do you want—jewellery?"
She didn't know what to say.

"Somefink to wear? Leathers?" said Mick.

"There's no need," said Gloria. "You don't have to get
me anything."

He reduced speed. They were coming to a slip-road that
would take them off the by-pass.

"Have you got a telly? Portable?"

"Look, I don't want anything, Mick. If you want to get
me a drink—"

"A drink? All right. You like fizz?"

"Fizz?"

"Champagne. You can have champagne if you want."
She laughed. "All right." If he wanted to be extravagant,
she'd settle for a glass of champagne. Immediately she
wondered if she'd made a wise choice. With some drink
inside him, Mick might take even bigger risks with the car.
Maybe she'd be wise to walk home.

They cruised at a mere seventy along the main road into
town, ignoring several pubs. Gloria decided that Mick was
driving them to his favourite haunt, some place where
punks and rockers met, with wood floors and music and
one-arm bandits.

In the High Street, he slowed and turned his head, as if
looking for someone. He cruised quite slowly, past
Woolworth's and Boot's and the Laundromat. Gloria
didn't know of any pub along here. There was just the
County Arms Hotel, with four stars in the RAC Guide, and
that, surely, wasn't the sort of place Mick would frequent.

Like a mind-reader, he said, "We'll get it in the Wine
Mart."

"Fine," said Gloria.

"Put your head down, right down, like you had it before."

"Why?"

"Why do you fink? We're going to ram-raid the place. These fings are built like bloody tanks."

She was horrified. "No, Mick!"

"Do what I say—if you want to keep your face." He spun the wheel sharply right.

She had a glimpse of the shop window of the Wine Mart straight ahead. She plunged her head between her knees. She felt the wheels mount the curb and then the terrific impact as the shop front was ripped apart. An alarm bell jangled.

Mick forced open his door and stepped through shattered glass into the shop's interior. Gloria sat up, twitching with fear and shock. The car's bonnet was covered in glass.

Mick was back, brandishing a bottle of champagne that he'd taken off a shelf at the rear of the shop. This was a nightmare.

Gloria said in a voice shrill with panic, "You're crazy!"

Mick shouted above the blare of the alarm, "Burst tyre. We got to run for it!" He opened the car door, grabbed Gloria's arm and tugged her out. "Come on! Let's get out of here."

They abandoned Mr Hibbert's car, still blocking the pavement with its front wheels inside the Wine Mart. Regardless of the people who must have heard and were certain to be watching from flats above the shops, Mick dashed up the High Street with Gloria following. At the first opportunity they turned left up a side-street.

Gloria leaned against a doorway to recover her breath.

Mick swung around. "You can't stop here. We got to go on."

If she'd had any breath left, she'd have shouted back at him, told him he must be a head-case to have done such a thing, made it clear that she would never have consented to it. That—far from impressing her—it proved that he was a pathological idiot.

A police siren frighteningly close interrupted her resentment. She forced herself to run again. They were coming into a paved area where cars couldn't normally pass, but she was sure the police car would pursue them if they were spotted. A couple of derelicts shouted at them from a shop doorway. They'd seen the bottle that Mick was still carrying and they were asking him to share it. Mick was too fast, but one of them stepped out to try and grab Gloria. He caught hold of her wrist with a filthy hand, and his face came close to hers, unshaven, bright pink and foul of breath. She screamed, pushed at his chest and managed to wriggle free. He stood in the middle of the walkway yelling obscenities as she dashed on.

Mick waited for her by the parish church beyond the shopping mall, a pathetic figure now with his stupid green hair in disarray like daffodil stalks after the flowers were picked. "Over the top, right?"

She nodded, too breathless to speak.

The wall around the churchyard was about four feet high. She put her hands on the coping and half-jumped, half-hauled herself off the ground. Mick shoved her backside unceremoniously higher and she scrambled onto the wall and jumped down. He followed, then stooped to pick up the champagne, which he must have tossed over first. Why he bothered with it, she couldn't imagine.

"Come on."

Stumbling between ancient headstones in the near-darkness they made their way as well as they could across the churchyard to the accompaniment of the police siren. At one point Gloria thought she could make out the sound of running footsteps quite close, but Mick was unconvinced. He'd stopped from sheer exhaustion, leaning against a tombstone. "They'd have searchlights and torches if they was trying to follow us."

Gloria said, "I can't run any more."

"Have some of this." He started fiddling with the foil wrapping on the champagne.

"I don't want any, you moron. I didn't want it in the first place."

He was loosening the wire around the cork. "You did. You said." He sounded like a six-year-old now.

"I didn't know you were going to break into a shop to get it and ruin Mr Hibbert's car."

The cork popped and Mick's hands were covered in froth. "Have a swig."

"I don't want any."

"I don't want any," he mimicked her. "Snotty-nosed bitch."

"I'm the one who stands to lose most," she pointed out. "I've never been in trouble with the police."

"Who says you're in trouble? We got away, didn't we?"

"Yes, but I took the keys from his overcoat pocket when he was visiting my Mum. It's going to be obvious."

"He was visiting your house?"

"Yes, he's probably still there."

"What's he doing with your Mum?"

"That's my business."

"Is he staying long?"

"I don't know—a couple of hours."

Mick fumbled in his pocket and produced the car-keys, dangling them in front of her face.

"You've still got them?"

"Now who's a moron? You can stick them back in his pocket and he won't never know."

"Give them to me."

He closed his fingers around them and hid them behind his back. "Who's a moron?"

"I'm sorry, Mick. I didn't mean that. Please."

"Come here."

"Mick, I said I was sorry."

He curled his finger, beckoning.

She felt her stomach clench. He wanted her. This was what it had all been leading up to, the joy-ride, the ram-raid, the champagne. Almost every day of her life since she had first learned about sex she had tried to imagine how it would happen to her the first time—the situation in which she would consent. Never, remotely, had she pictured it like this, among the gravestones in the bitter cold, with the police searching for her.

She said, "There isn't time." She could have added that it was dangerous and squalid and unromantic, but those were concepts that would make no impression on a punk. In his scale of values they might actually be incentives. And—in spite of everything that had governed her life until this moment—Gloria herself was being swayed. She was a different person now, a law-breaker.

Impulsively she stepped towards him and offered her lips.

He jammed his mouth against hers so hard that their teeth scraped. She could feel his hand fumbling low down at the front of her coat.

He said, "Take 'em, then."

It was a moment before she understood that he was trying to hand her the car keys. He pushed them into her hand.

Then he drew back and so did she, bewildered. Apparently all he'd wanted was the kiss.

"You'd better leg it now," he told her.

"Yes."

"See you." He turned and walked away.

She put her hand to her mouth as if the act of touching her slightly numb lips would somehow preserve the kiss. She didn't want him to leave her. She knew it was the sensible thing, the safe thing, but tonight she'd stopped being sensible and safe.

"Mick!"

He turned his head and said, "Leave it out, will you?"

Despairingly, she echoed the words he had used. "See you."

He walked on.

She bit back her distress. If she really wanted to be accepted by people like Mick she had to be tough with herself. She left the churchyard by a different route from Mick's and—to borrow his terminology—"legged it" through the streets towards home. So much had happened that she hardly expected to see the houses still lit—but they were—almost every one she passed. She couldn't believe that Mr Hibbert would still be in the house with his coat hanging in the hall, but in fact the entire adventure had lasted less than an hour and twenty minutes. It might still be possible to return the keys and pretend she had been at choir practice.

But when she turned the corner of King George Avenue she had a horrible shock. A police car was parked in the space where Mr Hibbert's car had been. The police? Already?

In two minds whether to run back and search the streets for Mick, she stopped at the corner and waited, going over in her mind what she could say if the police were with her mother now. She was in an appalling position. If she told the truth, she'd have to betray Mick. Then it occurred to her that the police might not yet have connected her with the theft of the car. It was possible that they were there for no other reason than to inform Mr Hibbert what had happened.

She was going to have to find the courage to walk into the house and act as if she knew nothing at all. It was no use waiting for them to leave, because Mr Hibbert was sure to leave as well. The only chance she had of returning the keys to his overcoat pocket was now.

With her heart pounding, she stepped up the street to the house. The light was on in the front room and she could hear the faint murmur of voices, but the curtains were too thick for her to see anything. Under the porch light she checked her clothes. Her shoes were muddy at the heels and her coat was dusty where she'd climbed over the church wall, so she did some rapid grooming with a paper tissue. She couldn't do anything about her hair; she'd just have to say that one of the plaits had come undone and she'd unfastened the other one. She took a deep breath, slotted her own key into the front door and let herself in.

The coat was still hanging on the hallstand, but there were others as well. And she didn't have time to do anything about the car-keys because the door of the front room opened and Mr Hibbert came out, followed by a police sergeant in uniform.

"You must be Gloria," said Mr Hibbert. "I've seen you several times, but we've never spoken. Your hair's different, isn't it?"

She murmured some bland response.

"Mrs Palmer's daughter," Mr Hibbert explained to the policeman. "Just back from choir practice, I believe." He sounded surprisingly chirpy for a man whose car had been stolen and wrecked.

Other people were coming out of the front room. Two women from up the street and old Mr and Mrs Chalk, from next door. Even the obnoxious Mrs Mackenzie from the house opposite, a woman her mother detested. So many witnesses?

And now her mother was there. "Gloria, help Mrs Mackenzie with her coat, there's a dear."

Nobody seemed unduly alarmed.

"I'll be off, then," announced the police sergeant, opening the front door. "Thanks for the coffee, Mrs Palmer."

Gloria reached for the fur coat that she recognized as Mrs Mackenzie's, just as Mr Hibbert was lifting his overcoat off the hook. He was saying something to her mother about coming again. In a swift movement, using Mrs Mackenzie's fur as a shield, Gloria succeeded in dropping the car keys into Mr Hibbert's coat pocket. Only just in time.

"Goodbye all." He'd put on the coat and was gone.

Some of the others were not so quick to leave. There was no sense of urgency. They were talking about what they would be doing for Christmas.

When Mrs Palmer finally closed the door on the last of them, she breathed a sigh of relief and said, "Let's have a fresh cup of tea, love. Have you had a nice evening? You're back early, aren't you? What have you done with your hair? I rather like it down. It suits you."

"Mum, whatever were all those people doing here—and the police?"

"Didn't I tell you? This is the third meeting we've had. We're setting up a Neighbourhood Watch. You know—keeping an eye on each other's property. It's becoming essential with all the crime round here. Sergeant Middleton was telling us how dreadful it is. He's the community liaison officer. It's his job to advise people like ourselves how to get organised."

"That's why they were here?"

"Well, yes."

"Mr Hibbert?"

"He *is* a neighbour, dear, and quite well off, I believe. He's got an interest in protecting his property. He's one of the moving forces. He's always the first to arrive."

"Yes, I noticed," said Gloria, wishing the earth would swallow her up.

The kettle had boiled. Mrs Palmer made the tea. "Of course, that Mrs Mackenzie from across the way came, and I'm convinced the only reason is that she wanted to see inside the house. She's so nosy, that woman. Do you know, when I made the coffee she insisted on coming out here to help me, as she put it. Of course, all she wanted was to get a look at my kitchen. Oh, and Gloria, darling, I'm *so* grateful to you for putting my thermal undies out of sight. Imagine if that woman had clapped eyes on them. I'd have died, I really would. I suddenly thought of them when she was opening the biscuits. The relief when I looked at the towel rail and they weren't there. I mean, they're not the most flattering things to have on display—my enormous bloomers."

Gloria tried to give the smile that her mother obviously expected.

Mrs Palmer added, "Tell me, where did you put them, dear?"

The doorbell chimed.

The Proof of the Pudding

Frank Morris strode into the kitchen and slammed a cold, white turkey on the kitchen table. "Seventeen pounds plucked. Satisfied?"

His wife Wendy was at the sink, washing the last few breakfast bowls. Her shoulders had tensed. "What's that, Frank?"

"You're not even bloody looking, woman."

She took that as a command and wheeled around, rubbing her wet hands on the apron. "A turkey! That's a fine bird. It really is."

"Fine?" Frank erupted. "It's nineteen forty-six, for Christ's sake! It's a bloody miracle. Most of them round here will be sitting down to joints of pork and mutton—if they're lucky. I bring a bloody great turkey in on Christmas morning, and all you can say is 'fine'?"

"I just wasn't prepared for it."

"You really get my goat, you do."

Wendy said tentatively, "Where did it come from, Frank?"

Her huge husband stepped towards her and for a moment she thought he would strike her. He lowered his face until it was inches from hers. Not even nine in the morning and she could smell sweet whisky on his breath. "I won it, didn't I?" he said, daring her to disbelieve. "A meat raffle in The Valiant Trooper last night."

Wendy nodded, pretending to be taken in. It didn't do to challenge Frank's statements. Black eyes and beatings had taught her well. She knew Frank's rule of fist had probably won him the turkey, too. Frank didn't lose at anything. If he could punch his way to another man's prize, then he considered it fair game.

"Just stuff the thing and stick it in the oven," he ordered. "Where's the boy?"

"I think he's upstairs," Wendy replied warily. Norman had fled at the sound of Frank's key in the front door.

"Upstairs?" Frank ranted. "On bloody Christmas Day?"

"I'll call him." Wendy was grateful for the excuse to move away from Frank to the darkened hallway. "Norman," she gently called. "Your father's home. Come and wish him a Happy Christmas."

A pale, solemn young boy came cautiously downstairs, pausing at the bottom to hug his mother. Unlike most children of his age—he was nine—Norman was sorry that the war had ended in 1945. He had pinned his faith in the enemy putting up a stiff fight and extending it indefinitely. He still remembered the VE Day street party, sitting at a long wooden bench surrounded by laughing neighbours. He and his mother had found little to celebrate in the news that "the boys will soon be home."

Wendy smoothed down his hair, whispered something and led him gently into the kitchen.

"Happy Christmas, Dad," he said, then added, unprompted, "Did you come home last night?"

Wendy said quickly, "Never you mind about that, Norman." She didn't want her son provoking Frank on this of all days.

Frank didn't appear to have heard. He was reaching up

to the top shelf of a cupboard, a place where he usually kept his old army belt. Wendy pushed her arm protectively in front of the boy.

But instead of the belt, Frank took down a brown paper parcel. "Here you are, son," he said, beckoning to Norman. "You'll be the envy of the street in this. I saved it for you, specially."

Norman stepped forward. He unwrapped his present, egged on by his grinning father.

He now owned an old steel helmet. "Thanks, Dad," he said politely, turning it in his hands.

"I got it off a dead Jerry," Frank said with gusto. "The bastard who shot your Uncle Ted. Sniper, he was. Holed up in a bombed-out building in Potsdam, outside Berlin. He got Ted with a freak shot. Twelve of us stormed the building and took him out."

"Outside?"

"Topped him, Norman. See the hole round the back. That's from a Lee Enfield .303. Mine." Frank levelled an imaginary rifle to Wendy's head and squeezed the trigger, miming both the recoil and report. "There wasn't a lot left of Fritz after we'd finished. But I brought back the helmet for you, son. Wear it with pride. It's what your Uncle Ted would have wanted." He took the helmet and rammed it on the boy's head.

Norman grimaced. He felt he was about to be sick.

"Frank dear, perhaps we should put it away until he's a bit older," Wendy tried her tact. "We wouldn't want such a special thing to get damaged, would we? You know what young boys are like."

Frank was unimpressed. "What are you talking about—'special thing?' It's a bloody helmet, not a thirty-piece tea service. Look at the lad. He's totally stunned. He loves it. Why don't you get on and stuff that ruddy great turkey, like I told you?"

"Yes, Frank."

Norman raised his hand, his small head an absurd sight in the large helmet. "May I go now?"

Frank beamed. "Of course, son. Want to show it off to all your friends, do you?"

Norman nodded, causing the helmet to slip over his eyes. He lifted it off his head. Smiling weakly at his father, he left the kitchen and dashed upstairs. The first thing he would do was wash his hair.

Wendy began to wash and prepare the bird, listening to Frank.

"I know just how the kid feels. I still remember my old Dad giving me a bayonet he brought back from Flanders. Said he ran six men through with it. I used to look for specks of blood, and he'd tell me how he stuck them like pigs. It was the best Christmas present I ever had."

"I've got you a little something for Christmas. It's behind the clock," said Wendy, indicating a small package wrapped in newspaper and string.

"A present?" Frank snatched it up and tore the wrapping away. "Socks?" he said in disgust. "Is that it? Our first Christmas together in three bloody years, and all you can give your husband is a miserable pair of socks."

"I don't have much money, Frank," Wendy reminded him, and instantly wished she had not.

Frank seized her by the shoulders, practically tipping the turkey off the kitchen table. "Are you saying that's my fault?"

"No, love."

"I'm not earning enough—is that what you're trying to tell me?"

Wendy tried to pacify him, at the same time bracing herself for the violent shaking that would surely follow. Frank tightened his grip, forced her away from the table and pushed her hard against the cupboard door, punctuating each word with a thump.

"That helmet cost me nothing," he ranted. "Don't you understand, woman? It's the thought that counts. You don't need money to show affection. You just need some savvy, some intelligence. Bloody socks—an insult!"

He shoved her savagely towards the table again. "Now get back to your work. This is Christmas Day. I'm a reasonable man. I'm prepared to overlook your stupidity. Stop snivelling, will you, and get that beautiful bird in the oven. Mum will be here at ten. I want the place smelling of turkey. I'm not having you ruining my Christmas."

He strode out, heavy boots clumping on the wooden floor of the hallway. "I'm going round Polly's," he shouted. "She knows how to treat a hero. Look at this dump. No decorations, no holly over the pictures. You haven't even bought any beer, that I've seen. Sort something out before I get back."

Wendy was still reeling from the shaking, but she knew she must speak before he left. If she didn't remind him now, there would be hell to pay later. "Polly said she would bring the Christmas pudding, Frank. Would you make sure she doesn't forget? Please, Frank."

He stood grim-faced in the doorway, silhouetted against the drab terraced houses opposite. "Don't tell me what to do, Wendy," he said threateningly. "You're the one due for a damned good reminding of what to do round here."

The door shook in its frame. Wendy stood at the foot of the stairs, her heart pounding. She knew what Frank meant by a damned good reminding. The belt wasn't used only on the boy.

"Is he gone, Mum?" Norman called from the top stair.

Wendy nodded, readjusting the pins in her thin, blonde hair, and drying her eyes. "Yes, love, You can come downstairs now."

At the foot of the stairs, he told her, "I don't want the helmet. It frightens me."

"I know, dear."

"I think there's blood on it. I don't want it. If it belonged to one of our soldiers, or one of the Yankees, I'd want it, but this is a dead man's helmet."

Wendy hugged her son. The base of her spine throbbed. A sob was building at the back of her throat.

"Where's he gone?" Norman asked from the folds of her apron.

"To collect your Aunt Polly. She's bringing a Christmas pudding, you know. We'd better make custard. I'm going to need your help."

"Was he there last night?" Norman asked innocently. "With Aunt Polly? Is it because she doesn't have Uncle Ted any more?"

"I don't know, Norman." In truth, she didn't want to know. Her widowed sister-in-law was welcome to Frank. Polly didn't know the relief Wendy felt to be rid of him sometimes. Any humiliation was quite secondary to the fact that Frank stopped out all night, bringing respite from the tension and the brutality. The local gossips had been quick to suspect the truth, but she could do nothing to stop them.

Norman, sensing the direction her thoughts had taken, said, "Billy Slater says Dad and Aunt Polly are doing it."

"That's enough, Norman."

"He says she's got no elastic in her drawers. What does he mean, Mum?"

"Billy Slater is a disgusting little boy. Now let's hear no more of this. We'll make the custard."

Norman spent the next hour helping his mother in the kitchen. The turkey barely fitted in the oven, and Norman became concerned that it wouldn't be ready in time. Wendy knew better. There was ample time for the cooking. They couldn't start until Frank and Polly rolled home from the Valiant Trooper. With last orders at a quarter to three, it gave the bird five hours to roast.

A gentle knock at the front door sent Norman hurrying to open it.

"Mum, it's Grandma Morris!" he called out excitedly as he led the plump old woman into the kitchen. Maud Morris had been a marvellous support through the war years. She knew exactly when help was wanted.

"I've brought you some veggies," Maud said to Wendy, dumping a bag of muddy cabbage and carrots onto the table and removing her coat and hat. "Where's that good-for-nothing son of mine? Need I ask?"

"He went to fetch Polly," Wendy calmly replied.

"Did he, indeed?"

Norman said, "About an hour ago. I expect they'll go to the pub."

The old lady went into the hall to hang up her things. When she returned, she said to Wendy, "You know what people are saying, don't you?"

Wendy ignored the question. "He brought in a seventeen-pound turkey this morning."

"Have you got a knife?" her mother-in-law asked.

"A knife?"

"For the cabbage." Maud turned to look at her grandson. "Have you had some good presents?"

Norman stared down at his shoe-laces.

Wendy said, "Grandma asked you a question, dear."

"Did you get everything you asked for?"

"I don't know."

"Did you write to Saint Nick?" Maud asked with a side-ward glance at Wendy.

Norman rolled his eyes upwards. "I don't believe in that stuff any more."

"That's a shame."

"Dad gave me a dead German's helmet. He says it belonged to the one who shot Uncle Ted. I hate it."

Wendy gathered the carrots from the table and put them

in the sink. "I'm sure he was only doing what he thought was best, Norman."

"It's got a bullet hole."

"Didn't he give you anything else?" his grandmother asked.

Norman shook his head. "Mum gave me some chocolate and the Dandy Annual."

"But your Dad didn't give you a thing apart from the helmet?"

Wendy said, "Please don't say anything. You know what it's like."

Maud Morris nodded. It was pointless to admonish her son. He'd only take it out on Wendy. She knew from personal experience the dilemma of the battered wife. To protest was to invite more violence. The knowledge that her second son had turned out such a bully shamed and angered her. Ted, her dear firstborn Ted, would never have harmed a woman. Yet Ted had been taken from her. She took an apron from the back of the door and started shredding the cabbage. Norman was sent to lay the table in the front room.

Four hours later, when the King was speaking to the nation, they heard a key being tried at the front door. Wendy switched off the wireless. The door took at least three attempts to open before Frank and Polly stumbled into the hallway. Frank stood swaying, a bottle in his hand and a paper hat cocked ridiculously on the side of his head. His sister-in-law clung to his coat, convulsed in laughter, a pair of ankle-strap shoes dangling from her right hand.

"Happy Christmas!" he roared. "Peace on earth and goodwill to all men except the Jerries and the lot next door."

Polly doubled up in uncontrollable giggling.

"Let me take your coat, Polly," Wendy offered. "Did you remember the pudding? I want to get it on right away."

Polly turned to Frank. "The pudding. What did you do with the pudding, Frank?"

"What pudding?" said Frank.

Maud had come into the hall behind Wendy. "I know she's made one. Don't mess about, Frank. Where is it?"

Frank pointed vaguely over his shoulder.

Wendy said despairingly, "Back at Polly's house? Oh, no!"

"Stupid cow. What are you talking about?" said Frank. "It's on our own bloody doorstep. I had to put it down to open the door, didn't I?"

Wendy squeezed past them and retrieved the white basin covered with a grease-proof paper top. She carried it quickly through to the kitchen and lowered it into the waiting saucepan of simmering water. "It looks a nice big one."

This generous remark caused another gale of laughter from Polly. Finally, slurring her words, she announced, "You'll have to make allowances. Your old man's a very naughty boy. He's took me out and got me tiddly."

Maud said, "It beats me where he gets the money from."

"Beats Wendy, too, I expect," said Polly. She leaned closer to her sister-in-law, a lock of brown hair swaying across her face. "From what I've heard, you know a bit about beating, don't you, Wen?" The remark wasn't made in sympathy. It was triumphant.

Wendy felt the shame redden her face. Polly smirked and swung around, causing her black skirt to swirl as she left the room. The thick pencil lines she had drawn up the back of her legs to imitate stocking seams were badly smudged higher up. Wendy preferred not to think why.

She took the well-cooked bird from the oven, transferred it to a platter and carried it into the front room. Maud and Norman brought in the vegetables.

"Would you like to carve, Frank?"

"Hold your horses, woman. We haven't said the Grace."

Wendy started to say, "But we never . . ."

Frank had already intoned the words, "Dear Lord God Almighty."

Everyone dipped their heads.

"Thanks for what we are about to receive," Frank went on, "and for seeing to it that a skinny little half-pint won the meat raffle and decided to donate it to the Morris family."

Maud clicked her tongue in disapproval.

Polly began to giggle.

"I can't begin to understand the workings of your mysterious ways," Frank insisted on going on, "because if there really is someone up there he should have made damned sure my brother Ted was sitting at this table today."

Maud said, "That's enough, Frank! Sit down."

Frank said, "Amen. Where's the carving knife?"

Wendy handed it to him, and he attended to the task, cutting thick slices and heaping them on the plates held by his mother. "That's for Polly. She likes it steaming hot."

Polly giggled again.

The plates were distributed around the table.

Not to be outdone in convivial wit, Polly said, "You've gone over-board on the breast, Frankie dear. I thought you were a leg man."

Maud said tersely, "You should know."

"Careful, Mum," Frank cautioned, wagging the knife. "Goodwill to all men."

Polly said, "Only if they behave themselves."

A voice piped up, "Billy Slater says that—"

"Be quiet, Norman!" Wendy ordered.

They ate in heavy silence, save for Frank's animalistic chewing and swallowing. The first to finish, he quickly filled his glass with more beer.

"Dad?"

"Yes, son."

"Would we have won the war without the Americans?"

"The Yanks?" Frank scoffed. "Bunch of part-timers, son.

They only came into it after men like me and your Uncle Ted had done all the real fighting. Just like the other war, the one my old Dad won. They waited till 1917. Isn't that a fact, Mum? Americans? Where were they at Dunkirk? Where were they in Africa? I'll tell you where they were—sitting on their fat backsides a couple of thousand miles away."

"From what I remember, Frank," Maud interjected. "You were sitting on yours in the snug-bar of the Valiant Trooper."

"That was different!" Frank protested angrily. "Ted and I didn't get called up until 1943. And when we were, we did our share. We chased Jerry all the way across Europe, right back to the bunker. Ted and me, brothers in arms, fighting for King and country. Ready to make the ultimate sacrifice. If Dad could have heard what you said just then, Mum, he'd turn in his grave."

Maud said icily, "That would be difficult, seeing that he's in a pot on my mantelpiece."

Polly burst into helpless laughter and almost choked on a roast potato. It was injudicious of her.

"Belt up, will you?" Frank demanded. "We're talking about the sacred memory of your dead husband. My brother."

"Sorry, Frank." Polly covered her mouth with her hands. "I don't know what came over me. Honest."

"You've no idea, you women," Frank went on. "God knows what you got up to, while we were winning the war."

"Anyway," said Norman, "Americans have chewing gum. And jeeps."

Fortunately, at this moment Frank was being distracted.

Wendy whispered in Norman's ear and they both began clearing the table, but Maud put her hand over Wendy's. She said, "Why don't you sit down? You've done more than enough. I'll fetch the pudding and custard. I'd like to get up for a while. It's beginning to get a little warm in here."

Polly offered to help. "It is my pudding, after all." But she didn't mean to get up because, unseen by the others, she had her hand on Frank's thigh.

Maud said, "I'll manage."

Norman asked, "Is it a proper pudding?"

"I don't know what you mean by proper," said Polly. "It used up most of my rations when I made it. They have to mature, do puddings. This one is two years old. It should be delicious. There was only one drawback. In 1944, I didn't have a man at home to help me stir the ingredients." She gave Frank a coy smile.

Ignoring it, Wendy said, "When Norman asked if it was a proper pudding, I think he wanted to know if he might find a lucky sixpence inside."

With a simper, Polly said, "He might, if he's a good boy, like his Dad. Of *course* it's a proper pudding."

Frank quipped, "What about the other sort? Do you ever make an improper pudding?"

Before anyone could stop him, Norman said, "You should know, Dad." His reflexes were too quick for his drunken father's, and the swinging blow missed him completely.

"You'll pay for that remark, my son," Frank shouted. "You'll wash your mouth out with soap and water and then I'll beat your backside raw."

Wendy said quickly, "The boy doesn't know what he's saying, Frank. It's Christmas. Let's forgive and forget, shall we?"

He turned his anger on her. "And I know very well who puts these ideas in the boy's head. And spreads the filthy rumours all over town. You can have your Christmas Day, Wendy. Make the most of it, because tomorrow I'm going to teach you why they call it Boxing Day."

Maud entered the suddenly silent front room carrying the dark, upturned pudding decorated with a sprig of holly. "Be an angel and fetch the custard, Norman."

The boy was thankful to run out to the kitchen.

Frank glanced at the pudding and then at Polly and then grinned. "What a magnificent sight!" He was staring at her cleavage.

Polly beamed at him, fully herself again, her morale restored by the humiliation her sister-in-law had just suffered. "The proof of the pudding . . ." she murmured.

"We'll see if 1944 was a vintage year," said Frank.

Maud sliced and served the pudding, giving Norman an extra large helping. The pudding was a delicious one, as Polly had promised, and there were complimentary sounds all round the table.

Norman sifted the rich, fruity mass with his spoon, hoping for one of those coveted silver sixpenny pieces. But Frank was the first to find one.

"You can have a wish. Whatever you like, lucky man," said Polly in a husky, suggestive tone.

Frank's thoughts were in another direction. "I wish," he said sadly, holding the small coin between finger and thumb, "I wish God's peace to my brother Ted, rest his soul. And I wish a Happy Christmas to all the blokes who fought with us and survived. And God rot all our enemies. And the bloody Yanks, come to that."

"That's about four wishes," Polly said, " and it won't come true if you tell everyone."

Wendy felt the sharp edge of a sixpence in her mouth, and removed it unnoticed by the others. She wished him out of her life, with all her heart.

Norman finally found his piece of the pudding's buried treasure. He spat the coin onto his plate and then examined it closely. "Look at this!" he said in surprise. "It isn't a sixpence. It doesn't have the King's head."

"Give it here." Frank picked up the silver coin. "Jesus Christ! He's right. It's a dime. An American dime. How the hell did that get in the pudding?"

All eyes turned to Polly for an explanation. She stared wide-eyed at Frank. She was speechless.

Frank was not. He had reached his own conclusion. "I'll tell you exactly how it got in there," he said, thrusting it under Polly's nose. "You've been stirring it up with a Yank. There was a GI base down the road, wasn't there? When did you say you made the pudding? 1944?"

He rose from the table, spittle flying as he ranted. Norman slid from his chair and hid under the table, clinging in fear to his mother's legs. He saw his father's heavy boots turned towards Polly, whose legs braced. The hem of her dress was quivering.

Frank's voice boomed around the small room. "Ted and I were fighting like bloody heroes while you were having it off with Americans. Whore!"

Norman saw a flash of his father's hand as it reached into the fireplace and picked up a poker. He heard the women scream, then a sickening thump.

The poker fell to the floor. Polly's legs jerked once and then appeared to relax. One of her arms flopped down and remained quite still. A drop of blood fell from the table edge. Presently there was another. Then it became a trickle. A crimson pool formed on the wooden floor.

Norman ran out of the room. Out of the house. Out into the cold afternoon, leaving the screams behind. He ran across the street and beat on a neighbour's door with his fists. His frantic cries of "Help, murder!" filled the street. Within a short time an interested crowd in party hats had surrounded him. He pointed in horror to his own front door as his blood-stained father charged out and lurched towards him.

It took three men to hold Frank Morris down, and five policemen to take him away.

The last of the policemen didn't leave the house until long

after Norman should have gone to bed. His mother and his grandmother sat silent for some time in the kitchen, unable to stay in the front room, even though Polly's body had been taken away.

"He's not going to come back, is he, Mum?"

Wendy shook her head. She was only beginning to think about what happened next. There would be a trial, of course, and she would try to shield Norman from the publicity. He was so impressionable.

"Will they hang him?"

"I think it's time for your bed, young man," Maud said. "You've got to be strong. Your Mum will need your support more than ever now."

The boy asked, "How did the dime get in the pudding, Grandma Morris?"

Wendy snapped out of her thoughts of what was to come and stared at her mother-in-law.

Maud went to the door, and for a moment it appeared as if she was reaching to put on her coat prior to leaving, but she had already promised to stay the night. Actually she was taking something from one of the pockets.

It was a Christmas card, a little bent at the edges now. Maud handed it to Wendy. "It was marked 'private and confidential' but it had my name, you see. I opened it thinking it was for me. It came last week. The address was wrong. They made a mistake over the house number. The postman delivered it to the wrong Mrs Morris."

Wendy took the card and opened it.

"The saddest thing is," Maud continued to speak as Wendy read the message inside, "he is the only son I have left, but I really can't say I'm sorry it turned out this way. I know what he did to you, Wendy. His father did the same to me for nearly forty years. I had to break the cycle. I read the card, love. I had no idea. I couldn't let this chance pass by. For your sake, and the boy's."

A tear rolled down Wendy's cheek. Norman watched as the two women hugged. The card drifted from Wendy's lap and he pounced on it immediately. His eager eyes scanned every word.

My Darling Wendy,

Since returning home, my thoughts are filled with you, and the brief time we shared together. It's kind of strange to admit, but I sometimes catch myself wishing the Germans made you a widow. I can't stand to think of you with any other guy.

My heart aches for news of you. Not a day goes by when I don't dream of being back in your arms. My home, and my heart, will always be open for you.

Take care and keep safe,

Nick

Nick Saint (Ex-33rd US Reserve),
221C Plover Avenue,
Mountain Home,
Idaho

P.S. The dime is a tiny Christmas present for Norman to remember me by.

Norman looked up at his Grandmother and understood what she had done, and why. He didn't speak. He could keep a secret as well as a grown-up. He was the man of the house now, at least until they got to America.

The Pushover

During the singing of the Twenty-Third Psalm, the man next to me gave me a nudge and said, "What do you think of the wooden overcoat?"

Uncertain what he meant, I lifted an eyebrow.

"The coffin," he said.

I swayed to my left for a view along the aisle. I could see nothing worth interrupting the service for. Danny Fox's coffin stood on trestles in front of the altar looking no different from others I had seen. On the top was the wreath from his widow, Merle, in the shape of a large heart of red roses with Danny's name picked out in white. Not to my taste, but I wasn't so churlish as to mention this to anyone else.

"No handles," my informant explained.

So what? I thought. Who needs handles? Coffins are hardly ever carried by the handles. I gave a nod and continued singing.

"That isn't oak," the man persisted. "That's a veneer. Underneath, it's chipboard."

I pretended not to have heard, and joined in the singing of the third verse—the one beginning "Perverse and foolish oft I strayed"— with such commitment that I drew shocked glances from the people in front.

"She's going to bury Danny in the cheapest box she could buy."

This baboon was ruining the service. I sat for the sermon in a twisted position presenting most of my back to him.

But the damage had been done. My response to what was said was blighted. If John Wesley in his prime had been giving the Address I would still have found concentration difficult. Actually it was spoken by a callow curate with a nervous grin who revealed a lamentable ignorance about the Danny I had known. "A decent man" was a questionable epithet in Danny's case; "a loyal husband" extremely doubtful; "generous to a fault" a gross misrepresentation. I couldn't remember a time when the departed one had bought a round of drinks. If the curate felt obliged to say something positive, he might reasonably have told us that the man in the coffin had been funny and a charmer capable of selling sand to a sheik. I cared a lot about Danny, or I wouldn't be here, but just because he was dead we didn't have to award him a halo.

My contacts with the old rogue went back thirty years. Danny and I first met back in the sixties, the days of National Service, in the Air Force at a desolate camp on Salisbury Plain called Netheravon, and even so early in his career, still in his teens, Danny had got life running the way he wanted. He'd formed a poker school with a scale of duties as the stakes and, so far as I know, served his two years without ever polishing a floor, raking out a stove or doing a guard duty. No one ever caught him cheating, but his silky handling of the cards should have taught anyone not to play with him. He seduced (an old-fashioned word that gives a flavour of the time) the only WRAF officer on the roll and had the use of her pale blue Morris Minor on Saturdays to support his favourite football team, Bristol Rovers. Weekend passes were no problem. You had to smile at Danny.

I came across him again twelve years later, in 1973, on the sea front at Brighton dressed in a striped blazer, white flannels and a straw hat and doing a soft-shoe dance to an old Fred Astaire number on an ancient wind-up gramophone with a huge brass horn. I had no idea Danny was such a beautiful mover. So many people had stopped to watch that you couldn't get past without walking on the shingle. It was a deeply serious performance that refused to be serious at all. At a tempo so slow that any awkwardness would have been obvious, he shuffled and glided and turned about, tossing in casual gull-turns and toe-taps, dipping, swaying and twisting with the beat, his arms windmilling one second, seesawing the next, and never suggesting strain. After he'd passed the hat around, we went for a drink and talked about old times and former comrades. I paid, of course. After that we promised to stay in touch. We met a few times. I went to his second wedding in 1988—a big affair, because Merle had a sister and five brothers, all with families. They were a crazy bunch. The reception, on a river steamer, was a riot. I've never laughed so much.

Danny was fifty-seven when he died.

We sang another hymn and the curate said a prayer and led us out for the Committal. The pall-bearers hoisted the coffin and brought it along the aisle. I didn't need the nudge I got from my companion as they passed. I could see for myself that the wood was a cheap veneer. I wasn't judgmental. Quite possibly Danny had left Merle with nothing except his antique gramophone and some debts.

"She had him insured for a hundred and fifty K," Meanmouth insisted on telling me as we followed the coffin along a path between the graves. "She could have given him a decent send-off."

I told him curtly that I wasn't interested. God knows, I was trying not to be. At the graveside, I stepped away from him and took a position opposite. Let him bend someone else's ear with his malice.

Young sheep were bleating in the field beside the churchyard as the coffin was lowered. The clouds parted and we felt warmth on our skins. I remembered Danny dancing on the front that summer evening at Brighton. *Bon voyage*, old buccaneer, I thought. You robbed all of us of something, some time, but we came in numbers to see you off. You left us glittering memories, and that wasn't a bad exchange.

A few tears were shed around that grave.

As the Grace was spoken I became conscious of those joyless eyes sizing me up for another approach, so I gave him one back, raised my chin to the required level and stared like one of those stone figures on Easter Island. My twenty years of teaching fifteen-year-olds haven't been totally wasted. Then I turned away, said "Amen," and smiled benignly at the curate.

Mean-mouth walked directly through the lych-gate, got into his car and drove off. Why do people like that bother to come to funerals?

Most of us converged on the Red Lion across the street. A pub lunch. A corrective to nostalgia. It fitted my picture of Danny that his mourners should be forced to dip into their pockets to buy their own drinks. The only food on offer was microwaved meat pies with soggy crusts. Mean-mouth must have known. He would have told me that Merle was the skinflint, and on sober reflection it is difficult to believe otherwise. It seemed Danny had ended up with a tightwad wife. A nice irony.

And the family weren't partying at the house. They joined us, Merle leading them in while "Happy Days Are Here Again" came over the music system. Her choice of clothes left no one in any doubt that she was the principal lady in the party—a black cashmere coat and a matching hat with a vast brim like a manta that flapped as she moved. She was a good ten years younger than Danny, a tall, triumphantly slim, talkative woman who chain-smoked. I'd heard that she knew a lot about antiques; at their wedding, Danny had got in first with the obvious joke about his antiquity, and frankly the way Merle had eyed him all through the reception, you'd have thought he was a piece of Wedgwood. Yet we all knew he was out of the reject basket. Slightly chipped. Well, extensively, to be truthful. He'd lived the kind of free-ranging life he'd wanted, busking, bar-tending, running a stall at a fairground, a bit of chauffeuring, leading guided walks around the East End and for a time acting as a croupier. Enjoyable, undemanding jobs on the fringe of the entertainment industry, but never likely to earn much of a bank balance. With his innocent-looking eyes and deep-etched laughter lines, he had a well-known attraction for women that must have played a part in the romance, but Merle didn't look the sort to go starry-eyed into marriage.

Someone bought her a cocktail in a tall glass and she began the rounds of the funeral party, cigarette in one hand, drink in the other, giving and receiving kisses. The mood of forced bonhomie that gets people through funerals was well established. I overheard one formidably fat woman telling Merle, "Never mind love, you're not bad-looking. Keep your 'air nice and you'll be all right. Won't 'appen at once, mind. I 'ad to wait four years. But you'll be all right."

Merle's hat quivered.

She moved towards me and I gave her the obligatory kiss and muttered sympathetic words. She said, "Good of you to come. We never really got to know each other, did we? You and Danny go back a long way."

"To his Air Force days," I said.

"Oh, he used to tell wonderful tales of the RAF," she

said, calling it the 'raff' and clasping my hand so firmly that I could feel every one of her rings. "I don't know if half of them are true. The night exercises."

"Night exercises at Netheravon?" said I, not remembering any.

She took hold of my hand and squeezed it. "Come on, you know Danny. That was his name for that pilot officer whose car he used."

"Oh, her."

"Night exercises. Wicked man." She chuckled. "I couldn't be jealous when he put it like that. To Danny, she was just an easy lay. I envy you, knowing him when he was young. He must have been a right tearaway. Anyway, sweetie, I'd better not gossip. So many old mates to see." She moved on, leaving me in a cloud of cigarette smoke.

Another woman holding a gin and tonic sidled close and said, "What's she on, do you think? She's frisky for a widow."

"I've no idea."

"Danny's brother Ben must have given her some pills."

"Which one is Ben?"

"In the blue suit and black polo neck. Handy having a doctor for your brother-in-law."

"Yes." I glanced across at brother-in-law Ben, a taller, slimmer version of Danny. "He looks young."

"Fourteen years younger than Danny. They were stepbrothers, I think."

On an impulse I asked, "Was he Danny's doctor also?"

She nodded. "They never paid a bean for medicines."

Malice must be infectious. This wasn't Mean-mouth speaking. This was a short, chunky woman in a grey suit. She introduced herself as their neighbour. Not for much longer, it seemed. "Merle told me she'll be off to warmer climes now. She was always complaining about the winters here, was Merle."

"To live, you mean?"

She nodded. "Spain, I expect."

I remembered the life insurance payout. Merle's antique had, after all, turned out to be worth something if she was emigrating. Watching the newly-weds at their wedding reception, only four years ago, it hadn't crossed my mind to rate Danny as an insurance claim. Had it occurred to Merle?

What a sour thought to have at a funeral! I banished it. Instead I talked to the neighbour about the weather until she got bored and wandered off.

I did some circulating of my own and joined a crowd at a table in the main bar I recognized as more of Danny's close family. They all had large teeth and lop-sided grins like his. A man who looked like another younger brother was saying what a shock his death had been. "Fifty-seven. It's no age, is it? He was always so fit. I never knew Dan had a dicky heart."

"He didn't look after himself," a woman said.

"What do you mean—didn't look after himself?" the brother retorted. "He wasn't overweight."

"He didn't exercise. He avoided all forms of sport. Never learned to swim, hold a tennis racket, swing a golf club. He thought jogging was insane."

"He danced like a dream."

"Call that exercise? He never worked up a sweat. I tell you, he didn't look after himself."

"He had two wives," one of the men chipped in.

"Not at the same time," another woman said, giggling.

"What are you saying—that two wives strained his vital powers?"

There was some amusement at this. "No," said the man. "*You* said he didn't look after himself and I was pointing out that he had two women to do the job."

"That's what marriage is for, is it, Charlie?" the woman

came back at him. "So that the man's got someone to look after him?"

"Hello, hello. Have you turned into one of those feminists?" retorted Charlie.

"I'm sure being looked after wasn't in Danny's mind when he married Merle," said the giggly woman.

"We all know what was in Danny's mind when he married Merle," said the feminist.

Resisting the temptation to widen the debate by asking what had been in Merle's mind, I went back to the bar for a white wine. When I picked it up, my hand shook. A disturbing possibility had crept into *my* mind. The law allows a doctor considerable discretion in dealing with the death of a patient in his care. Provided that he has seen the patient in the two weeks prior to the death, and the cause of death is known to him and was not the result of an accident, or suspicious circumstances, he may sign the death certificate without reporting the matter to the coroner. Merle's brother-in-law Ben had treated Danny.

Across the bar, Ben was talking affably to some people who hadn't attended the funeral. This was his village, his local. Most of the family lived around here. He was at ease. Yet there was something more about his manner, a sense of relief; or perhaps it was triumph.

As for Merle, she was remarkably animated for a woman who had only just buried her husband. It must be an act, a brave attempt to get through the day without weeping, I tried telling myself. Watching her, I wasn't convinced. Her eyes shone like a bride's.

Another curious thing I noticed was that Merle spent time with everyone in that bar except her doctor brother-in-law, Ben. She kept away from him as if he were radio-active. Yet they were keenly aware of each other. Each time Merle moved, Ben would look across and check her position. Occasionally their eyes locked briefly. I was increasingly convinced that they had agreed not to be seen talking together. They weren't being hostile; they shared a secret.

When I left about six, the party was still going on. I didn't blame anyone for turning it into a wake. I was sure Danny would have approved. He would have been in the thick of the junketing, well pickled by this time, full of good humour, just as long as he didn't have to buy a round.

My unease about the circumstances of Danny's death dispersed within a week. I had more urgent things going on in my life that don't play any part in these events except that by February, six months after the funeral, I was tired and depressed. Then someone made things worse by breaking into my car and stealing my credit cards. The police were useless. The only positive thing they suggested was that I inform the people who issued the cards. When my shiny and pristine replacement cards arrived, I had an impulse to use them right away to give myself a boost. I walked into a travel agent's and booked two weeks in the sun. Immediately.

In Florida I spotted Merle Fox. By pure chance, or fate, I walked into the Guild Hall Gallery on Duval Street in Key West and there she was, looking at stained glass pictures of fish. She'd bleached her hair and cut it short and she was deeply tanned and wearing a skimpy top and white trousers that fitted like a second skin. Something new in widow's weeds, I thought unkindly—for I recognized her straight away. Of course she hadn't altered her features, but her stance was the giveaway, the suggestion of swagger in the shoulders. It was no different from the way she'd swanned around the bar of the Red Lion after Danny's funeral.

I didn't speak to Merle. In fact, I moved out of range,

hidden from her view by a rotating card-stand. But when she came out of the shop I followed, intrigued, you may say, if you don't call me nosy. I was pretty inconspicuous in T-shirt and shorts like most of the tourists strolling along the street.

Halfway along Duval Street she turned up a side road that was mainly residential and lined with two-storey Bahamian-style wood-frame buildings shaded by palms and wild purple orchid trees and fronted by white picket fences. She walked two blocks (with me in discreet attendance) and let herself into an elegant three-bay house with a porch and—more irony here—a widow's walk. Had I really seen Merle? The moment she'd stepped out of my view I became doubtful. It isn't the custom in Key West to have one's name on the mailbox, so it was difficult to make certain without speaking to the woman. I wasn't sure I wanted a face-to-face.

I crossed the street for a longer view of the house. The shutters were open, but the louvred windows effectively screened the interior.

You wouldn't believe that a leafy street bathed in sunlight could make you feel uneasy. After the crowds on Duval Street, this was eerie in its quietness.

A cat leaned against my shin and made a plaintive sound. I stooped to stroke it.

A voice startled me. "We call him Rocky, after the boxer. He has the most formidable front paws."

I looked behind me. This elderly woman had been sitting unnoticed in her porch swing in front of a small white house.

"He's a champion," I remarked, wondering if my luck was still running. "I was looking for a friend of mine who came to live in Key West. Mrs Fox. Do you know her?"

She paused some seconds before answering, "I can't say I do."

"She must have arrived some time in the last three months," I ventured. "She's a widow."

"The only lady who came to Southard Street since the summer is Mrs Finch in the house across the street and she's no widow," she informed me.

My confidence ebbed. "Mrs Finch, you said?"

"Mrs Merle Finch, from England. They're both from England."

"Ah. That wouldn't be the lady I know," I said, mentally turning a back-flip of triumph. "But thank you for your help, ma'am. Rocky is a cat in a million." I walked away, reflecting that Merle must have kept her hair extra nice to have charmed Mr Finch, whoever he was, into such a quick marriage. A little over six months since she had buried Danny she was re-married, settled in her new home. If her tan was any guide, she had already been in Florida some time.

The big insurance payout, the death certificate provided by her brother-in-law, the quick marriage and the escape to Florida. Had they all been planned? Was it any wonder I felt suspicious?

My holiday routine altered. Next morning I made sure of passing the house on my way to the shops. I lingered across the street for ten minutes or so. Wherever I went in Key West I was hawk-eyed for another sighting.

It came the next evening. Merle stepped out of Fausto's Food Palace on Fleming Street, crossed my path to a moped and put her bag on the pannier. My heart-rate stepped up. The hours of watching out for her, passing the house and so on, had made me feel furtive. Now I was ready to panic. Ridiculous.

I don't like being sneaky. That isn't my nature. I like to be straight with people. Confrontation is the honest way. So I steeled my nerves, stepped towards her and said, "Hi, Merle."

She stopped and stared.

"Remember me?" I said. "Danny's oppo from his Air Force days. Isn't this amazing? I must buy you a drink."

She couldn't deny her identity. Recovering her poise, she said in her very British accent that she would have been delighted, but she had to get back to the apartment. She had something cooking.

I almost laughed out loud at the phrase. Instead I insisted we must meet and suggested a nightcap later at one of the quieter open-air bars. She had a hunted look, but she agreed to see me there at ten.

"You got your wish, then," I said when we shared a table in a dark corner of the bar drinking margaritas.

"What do you mean?" She was tense.

"A warm place to live. I presume you live here."

"Yes, I do."

"And not alone. You're Mrs Finch now."

She frowned. "How did you know that?"

"I was told. Is he British, your husband?"

She gave a nod.

"Anyone I know?"

She said, "Why are you asking me these things?"

I said, "What's the matter? Don't you want to talk about them?"

She said, "I left all that behind. It's painful. I don't want to be reminded."

"I wasn't reminding you about the past, Merle. I was enquiring about the present. Your present husband. What's his name?"

She took a long sip of her drink. "Have you seen him?"

"No. But I'd love to meet him—if you let him out."

She pushed aside the drink. "I'll pay for these. I'm leaving."

I put a hand on her arm. "I'm sorry. That was insensitive. Don't take offence."

She brushed my hand away and got up. I didn't follow. I knew it would be no use. I *had* been insensitive. But she had fuelled my suspicions. She had behaved like a guilty woman. Meeting me had been an unpleasant shock. The geography of the Florida Keys—the long drive south from Miami over bridges that span the sea—fosters a feeling of escape, of reaching a haven in Key West bathed in sun and good will. You don't expect sharp questions about your conduct.

I believed Merle and her brother-in-law Ben had conspired to murder Danny. A lethal injection seemed the most likely means. Ben had written something innocuous on the death certificate and Merle had claimed the insurance, paid Ben for his services and escaped to Florida to marry her lover, the fascinating Mr Finch.

I believed this, yes. But it was only belief so far. The evidence I had was circumstantial. A cheap funeral, an alleged insurance payout, some sly glances and a quick marriage. None of this was sufficient to justify fingering Merle for murder.

Unable to sleep that night, I asked myself why I wanted to pursue the matter, for it was taking over my holiday. Was it anything as highminded as a concern for justice? Or was it morbid curiosity?

No.

It was more personal. Danny had been important in my life. The link between us was stronger than I'd admit to anyone. I was angry, deeply angry, at what I believed had happened. Our lives had touched only intermittently since 1961, and I regretted that. Face it, I thought. His murder killed a part of you.

Yet I knew if I pursued this, I was putting myself at risk. If I threatened Merle with exposure I would give her a reason for killing me. Or having me killed.

These were the thoughts I grappled with next day. They

made me sick with self-disgust because I had discovered I was a coward. I was scared to do any more about my suspicions. I despised myself.

So I became a tourist again, instead of a snoop. I lounged by the hotel pool in the morning and later took a trip to the coral reef in a glass-bottomed boat. I spent an hour in the cemetery. Morbid, you may think, but the gravestones are on the tourist trail. I found the famous epitaph "*I told you I was sick.*" It didn't seem funny when I saw it.

Late in the afternoon, I had a quiet drink in one of the smaller bars on Duval Street watching the movement of people towards Mallory Square. There's a tradition in Key West that people converge on the dock to celebrate the sunset. When I'd finished my drink, I joined them.

I didn't expect to meet Merle there. As a resident, she'd regard the sunset spectacle as a sideshow for tourists. Even so, as I sidled through the good-natured crowd I caught myself looking more than once at women who resembled her and the men they were with. I still wanted keenly to catch a glimpse of Mr Finch, the new husband.

The sky became pastel blue and the sun dipped towards the sea, becoming ever more red. The heads of some of the crowd were in silhouette. At one end a tightrope was slung between tripod posts and the performer was teasing his audience, keeping *them* in suspense with patter and juggling. I ambled on, past a guitarist and a dog-trainer. Ahead, someone else had drawn a fair crowd. A fire-eater, I guessed. There's something hypnotic about the sight of a flame, particularly in the fading light. But I decided the aerialist would be better value and I turned back. I was actually retracing my steps when I heard a scratchy sound that froze my blood, an old 78 record of a band playing some song from way back. It was coming from behind the crowd at the end.

I returned, fast.

I couldn't see for the tightly packed people. I circled the crowd in frustration while that infernal tune blared out. Unable to contain my feelings I scythed through the crowd saying, "I'm sorry, I have to get through"—until I had a view.

Danny was wowing them in his straw hat, blazer and flannels, hoofing it just as smoothly as he had in the old days. Far from dead, he had a better colour than most of his audience. The old gramophone was behind him on the ledge, grinding out "Let's Face the Music."

He saw me and winked.

I stared back, stunned. Maybe I should have rejoiced, but I'd grieved for this fraudster. I was more angry than relieved. It was a kind of betrayal.

Coward that I am, afterwards, when the sun had set and the crowds had dispersed I sat tamely with Danny on a ledge of the sea wall at the south end of the dock, our backs to the sea. He had a six-pack of Coors that he systematically emptied. Dancing, he explained, was thirsty work. He offered me some, and I declined.

"Merle told me she met you," he admitted. "She didn't want me to come out tonight, but I'm a performer, damnit. The show goes on. She doesn't understand that you and I go back a long way. You wouldn't blow the whistle on your old RAF buddy."

I didn't rise to that. "You've played some cool poker hands in your time, Danny, but this beats everything. I don't know how you managed it."

He grinned. "No problem. My stepbrother Ben is my doctor. He signed the death certificate. Merle picked up the life insurance and here we are—Mr and Mrs Finch. The fake passports cost us a packet, but we could afford them. Isn't this a great place to retire?"

"But there was a funeral."

"That didn't cost much."

"Too true."

"A lot of them were in on this," he confessed. "My cousin Jerry runs an undertaking business in the next village. He supplied the coffin."

"And a corpse?" I said, appalled.

"A couple of sandbags."

"You're a prize bastard, Danny Fox."

He chuckled at that. "Aren't I just? And the prize is in the bank."

"What you did is sick."

"Oh, come on," he said. "Who loses out? Only the insurance company. I had to pay huge premiums."

"There were people in that church who genuinely grieved for you."

"Horseshit."

That hurt. "I grieved."

"Jesus—what for?" His eyebrows jutted in genuine puzzlement.

I started to say, "If you don't remember—"

Danny cut me off with, "All that was thirty years ago. And then it was only—"

"Night exercises," I completed the statement for him.

"What?"

"Night exercises. That's what you thought of me, didn't you?" I stood up and faced him. "Admit it. Say it to my face, you skunk."

There was a pause. The night had virtually closed in. Danny up-ended his last can of beer. "All right, if that's what you heard from Merle, it must be true." He laughed. "Let's face it, Susan—that's what you were. P.O. didn't stand for Pilot Officer in your case, it stood for pushover."

I said, "That's unbelievably cruel."

Unmoved, Danny told me, "If you really want to know, I couldn't even remember your name that day we met in Brighton. I remembered your car, though."

That was one injury too many—even for a coward like me. The precious flame I'd guarded for thirty years was out. Our relationship had been the one experience in my life that I thought I could call truly romantic. Nothing since had compared to it. Danny had made me feel beautiful, desired, a woman fulfilled.

He knew the pain he had just inflicted. He *must* have known.

"Danny."

"Yes?" He looked up.

By that time Mallory Dock was deserted except for us. The water there is deep enough to moor a cruise liner.

The body of the middle-aged male washed up on Key West Bight a week or so later was identified as that of the man who sometimes danced on the dock at sunset. Nobody knew his name and nobody claimed the body for burial.

Quiet Please—
We're Rolling

A naked man on a tropical beach was chasing a small white dog that had just run off with his swimming trunks. The scene was shot from the rear. Once in a while, a bare bum is acceptable for early evening viewing.

Albert Challis, in his bedsit in Reading, reached for another can of lager, his eyes never leaving the screen of the small portable TV.

"Jesus! I don't know how they get away with this. It's bloody obvious most of it is faked."

His wife Karen continued mending the jumper on her lap, oblivious to Albert's ranting. She didn't enjoy the programme, and she had a long evening in prospect, repairing clothes. There was no escape from the TV when you lived in a bedsit.

Albert continued, after a belch, "When this show first went out, I reckon most of the clips were genuine. Then they started offering a few hundred quid for new material. Stands to reason people are going to fake the incidents. They set up someone making a fool of himself, roll the camera and cash in."

He watched in cynical expectation as a grey man in a

grey room began painting a door frame. A second later the door opened and the hapless decorator was dowsed in red.

"Well, knock me down with a feather," said Albert with heavy sarcasm. "I never saw that one coming. It's like I say, Karen. The whole thing's a set-up."

Karen folded the jumper and placed it on her 'done' pile, then turned her attention to a black woollen sock. It was one of Albert's, the survivor of a pair he had worn so proudly on their wedding day, eighteen years ago. Now it contained as much darning wool as original thread, but Albert insisted it wasn't ready for the rag-box yet.

On the screen a well-dressed woman in a stable yard started walking beside the half-doors where the horses were kept.

"Ay up!" said Albert. "Watch what happens to her big straw hat. There it goes!"

Sure enough, a horse's head appeared suddenly from one of the stables and got the woman's hat between its teeth and whipped it off her head and out of reach.

"I bet they rehearsed it three times."

Karen had looked up and watched the clip, prompted by Albert's "Ay up!" "If they did," she said, "they must have got through more than one hat. It's very destructive. I've never had a hat as nice as that."

Albert said, "It seems to me all you have to do is buy one of these bloody camcorders and the money's yours. They'll take anything, slipping on some ice, falling into a pond, being hit on the head by a football, any bloody thing. You could make one a week, I reckon. Shoot it on Saturday, send it to the television people on the Monday, and, bingo, the cheque arrives on Wednesday. We could live like kings on that sort of money, Karen."

Karen looked down at her darning again. "Well why not, if it's so simple? Why not get one of those cameras and try it?"

Albert had no immediate answer. He placed his can on the aged carpet and folded both arms across his ample beer-belly. The best he could manage in response was a smile that was meant to be superior.

Karen said, "You're all mouth and trousers, Albert Challis. You say it's all a con, but you don't have the bottle to prove it."

Albert found his voice. "I'm not sure I heard you correctly, my sweet," he said. "You did just suggest buying one of those camcorders, didn't you? When was the last time you looked in the bloody shop window? Have you any idea of the price of those things?"

Karen shook her head. They didn't have the sort of money most other people seemed to have. Nothing in their household had been bought new. They got it all second-hand. Whatever broke, burst or wore out had to be repaired.

"They cost a bloody fortune, woman," Albert ranted. "Hundreds of pounds. Can you imagine that, a little piece of black plastic costing five hundred quid?"

Karen shook her head, returning to the rhythmical comfort of needle and thread.

Albert finished his lager, watching a fat woman being chased across a field by a goat while the studio audience guffawed. "The point is," he said in support of his apparent caution, "I'm not prepared to splash out five hundred on a camcorder when we only stand to make two hundred and fifty back."

"But you just said you could make one a week and we could live like royalty," Karen reminded him. "Soon as I call your bluff, you back off."

Albert shot her a filthy look. "Don't you provoke me."

"It's not as if we haven't got the money," Karen persisted. "We must have more than five hundred in the bank."

"Never you mind what we have or haven't got in the bank, Karen."

"I do mind," she said. "It's mine as much as yours. I work to keep us going, same as you. The cooking, the cleaning, the mending. I think we ought to have a joint account and then I'd know how much we're worth."

"You'd spend it in a week," said Albert. "Look, if anything happened to me, God forbid, that money goes to you, right? All my worldly goods. Satisfied?"

The programme was coming to an end. The grinning host was saying, ". . . be sure to keep your home-movie clips coming in, because you could be the winner of our clip of the series prize, and that's worth a cool ten thousand pounds."

"Ten grand!" said Albert, deeply impressed. "Now that might be worth lashing out for. The clip of the series. We'd have to think of something really brilliant. Get me a pen and paper, quick. I'm taking down the address."

In bed, Karen was trying her best to sleep, drawing the thin blankets tightly around her, thinking of continental quilts, double glazing and central heating. She wondered how much they really had in that bank account.

Albert's voice broke into her fantasies. "It would have to be a really great caper. Something completely fantastic. They wouldn't give the money for one more silly kid messing about with a hosepipe."

Karen said, "Are you still on about that programme?"

"I'm on about ten grand."

There was an interval of silence before Karen spoke again.

"It would have to be believable."

"What do you mean?"

She raised herself onto her elbows, any hope of sleep impossible as long as Albert was preoccupied with the big prize. "Well," she said, "when you see most of those clips, the situation is just unreal. You couldn't believe in it."

The bed creaked and Albert rolled towards her. "Go on. I'm listening."

"Tonight, for instance," Karen said. "The chap who ended covered in paint. You yourself said it was probably all set up for the programme. I mean, who would want to film a door being painted?"

Albert clutched her arm. "You've hit the nail on the head. It's hardly a prime home-movie subject."

Karen explained, "That's why the ones they show at weddings work so well. You know, when they can't get the knife into the cake and they knock it off the stand. Or a breeze gets under the bride's gown and lifts it up to her waist. Stuff like that. People accept them as genuine accidents because a wedding is the place where you take your video camera."

"But you can't mess up someone's wedding just to get a laugh on video," Albert said, misreading the plot.

"That's just an example," said Karen. "All I'm telling you is that to win the big prize you'd have to find a situation when it would be perfectly normal to be filming. Then it looks genuine, and it's funnier, too."

Albert pondered the matter further. "Weddings, kiddies' parties, barbecues, village fetes. Where else do people take these little cameras?"

"Holidays," Karen dreamily replied. She yawned. "Night, night." She turned over, trying to find a comfortable spot between the thinly-covered mattress springs.

Albert's eyes were gleaming in the dark. He reached out and fondled Karen's rump. "You're brilliant."

"Shove off," she said, pushing his hand away.

"What I have, I hold," said Albert, replacing it. "You and I are going to take a holiday, my sweet. A caravan holiday."

"A *caravan*, did you say?"

"And I know where to get one. That bloke across the street who keeps it on his drive."

"Mr Tinker? He wouldn't let us borrow his caravan."

"I bet he will. He doesn't use it himself. Since the divorce, it's been stuck on that drive for two years. He'll be glad to be rid of it."

"*Rid* of it?" said Karen, failing to understand.

"We'll be doing him a favour," said Albert. "What does he want with a caravan? He'll make a few quid on the insurance. I'll speak to him tomorrow."

When Albert returned from his chat with Joe Tinker, he was practically turning cartwheels of joy. "He couldn't be more helpful," he told Karen. "Like I said, he's got no more use for the caravan. We're welcome to do just whatever we like with it."

"Take it on holiday?"

"We're doing him a favour," said Albert. "He won't have to park his car on the street any more. But that isn't all. I told him what this is about."

"You told him?" said Karen, horrified.

"Everything. To get his co-operation," said Albert. "He's seen the programme and he thinks the same as us. He says this is one hell of a stunt and he reckons we can't fail to win the big money. I've told him I'll give him a couple of hundred if we do. Fair enough, eh?"

"I suppose so," said Karen, "but can we trust him to stay quiet about it?"

"That's why he gets a cut. He's part of the conspiracy, then," said Albert. "But I haven't told you the best part. Joe Tinker also owns a camcorder. Yes, I'm not kidding. He's going to lend it to us for nothing. For nothing, Karen! What's more, he'll show you how to use it."

"Me?" said Karen.

"Unless you want to be making an idiot of yourself on television, you've got to be holding the camera, pointing it at me. And it's got to be done properly. Good focusing. No shaking. You only get one take, remember. It's got to be right first time, and it's got to be up to professional standard to win the ten grand."

She said nervously, "I don't think I can do it, Albert."

"Course you can! They're simple, these camcorders, dead simple. I told Joe you'll be over for some instruction this afternoon. He's a good bloke, and he fancies you anyway. He'll give you all the confidence in the world."

"What is this stunt, anyway?" said Karen.

"We take a holiday, like I said, towing Joe's caravan."

"Where to?"

"Some remote part of Wales. I'm going to study the map this afternoon while you're learning to be an ace camerawoman. If you get your certificate of competence we can drive down there next Saturday for the shoot."

"The shoot?"

"Of the film," Albert explained. "Get with it, love. We're shooting a film, remember? Like I say, we hook the caravan to my old Cortina. Joe's lending me his towbar as well. He's great."

"Is it strong enough?"

"The towbar?"

"Your car. Those caravans are big things to tow."

"No problem," said Albert. "We can take it gently, just tootling along. We'll be stopping every few miles filming bits and pieces of our journey."

"What for?"

Albert sighed. Everything always had to be explained to Karen. "Because it has to look like we're on a proper holiday. We need about twenty minutes of boring holiday stuff to divert suspicion from our real intentions. Can't you see how phony it will look if the only thing on the tape is the caravan going over the cliff?"

Karen gasped in horror. "Over the cliff? Mr Tinker's caravan?"

Albert smiled. "With only the seagulls as witnesses—apart from the camera and fifteen million viewers."

"It's insane!"

"That's why it's going to win ten grand. What a spectacle! I'm going to look at the Ordnance Survey and find a bit of the coast with a gentle slope leading to the cliff edge, and a good long drop to the rocks below. We park the caravan thirty yards up the slope. That way I have time to get out."

"Get out?"

"Before it rolls over. It's going to be sensational. You'll be outside filming the scenery from the cliff top. You pan around to me at the window of the caravan. I'll hold up a bit of metal and say, 'What's this, love?' The caravan will start to move. I'll shout something the TV people will have to bleep out—the audience always loves that—then I leap from the door holding the broken hand-brake of the caravan, to watch the thing roll over the edge." He laughed out loud and raised his arms like a boxer who has just heard his opponent counted out.

"It's so dangerous," said Karen. "I mean, it's a tremendous idea, but . . ."

Albert brushed the objection aside. "No risk at all," he said. "If you're nervous, we'll give the van fifty yards to roll, instead of thirty."

In the week that followed, Albert planned the "shoot," as he called it, with military precision. Having selected several possible clifftop sites, he drove down to Wales to make a decision on the most suitable. He found one on the Pembrokeshire Coast that was wonderfully remote, with a grassy slope leading straight to a two-hundred foot drop. In his spare moments he worked diligently on the script that he and Karen would have to follow, complete with stage directions.

"We only get one shot at this," he told her when he returned from scouting the locations. "It has to go like clockwork, while appearing totally unplanned. How are the lessons going?"

"All right," Karen said.

"You've been clocking in with Joe, have you, while I was away?"

She nodded.

"Mastered it yet?"

"I hope so."

"Hope isn't good enough," said Albert. "You've got to be certain. Are you going over to see him again?"

"This afternoon."

"Excellent. He's a good bloke, isn't he?"

"He's very good," said Karen, and she meant it.

"While you're in there, I'm going to do a bit of work on the old caravan. It could do with a clean. The smarter it looks, the better the effect."

So whilst Albert sponged and polished, preparing the caravan for its TV debut, Karen had more tuition from Joe. Really, as Joe explained, the camcorder was a simple machine that almost anyone could use, but if the attractive Mrs Challis wanted more practice with the thing, he was only too pleased to show her how to hold it. No woman had been inside his house since his wife had divorced him two years ago.

For her part, Karen was not displeased to feel Joe's arm around her shoulders steadying the camera from time to time. He was a most considerate man, and not bad looking, either. And he had double-glazing and central heating. "It seems a real shame that you're going to lose your caravan through this," she said.

"Not at all," said Joe cheerfully. "It's had its day. I've no more use for it. Besides, it's not in very good condition any more. The door has warped in the damp. You have to give it quite a tug to open it. Better mention that to Albert. A little grease around the sides will ease it."

Extremely early Saturday morning, when it was still dark and nobody was about, Albert went over to Joe's to attach the towbar. He'd arranged to collect Karen at the last minute. She sat in their front room with the lights off, mentally revising the instructions for the video camera. She had collected the camera from Joe after one last session of instruction the previous afternoon. Joe had been a tower of strength.

After what seemed like a couple of hours, Albert drew the caravan from its mooring and swung the car across the street. Karen climbed in, camcorder in hand.

"You'll do no filming in this light," Albert said tensely. "I don't know what you're holding it for. Chuck it on the back seat."

"It doesn't belong to us," said Karen.

Instead of "tootling along" as he'd promised, Albert drove fast for the first two hours. Two or three times Karen said she was nervous about the car, but he didn't slow down. Near the Welsh border, as dawn came up, she suggested a stop for filming. Albert said there would be opportunities later.

She reminded him of the reason for having some footage of other places as well as the clifftop, and he relented and let her film some sheep sheltering at the side of the road.

Albert looked at his watch. "I want to get on," he told her. "The light isn't so good in the middle of the day. It gets too bright."

"Joe said it doesn't matter what time of day you film with one of these."

"Will you shut up about Joe?"

As they neared their destination, Albert made a couple

of short stops to consult the map. The area was very remote.

About ten in the morning, the cliff came up on their left. Albert steered the car off the road and towed the caravan across the turf to the position he'd selected. He secured the brake on the caravan, uncoupled the car and drove back to a point near the road. They had a good view for miles around and no one was in sight.

"Smell it, love?" said Albert.

"The sea air?" said Karen.

"Money, stupid. Ten bloody grand."

"It's a good thing there's no wind," Karen pointed out as they walked towards the caravan. "This should be good for sound."

"You talk like you work for the BBC."

Albert walked towards the cliff edge and peered over. "Perfect," he enthused. "The tide's in. There's a thumping great drop, and it's going to get smashed to little bits and washed away and turn to driftwood." He came back to where Karen was standing with the camcorder. "Want to run over your lines?"

"It's all right," she said nervously. "Let's get on with it."

"Make sure it's working first."

She switched on and checked the battery level for the umpteenth time. She took some footage of Albert standing with his back to the cliff edge and they played it back through the eyepiece to check. The clarity was wonderful.

Albert seemed to be getting his confidence back. "Isn't it just like I promised? The gentle grassy slope, the impressive visual panorama, the sheer bloody suspense of the thing? And just look at that caravan!"

"Like ten thousand grand," she said, admiring the polished chrome and freshly-cleaned surface.

Albert walked her to her position. "Now you do know what to do?"

She nodded.

"And what to say?"

"Mm."

"Let's get on with it, then."

She watched him walk to the caravan. He had some difficulty opening the door, but he managed it at the second attempt, climbed inside, slammed the door and took his place by the window, opening it wide.

"Can you hear me all right?"

"Perfectly, Albert."

"Are we ready to roll, then?"

"Yes."

"Remember what I said. Establish the shot with a view of that cliff to your left, showing just how big the drop is, then pan around slowly along the cliff edge and across the grass to me. Right?"

"Right."

"Start the camcorder now. Action."

Heart thumping, Karen pressed the red *record* button, swinging slowly around to encompass the impressive-looking cliff. She didn't care any more that her hands were shaking. She watched the grass in the lens, then the white gleam of the caravan, then Albert at the window.

True to his "script," he held up a piece of metal. The caravan lurched on its mooring feet and for a second, Karen feared that it wasn't going to move.

Albert spoke his words: "Do you know what this is, love?"

The caravan began to roll.

"It's the brake, Albert! What is it doing in your hand? Get out—the van's moving!"

"Bloody hell!"

She saw Albert move fast towards the door and waited for the panic to set in for real.

Thirty yards to the edge.

She screamed his name as loudly as possible, mainly

to obscure his shouting. She had stopped filming, of course.

The caravan moved sedately on its way.

He was desperately trying to open the jammed caravan door. How many times had Joe stressed to her that she should tell Albert to grease the edges? Not once had she considered passing on the information. She wanted Albert to die.

Twenty yards to go, and it was picking up a little speed.

The worst thing would be finding a phone in this God-forsaken place. The closest must be miles away. Everything else would be simple. A few tears for the police. Then hand over the tape. "It must be all on here, officer. It's been the most awful accident."

Karen continued to scream, thinking of her future with Joe Tinker with his double-glazing and his central heating and his modern fully-sprung bed with the continental quilt.

Ten yards.

Five.

A moment before the caravan disappeared from view, the caravan door burst open, Albert flung himself out and hit the turf a yard from the edge. He had survived.

Karen was devastated. She flung down the camcorder and stamped her foot.

Fortunately, Albert was too shaken to notice. He still lay face down, panting.

Eventually she drew herself together and went to him. She could probably have pushed him over, he was so near, but she couldn't bring herself to do it. That would be too direct, a hands-on murder.

Albert said, "That was a bloody near thing."

"What went wrong?" said Karen as innocently as she was able.

"Couldn't get the bloody door open. I knew it was difficult. Found that out when I was cleaning the thing. Put some grease on it yesterday, but it wasn't enough, obviously. Ended up kicking my way out." He got to his feet. "Look at me. I'm shaking like a leaf."

Karen said, "Let's get you to the car."

"Where's the camera?"

"Oh, I dropped it over there," she said. "I'm not sure how much I got. God, I was frightened!"

"Doesn't matter, love," said Albert with unusual tenderness. "We can't use the video anyway."

"Why not?"

"Evidence. If they ever find anything at the bottom of that cliff and come knocking on our door, the last thing we want is a bloody video of the event."

She frowned. "They could only find the caravan."

Albert was shaking his head. "There's something else. With luck, the sea will take care of it."

"What on earth are you talking about?"

"Bloody Joe Tinker. When I went in to see him this morning, he said he wanted a half-share of the profits. *Five grand!* You know me, love. Mean as hell. I lashed out. Hit the bleeder against the kitchen stove and cracked his skull. Killed him outright. What could I do but shove him into his own bloody caravan and bring him down here for disposal?"

"Oh, God, no!" wailed Karen.

"Don't shed tears over him," said Albert. "Didn't you ever notice he fancied you something rotten, the jerk? Like I told you the other night, what I have, I hold."

Wayzgoose

A slight, worried woman in a leather jacket walked into Bath police station.

The desk sergeant eyed her through the protective glass. "Yes, ma'am?"

"Can I speak to someone?"

"You're speaking to me, ma'am."

"Someone senior."

The sergeant had been dealing with the public across this desk for twelve years. "I'm the best on offer."

Unamused, the woman waited. Her hair was dark and short, shaped to her head. She wore no make-up.

The sergeant coaxed her, "Why don't you give me some idea what it's about?"

"I just killed my husband."

The sergeant bent closer to the glass. "You what?"

"I came in to confess."

"Hang about, ma'am. Where did this happen?"

"At home. 32, Collinson Road."

"He's there now?"

"His body is."

"Collinson Road. I ought to know it."

"Twerton."

The sergeant gestured to a woman police officer behind him and told her to get a response car out to Twerton. Then he asked the woman, "What's your name, ma'am?"

"Trish Noble."

"Trish for Patricia?"

"Yes"

"And your husband's name?"

"Glenn."

"What happened, Mrs Noble?"

"He was in a drunken stupor at four in the afternoon when I came in from work, so I was that mad that I threw a teapot at him. Cracked him on the head. It killed him. Is that murder? Will I go to prison?"

"A china teapot?"

"Half full of tea. I've always had this wicked temper."

"Are you sure he's dead? Maybe you only stunned him."

She shook her head. "He's gone all right. I'm a ward sister, and I know."

"A *nurse?*"

"Shocking, isn't it?"

"You'd better come in and sit down," said the sergeant. "Go to the door on your right. Someone will see you right away."

The someone was Superintendent Peter Diamond, the senior detective on duty that afternoon. Diamond was head of the murder squad and this looked like a domestic incident, but as homicide had apparently occurred, he was in duty bound to take an interest. He made quite a courtesy of pulling forward a low, upholstered chair for the woman, then spoilt the effect by seating himself in another with a bump as his knees refused his buttocks a dignified descent. He had a low centre of gravity. A rugby forward in years past, he was better built now for anchorman in a tug-of-war team. "You're a nurse, I understand, Mrs Noble?"

"Sister on one of the orthopaedic wards."

"Locally?"

"The Royal United."

"So . . . ?"

"I came off duty and when I got home Glenn—that's my husband—was the worse for liquor."

"You mean drunk?"

"Whatever you want to call it." She closed her eyes, as if that might shut out the memory.

Mild as milk, Diamond said, "You came in from work and saw him where?"

"In the kitchen."

"Did you have words?"

"He wasn't capable of words. I saw red. That's the way I am. I picked up the teapot—"

"You'd made tea?"

"No. I'd only just come in."

"So he'd made tea?"

"No, it was still on the table from breakfast, half-full, really heavy. It's a family sized pot. I picked it up and swung it at him. Hit him smack on the forehead. The pot smashed. There was tea all over his face and chest. He collapsed. First, I thought it was the drink. I couldn't believe I'd hit him that hard. He'd stopped breathing. I could get nothing from his pulse. I lay him out on the floor and tried mouth-to-mouth, but it was no good."

She conveyed a vivid picture, the more spectacular considering what a scrap she was. She spoke calmly, her pale blue eyes scarcely blinking. I wouldn't mind mouth-to-mouth from you, sister, Diamond incorrectly thought.

The door behind him opened and someone looked in, a sergeant. "A word in your ear, sir."

Diamond wasn't getting out of that chair. He put a thumb and forefinger to the lobe of his right ear.

The sergeant bent over and muttered, "Report just in from the house, sir. Body in the kitchen confirmed."

Diamond nodded and asked Mrs Noble, "You said this happened at four in the afternoon?"

"Yes."

"It's twenty to six now."

"Is it?"

"Quite a long time since it happened."

"I've been walking the streets, getting a grip on myself."

"You're doing OK," Diamond told her, and meant it. She was a nurse and used to containing her feelings, but this was a stern test. He admired her self-control and he was inclined to believe her story, even if it had strange features. "You didn't think of phoning us?"

"I'm here, aren't I?"

"Earlier, I mean. When it happened."

"No point. He was beyond help."

He offered her a hot drink for the shock—and just stopped short of mentioning tea.

She declined.

"You said you saw red at finding him drunk," he recapped.

Her face tensed. "I disapprove of drink."

"Was he in work?"

She shook her head. "He was one of those printers laid off from Regency Press a year ago."

"Was he still unemployed?"

"Yes."

"Depressed?"

"Certainly not."

"It must have been difficult managing after he lost his job," Diamond said, giving her the chance to say *something* in favour of her dead husband.

"Not at all. He got good redundancy terms. And I'm earning as well."

"I meant perhaps he was drowning his sorrows?"

"What sorrows?"

"This afternoon bout was exceptional?"

"Very."

"Which was what upset you?"

She gave a nod. "It's against my religion."

Diamond treated the statement as if she were one of those earnest people in suits who knock on doors and ask whether you agree that God's message has relevance in today's world. He ignored it. "You're a nurse, Mrs Noble, and I imagine you're trained to spot the symptoms of heavy drinking, so I don't want you to be insulted by this question. What made you decide that your husband was drunk?"

"The state of him. He was slumped in a chair, his eyes were glazed, he couldn't put two words together. And the brandy bottle was on the table in front of him. The brandy he was given as a leaving present. He promised me he'd got rid of it."

"Didn't he like brandy?"

"It's of the devil."

"Had he drunk from the bottle?"

"Isn't that obvious?"

"Had he ever used drugs in any form?"

She frowned. "Alcohol is a drug."

"You know what I mean, Mrs Noble."

"And I've seen plenty of drug-users," she riposted. "I know what to look for."

"No question of drugs?"

"No question."

"Did he look for another position after the printing came to a stop?"

"There wasn't much point. All the local firms were laying people off."

"So how did he spend the days?"

"Don't ask me. Walks in the park. Television. Have you ever been out of work?"

He nodded. "And my wife couldn't find a job either."

"Then you ought to know."

"Unemployment hits people in different ways. I'm trying to understand how it affected your husband."

"You're not," she said bluntly. "You're trying to find out if I murdered him. That's your job."

Diamond didn't deny it.

"It wasn't deliberate." She raised her chin defiantly. "I wouldn't dream of killing him. Glenn and I were married eleven years. We had fights. Of course we had fights, with my temper. That's my personal demon—my temper. I threw things. Mostly I missed. He could duck when he was sober." Her lips twitched into a sad smile. "We always made up. Some of the best times we had were making up after a fight."

Trish Noble's candour was touching. Diamond sympathised with her. There was little more he could achieve. "We'll need a statement, Mrs Noble, a written one, I mean. Then you can go. Do you have someone you can stay with? Family, a friend?"

"Can't I go home?"

"Our people are going to be in the house for some time. You'd be better off somewhere else."

She told him she had a sister in Trowbridge. Diamond offered to make the call, but Trish Noble said she'd rather break the news herself.

2

To most of the staff at Manvers Street Police Station this room on the top floor was known as the eagle's nest. John Farr-Jones, the Chief Constable, greeted Diamond, who had arrived for a meeting of the high fliers. "You're looking fit, Peter."

"I used the lift."

"What's it like to be back in harness?"

The big detective gave him a pained look and said, "I gave up wearing harness when I was two years old." He took his place in a leather armchair and nodded to a chief inspector he scarcely knew. The wholesale changes of personnel in the couple of years he had been away had to be symptomatic of something.

"Mr Diamond's problem is that we haven't had a juicy murder since he was reinstated," Farr-Jones told the rest of the room. Since it was thanks to Farr-Jones's recommendation that Diamond had got his job back, he may have felt entitled to rib the man a little. But really the recommendation had been little more than a rubber stamp. In October 1994, a dire emergency had poleaxed Avon and Somerset Constabulary. The daughter of the Assistant Chief Constable had been taken hostage and her captor had insisted on dealing only with Diamond. The old rogue elephant, boisterous as ever, was now back among the herd.

"What about this teapot killing?" Farr-Jones persisted. "Can't you get anything out of that?"

There were smiles all round.

John Wigfull unwisely joked, "A teabag?" There was a history of bad feeling between Wigfull and Diamond. Many a time Diamond had seriously contemplated grabbing the two ends of Wigfull's ridiculously overgrown moustache and seeing if he could knot them under his chin. Now that Diamond was back, Wigfull had been ousted as head of the murder squad and handed a less glamorous portfolio as head of CID operations. He would use every chance to point to Diamond's failings.

Tom Ray, the Chief Constable's staff officer, hadn't heard about the teapot killing, so Diamond, wholly against his inclination, was obliged to give a summary of the incident.

When he had finished, it was rather like being in a staff college seminar. Someone had to suggest how the law should deal with it.

"Manslaughter?" Ray ventured, more in politeness than anything else.

"No chance," growled Diamond.

Wigfull, who knew *Butterworth's Police Law* like some people know the Bible, seized the moment to shine. "Hold on. As I remember, there are four elements necessary to secure a manslaughter conviction. First, there must be an unlawful act. That's beyond doubt."

"Assault with a teapot," contributed Ray.

"Right. A half-full teapot. Second, the act has to be dangerous, in that any sober and reasonable person would recognize it could do harm."

"Clocking a fellow with a teapot is dangerous," Ray agreed, filling a role as chorus to Wigfull.

"Third, the act must be a cause of the death."

"Well, he didn't die of old age."

"And finally, it must be intentional. There's no question she meant to strike him."

"No question," Ray echoed him.

Diamond said flatly, "It was a sudden death."

"We can't argue with that, Peter," said Wigfull, and got a laugh.

"I'm reporting it to the coroner. It's going in as an occurrence report."

Wigfull said, "I think you should do a process report to the CPS."

"Bollocks."

"It would be up to them whether to prosecute," Wigfull pointed out.

Diamond's patience was short at the best of times and it was even shorter when he was on shaky ground. He stabbed a finger at Wigfull. "Don't you lecture me on the

CPS. I refuse to dump on this woman. She's a nurse, for pity's sake. She walked all the way here from Twerton and reported what she'd done. If the coroner wants to refer it, so be it. He won't have my support."

Ray asked, "Have you been out to Twerton yourself?"

"I haven't had a chance, have I?" said Diamond. "I'm attending a meeting, in case anyone hadn't noticed. Julie is out there."

"Inspector Hargreaves?" said Farr-Jones. "Is that wise? She isn't so experienced as some of your other people."

"She was my choice for this, sir." He didn't want to get into an argument over Julie's capability, or his right to delegate duties, but if necessary he would.

He was first out of the meeting, muttering sulphurous things about John Wigfull, Farr-Jones and the whole boiling lot of them. He stomped downstairs to his office to collect his raincoat and trilby. He'd had more than enough of the job for that day.

Someone got up as he entered the room, a stocky, middle-aged man with black-framed bifocals. Dr Jack Merlin, the forensic pathologist. "What's up?" Merlin said. "You're looking even more stroppy than usual."

"Don't ask."

"Have you got a few minutes?"

"I was about to leave," said Diamond.

"Before you do, old friend, I'd like a quiet word. Why don't you shut that door?"

The "old friend" alerted Diamond like nothing else. His dealings with Merlin—over upwards of a dozen corpses in various states of decomposition—were based on mutual respect. Jack was the best reader of human remains in Britain. But he rarely, if ever, expressed much in the way of sentiment. Diamond grabbed the door-handle and pulled it shut.

"This one at Collinson Road, Twerton," said Merlin.

"The man hit with a teapot."

"Yes?"

"You don't mind me asking, I hope. Did you visit the scene yourself?"

Diamond shrugged. "I was tied up here. I sent one of my younger inspectors out."

"Good," said Merlin. "I didn't think you had."

"Something wrong?"

"You interviewed the wife, I believe?"

"Yes."

"She claimed to have topped him with a teapot?"

He nodded. "She's a ward sister at the RUH. Bit uptight, got religion rather badly, I think, which makes it harder for her."

Merlin fingered the lobe of his left ear. "The thing is, matey, I thought I should have a quiet word with you at this stage. Shan't know the cause of death until I've done the PM, of course, but . . ."

"Give it to me, Jack."

". . . a first inspection suggests that the victim suffered a couple of deep stab wounds."

"*Stab* wounds?"

"In the back."

Diamond swore.

"Not a lot of blood about," the pathologist added, "and he was lying face up, so I wouldn't be too critical of that young inspector, but it does have the signs of a suspicious death."

3

Collinson Road, Twerton, backs on to Brunel's Great Western Railway a mile or so west of the centre of Bath. Diamond drove into a narrow street of Victorian terraced housing, the brickwork blackened by all those locomotives steaming by in years past. Several of the facades had since been cleaned up and gentrified with plastic guttering, picture windows and varnished oak front doors with brass fittings, but Number 32 was resolutely unaltered, sooty and unobtrusive behind an overgrown privet hedge and a small, neglected strip of garden. The door stood open. The Scenes of Crime Officers had received Diamond's urgent instruction to step up the scale of their work and were still inside. Most of them knew him from years back and as he went in he had to put up with some good-natured chaffing over his intentions. It was well known that he'd been moodily waiting for a murder to fall in his lap.

The team had finished its work downstairs, so he went through the hallway with the senior man, Derek Bignal, and looked inside the kitchen. Almost everything portable had been removed for inspection by the lab. Strips of adhesive tape marked the positions of the table and chairs and the outline of the body.

Diamond asked if the murder weapon had been found.

"Who knows?" said Bignal with a shrug, practically causing paranoia in Peter Diamond so soon after his conversation with Merlin, the laid-back pathologist. "We made a collection of kitchen knives. See the magnetic strip attached to the wall over the draining-board? They were all lined up there, ready to grab. Some of them had blades that could have done the business."

"No other knife in the sink, or lying on the floor?"

"With blood and prints all over it? You want it easy, Mr Diamond."

He tried visualising the scene, which was no simple task with the furniture missing. According to her story, Trish Noble had returned from the hospital at four in the afternoon. If she was speaking the truth she must have let herself in at the front door, stepped through the hallway and found her husband seated facing her at the small table against the wall to her left as she entered the kitchen. In a fit of anger, believing him to be drunk, rather than mortally injured, she would have taken a couple of steps towards the table, where the teapot was, snatched it up and hit him with it. He had fallen off to the right of the chair—her right—and lay on his back on the floor, where she had tried resuscitation. That, anyway, was her version. The taped outline of the body didn't conflict with what she had stated.

To Diamond's left was a fridge-freezer. The doors were decorated with postcards and photos. The shiny surfaces bore traces of powder, where they had been dusted for prints. Holiday snaps of Glenn Noble, deeply tanned, in shorts and sandals, his arms around the shoulders of his pretty, bikini-clad wife. More of Trish Noble in her nurse's uniform, giggling with friends. A sneaky shot of her taken in a bathroom, eyes wide in surprise, holding a towel against her breasts, evidently unaware that her right nipple wasn't covered. Surprising that a woman who claimed to be religious kept such a picture on her fridge door, Diamond mused, then decided that nurses must have a different perception of embarrassment. Another that took his attention was clearly taken on some seaside promenade. Glenn and an older, stocky man were giving piggyback rides to two women in swimsuits, one of them Trish—but it wasn't Glenn's back she was riding.

Diamond sighed. To study people's private snaps systematically like this was an invasion of privacy, an odious but necessary part of the job. He wasn't in the house to look for evidence. Others had already been through for that. He was getting a sense of how the couple had lived and what their relationship had been. Having thought what a liberty it was, he stripped every photo off the fridge door.

"What's a wayzgoose when it's at home?" he asked Bignal.

"Come again."

"A wayzgoose. This picture of the two couples horsing about on the seafront has a note on the back. Wayzgoose, 1993, Minehead."

"Is it a place?"

"Minehead is."

"Could it be the name of some game, do you think?"

"I doubt it."

He looked into the other rooms downstairs. One was clearly the living room, with two armchairs, a TV and video, a music centre and a low table stacked with newspapers. The Nobles read the *Daily Mirror* and possessed just about every recording Freddie Mercury had made. On the wall were a bullfight poster and an antique map of Somerset. He picked an expensive-looking art book from a shelf otherwise stacked with nursing magazines. "Who's Eugene Delacroix?"

"A French romantic painter," Bignal informed him.

Diamond flicked the pages over. "Doesn't seem to go with Freddie Mercury and the Mirror."

"There were also two coffee mugs on the table," Bignal told him. "By the look of them, they were left over from last night. They're going to the lab."

It was not vastly different from his own living room. He moved on. The front room was used as a workroom by the couple, for sewing, typing and storing household bills and bank statements. They had a joint account and seemed to be steadily in credit, which was better than the Diamonds managed.

In another ten minutes the team finished upstairs. No signs of violence there, they informed Diamond. The aggro seemed to have been confined to the kitchen.

He went to see for himself.

The Nobles favoured a rather lurid pink for their bedroom, slept in a standard size double bed and had a portable TV on the chest of drawers Glenn used for most of his clothes. Trish Noble had a wardrobe and a dressing table to herself. She was reading Catherine Cookson and the Bible and Glenn had been into one of the Flashman books. If the quantity and variety of condoms in Glenn's bedside cabinet was any guide, their sex life hadn't been subdued by Trish's religion.

The second bedroom contained a folding bed, an ironing board and various items the couple must have acquired and been unwilling to throw away, ranging from an old record-player to a dartboard with the wire half detached.

He glanced into the bathroom. Nothing caught his attention.

"What's in the back garden?" he asked Bignal.

"Plants, mostly."

"Don't push me, Derek. Have you been out there?"

"Personally, no."

"Has anyone thought of looking for a murder weapon, footprints, a means of escape?"

"Not systematically," Bignal admitted. "It was already dark when we got here."

"Not systematically," muttered Diamond with heavy sarcasm. "It backs onto the railway, doesn't it?"

"Yes."

"Tomorrow, early, I want a proper search made. In particular, I want to know if there are signs that anyone got in or out by way of the railway embankment."

Bignal's eyebrows peaked in surprise. "You think someone else is involved, as well as the wife?"

"That's the way they would have escaped."

"*They?*"

"He, she, they or nobody at all. Let's keep an open mind, shall we?"

4

Julie Hargreaves may have expected a roasting for having
failed to notice the stab wounds, but she need not have
troubled. Diamond was more interested in roasting Trish
Noble. "She had the kid-glove treatment from me yesterday," he summed up as they drove out to Trowbridge.
"Today she's got to be given a workover."

"Do you see her as the killer?"

"Do you?"

She paused for thought. "It would be unusual, a woman
using a knife as a weapon. The teapot, I can believe—but
why would she hit him with the teapot if she'd already
stuck a knife in his back?"

"To finish him off."

"Ah."

"However, there could be a second person involved."
Diamond casually tossed in some information he'd
received that morning from the SOCOs combing the back
garden at Twerton. "There's evidence that someone
climbed over the fence to the railway embankment. Two
slats are freshly splintered at the top."

"An intruder? Nothing was stolen."

"Yes, but if she had an admirer, for instance . . ."

Julie didn't buy the idea. "That's pretty unlikely, isn't
it?"

"You mean with her religious convictions? I said
'admirer,' not 'lover'."

"No, I mean he wouldn't need to climb over the fence.
She'd let him in. And they would have to be real thickos to
stab the husband and then go down to the nick and report
it."

He responded huffily, "I didn't say it was a conspiracy.
Unrequited love, Julie. The admirer is obsessed with Trish.
She's unattainable while her husband is alive, so this nutter

breaks into the house and knifes him. Trish comes home and finds Glenn dying, but mistakenly thinks he's drunk."

"And bashes him with the teapot?"

"Exactly. I think she told the truth yesterday. By now she may have something else to tell us."

"I wonder," said Julie. "I find it difficult to believe in this crazy admirer."

Diamond said loftily, "You may understand better when you meet Trish Noble. She's on the side of the angels and bloody attractive. Dangerous combination."

"That would explain everything," murmured Julie in a bland tone. "Shall I organize house-to-house to find out if anyone was spotted on the railway embankment yesterday afternoon?"

"It's under way," he told her. "Two teams."

Trish Noble's sister lived in a semi-detached on a council estate north of Trowbridge. But it was the bloody attractive young widow herself who answered their knock. In jeans and a white tee-shirt, with the height and figure of a pre-teen schoolgirl, she looked too frail to use a knife on a chocolate cake, let alone a man. The hours since the killing had taken a toll. Her big eyes were red-lidded and they seemed to have sunk deeper into her skull. Julie must have wondered at Diamond's ideas of attractiveness.

He introduced her and said there were things he needed to ask. Trish calmly invited them in, explaining that she had the house to herself because her sister was at work. In a narrow sitting room, watched by two unwelcoming spaniels, Diamond took the best armchair and launched straight into the workover. "You didn't kill your husband with the teapot, Mrs Noble. He was stabbed in the back."

She frowned and stared.

Julie said, "Why don't you sit down?" She stood behind the second armchair until Trish Noble acted on the advice.

"Did you stab him?" Diamond asked.

Trish seemed to have difficulty taking in what she had just been told—or she was making a convincing show of being stunned by the news. She shook her head.

Diamond said, "If you'd like to explain how it happened, we're ready to listen."

She said, "Stabbed?"

"Twice, in the back."

"That's impossible. He was sitting in the kitchen."

"Your story."

"It's true! He was at the table when I got in. I've told you this."

"You didn't stab him yourself?"

"That's insulting."

"We'd like a clear answer, Mrs Noble."

She said vehemently, "No, I did not stab my own husband."

"That's clear, then." Diamond glanced across at Julie, who had found an upright chair by the sideboard. "Got that? She denies it."

Julie opened her notebook.

"If you didn't stab him yourself," Diamond plunged in again, "we've obviously got to look for someone who did. Was there anyone else in the house when you got home from the hospital?"

The tired eyes widened. "No one."

"You're sure? You can't be sure, can you? Let's take this in stages. Did you see anyone?"

"No. This is unbelievable."

"Or hear them?"

"No."

"Is there anyone else living in the house?"

"What do you mean—a lodger? No."

"Does anyone have a key?"

"What?"

"Some friend, perhaps?"

"We don't give keys to our friends."

"I'll tell you what I have in mind," Diamond offered. "If someone let himself into the house unknown to your husband, he could have taken him by surprise and stabbed him shortly before you came in."

"Who would do that?" she said, and there was a note of scorn in the voice. She was getting over the shock.

"Do you have a lover?"

She reddened, but that wasn't necessarily an admission. Almost anyone would have blushed at the question. She told him with a glare, "You should wash out your mouth."

"Would you like it rephrased?" Diamond said. "A boyfriend? A fancy man? A bit on the side? Come on, Mrs Noble, you work in a hospital. Life in the raw. I don't have to pick my words with you, do I?"

"I am a married woman—or was," she answered primly. "I took vows before the Lord."

"No need for a boyfriend?"

The look she gave him was her response and he was convinced by it. Moreover, he'd seen inside her husband's bedside drawer.

"In that case, we have to consider what used to be called unrequited love. To put it crudely, some nutter who fancies you. You see what I'm driving at, don't you? This man obsessed by you murders your husband to have you to himself."

She sighed like a scythe and said, "I can't listen to these serpent-words."

"No secret admirer you're aware of? Let's look at another possibility. Did your husband have any enemies?"

The change of tack brought a more measured response. "Glenn didn't have enemies."

"Then did he have friends? Encouraging him in bad habits, perhaps?"

She said, "I can do without your sarcasm."

"These are friends, presumably?" He took from his pocket the photo taken at Minehead, the piggyback picture. "Were these people in the printing trade?"

She snatched it possessively. "You were the one who stole them, then. My photos are personal."

"Who are the people?"

The resentment remained in her voice. "The Porterfields. Friends of ours. We had a day out with them."

"Is Mr Porterfield a printer?"

"No. Basil is a businessman. He sells car-parts."

"And the lady?"

"His wife Serena. She's an art teacher."

"That's Serena mounted on your husband's back?"

She gave him a cold stare. "That was for a silly photograph."

"At Minehead?"

"Yes."

"For a wayzgoose?"

She frowned. "I beg your pardon."

"Look on the back. My dictionary says that a wayzgoose is a works outing for those in a printing house. A silly photo at a wayzgoose makes sense to me."

She glanced at the words on the back of the photo and shrugged. "It doesn't make any to me. Basil and Serena had nothing to do with Glenn's job. Besides, he was already redundant when we went to Minehead. He'd been out of work for over a year."

"I noticed an art book in your living room. French painter."

"Delacroix?"

"Yes. Was that a gift from Mrs Porterfield?"

"No. Glenn bought it himself."

"So he was interested in art?"

"Only in Delacroix."

"Are the Porterfields local?"

"They live up by the golf course."

"What's the address?"

"I don't want them troubled. They've got nothing to do with this. They're decent people."

"In that case, they'll want to help me find your husband's killer."

She said openly, "I can't believe this is happening. I thought I killed him. I was sure of it."

If she is playing the innocent, Diamond thought, she's doing it with style. He tried to resist making up his mind. First impressions were so misleading. In his time he'd made more mistakes over women than King Henry the Eighth. And this one with her martyred eyes was taking the steam out of his workover.

"After you hit him with the teapot and he fell off the chair, what did you do? Tell me precisely."

"I went to him at once. I could tell from the way he fell that he was out cold when he hit the floor. I found he'd stopped breathing, so I tried to revive him. Tilted back his head and drew the chin upwards. I don't have to go through the drill, do I?"

"Mouth to mouth?"

"Of course."

"Think carefully. While you were doing it, did you hear any extraneous sounds?"

"What do you mean?"

"If anyone else was in the house, in that kitchen, even, they may have picked this moment to run out." It was a wily suggestion. He couldn't have handed her a better opportunity of shifting the suspicion to some mythical intruder.

She hesitated, then said, "I didn't notice a thing."

Innocent, or refusing to be drawn? He couldn't tell.

"After the resuscitation had no result, what did you do?"

She bit her lip. "It's difficult to remember. It's just a blur. I was deeply shocked."

"Did you stay in the kitchen?"

"For a bit, I think."

"You didn't go upstairs, or in the other rooms?"

"I don't think so. I was horrified by what I'd done. I got the shakes. I think I ran out of the front door and wandered up the street asking the Lord to forgive me. It took Him a long time to calm my troubled spirit. In the end I walked all the way to Bath to confess to you."

"Did you speak to anyone between leaving the house and coming to us?"

"No."

"See anyone you knew?"

"I wasn't noticing other people." She made it all sound plausible.

"If there was anyone," said Diamond, becoming reasonable in spite of his best efforts to be tough, "it would help us to account for your movements."

"I've told you my movements."

"And we only have your word for them."

"That was after he died. Why do you want to know what I was doing after he died?"

He declined to answer. "Is there anyone you can think of who ever threatened your husband?"

"No."

Julie looked up from her notes and said unexpectedly, "Was he seeing a woman?"

Trish Noble blinked twice and flicked nervously at her hair. "If he was . . ." she started to say, then stopped. "If he was, I'd be very surprised."

"The wife usually is," Diamond added, privately wishing he'd remembered to ask. Smart thinking on Julie's part. "Anyone you can think of who may have fancied him?"

"How would I know? Look, you're talking about the man I loved and married. He isn't in his grave yet. Do you have to be so cruel?"

Julie said, "You want us to find the person who stabbed him, don't you?"

She nodded.

"There is someone, isn't there?" said Julie.

"I don't know."

"But you had your suspicions?"

She looked down and fingered her wedding ring. Speaking in a low, scarcely audible voice, she said, "Sometimes he came home really late. I mean about two in the morning, or later. He was exhausted. Too tired for anything."

"Drunk?"

"No. I would have noticed."

"How long was this going on?"

"When it started, it was once every two months or so. Lately, it was about every ten days."

"Did you question him about it?"

"He snapped my head off when I did. Really told me to mind my own business. It made me think there might be someone, but I had no way of finding out. He didn't smell of scent, or anything."

Diamond told her to collect her coat.

She looked seriously worried. "Where are you taking me?"

"Home. Julie will take you home. I want you to look at the scene and tell Julie everything you remember."

"Aren't you going to be there?" A question that might have conveyed disappointment was actually spoken on a rising note of relief.

"I may come later." He turned to Julie. "On the way, you can drop me off at the hospital."

Trish's anxiety flooded in again. "The hospital? Do you mean the RUH? You don't have to talk to them. They can't tell you anything."

"It isn't about you," said Diamond. "It's another matter." And it wasn't about his weight problem either.

5

"Believe it or not, I didn't come here to admire your sewing," Diamond told Jack Merlin.

There was no reaction from the pathologist.

"May I see the other side?"

"Not *my* sewing. My assistant Rodney does the stitch-work." In the post-mortem room at the Royal United Hospital, Merlin had the advantage of familiar territory. No visitor was entirely comfortable in the mortuary. Attendance at autopsies is routinely expected of detectives on murder cases. Diamond ducked out whenever he could think up a plausible excuse. On this visit he arrived late. The gory stuff had already been got over. With only a sewn-up corpse to view, he was putting on a good show of self-composure, but it didn't run to treating these places like a second home.

The assistant Rodney stepped forward and helped Merlin turn the body of Glenn Noble. Two eye-shaped stab wounds were revealed.

Diamond's hands tightened behind his back. "Not much doubt about those."

Merlin watched him and said nothing.

"They don't look superficial, either."

Still nothing.

"I reckon they tell a story."

There was a long interval of silence before Diamond spoke again. "You're a helpful bugger, aren't you? You know I'm pig-ignorant, yet you're not going to help me out."

Merlin shot an amused look across the corpse and then relented. "This one to the right of the spine did the main damage. Penetrated the lung two inches above its basal margin."

Diamond bent closer to the body to examine the wounds. "Obviously you've cleaned him up."

"You don't get much external bleeding from stab wounds. There was a pint or so in the right pleural cavity."

"So was that what killed him?"

"It was a potentially fatal injury."

"The cause of death, in other words."

"The potential cause of death."

Diamond straightened up, frowning. "Am I missing something here?"

"I can't be specific as to the cause."

"With a couple of stab-wounds like this and massive internal bleeding? Come on, Jack. Give me a break."

Merlin said, "As I understand it, the wife admitted to you that she cracked him on the head with a teapot."

"I believe her. Somebody certainly smashed a teapot. His shirt-front was stained with tea, as I'm sure forensic will tell us in their own good time. Probably tell us if it was Brooke Bond or Tetley's and whether she warmed the pot."

"There's bruising here on the head, just above the hairline," Merlin confirmed.

"Look, what is this about the teapot? The man has two deep stab wounds."

"And a bruised cranium."

Diamond screwed his face into an anguished expression. "Are you telling me it's possible that the teapot actually finished him off?"

"It's an interesting question. I can't exclude the possibility of a fatal brain injury. Of course I'll examine the brain."

"Haven't you done that?"

"It has to be fixed and cut in sections for microscopic examination."

"How long will that take?"

"Three to four weeks."

"God help us." He complained because of his own

frustration. He knew Merlin would give him all the information he could as soon as it was available. He was the best.

"And even after I examine the brain, I may not have the answer."

"Oh, come on, Jack!"

"I mean it. I've examined people who died after blows to the head and I could find no perceptible damage to the brain. We don't know why it happens. Maybe the shock wave passing through the brain stem was sufficient to kill them."

"So even after four weeks, you may not have the answer?"

"I'm a pathologist, not an ace detective."

There was an interval of silence.

"Let me get one thing clear in my mind," said Diamond. "Is it possible that what Mrs Noble told me is true that he was still alive when she clobbered him?"

"Certainly."

"With stab wounds like this?"

"A victim of stabbing may survive for some time."

"How long?"

"How long is a piece of string?"

"Your middle name wouldn't be Prudence by any chance?"

Merlin smiled.

"A few seconds? A few minutes?"

"I couldn't possibly say."

"And how would he have appeared? Unsteady, like a drunk?"

"Your guess is as good as mine."

"A distressed drunk?"

"Distressed is probably right."

"Unable to speak?"

"That's possible. The knife cut through some of the

blood vessels and airways in the lung, so there was bleeding not only into the chest cavity but into the air passages. That would have affected his power of speech."

"You see what I'm getting at?" said Diamond.

Merlin grinned. "You're testing the woman's story. I was at the scene before you, remember," he rubbed it in. "I saw the brandy bottle on the table. But I'm not given to speculation, as you know."

"Jack, I could be making an arrest very soon. Someone entered that house and stabbed him. Not the wife. I'm convinced she's telling the truth."

"Do you have a suspect?"

"I'm getting close."

"I wouldn't get too close. If you nab them for murder at this stage, you could be torn to shreds by a good defence counsel. Mrs Noble admits that she clobbered her husband with the teapot. She may have killed him, stabbing or no stabbing."

6

It was a five minute drive, no more, from the hospital to the murder house in Collinson Road. Frustrated by his session with Jack Merlin, Diamond looked to Julie Hargreaves for some progress in the investigation. He had left her there with Trish Noble, ostensibly checking the contents to see if anything had been stolen. More importantly, she would have been working on drawing Trish out, putting her at her ease and gaining her confidence in the way that she did with women suspects almost without seeming to try. If there were secrets in the lives of the Nobles, Julie was best placed to unlock them.

When he looked in, the two women were waiting in that chintzy living room with the bullfight poster and the map of Somerset. The television was on and coffee and biscuits were on the table. There must be something wrong with my methods, Diamond thought. While I look at a dead body, my sidekick puts her feet up and watches the box.

"Am I interrupting?" he asked.

Julie looked up. "We were waiting for you."

"What are you watching—a kids' programme?"

"Actually we were looking out of the window at the SOCOs in the back garden." She reached for the remote control and switched off. "They look as if they're about to pack up. Would you like coffee?"

"Had a hospital one, thanks." In a paper cup from a machine and tasting of tomato soup, he might have added. He wouldn't want another drink for some time. He reached for the packet of chocolate digestives and helped himself. "What's the report, then? Anything missing?"

"Most of the furniture from my kitchen," Trish Noble said accusingly.

"That'll be the scenes of crime team," Diamond told her. "They must have left you a check-list somewhere. You'll get everything back eventually."

"They weren't the ones who pinched the photos from my fridge door."

He said smoothly, "You'll get them back." He reached for the art book he'd remarked on before and leafed through the pages. "Is anything of value missing? Money? Jewellery?"

Julie answered for her. "We checked. Everything seems to be there."

"Speaking of money," Diamond said to Trish as if she had brought up the subject herself, "we'll need to look at the bank account and your credit card statements. You do have a credit card? How are you placed financially? I'm not being nosy. We need to know." He knew, but he wanted to question her on the details.

"We're solvent," she answered without looking up.

He hadn't Julie's talent for easing out the information. "Your husband must have been given a lump sum when he was made redundant."

She only nodded, so he talked on.

"It seems generous at the time, but it soon goes, I dare say. Where do you keep the statements?"

"They should still be in the front room if your people haven't taken them away."

"Would you mind?" he asked her.

In the short interval when Trish was out of the room, Diamond asked Julie what she had learned of importance.

"Glenn was up to something that she didn't care for," said Julie. "I think we touched a raw nerve asking if he had been two-timing her with some other woman."

"You touched the nerve," he said. "That was your contribution."

Julie flushed slightly. She wasn't used to credit from Peter Diamond. "Anyway, she's suspicious, but she isn't sure."

"She wouldn't have stuck a knife in his back unless she was damned sure."

Trish returned and handed across the statements. He studied them. "High standard of living. Shopping at the best boutiques. Meals out at Clos du Roy and the Priory. A holiday in the south of France."

"That's the way we chose to spend our money."

"But it doesn't seem to have hit your bank balance."

"Glenn had his redundancy cheque."

"What's this restaurant in Exeter that you visited twice in August?"

"The Lemon Tree? We often eat there after visiting his brother. Alec's home is a working paper mill, a lovely old place in the country near Torquay, but he forgets that people need to eat."

"I can take a hint. We'll get you back to your sister's," said Diamond.

Seated in the front, whilst Julie drove, he tried drawing out Trish by talking about the pressures that nurses had to work under. "My own health is pretty good, thank God, but in this line of work you get to see the insides of hospitals all too often. The RUH is one of the better ones. I still wouldn't care to be a nurse."

She didn't comment. Perhaps she found it hard to imagine the big policeman nursing anyone.

"How long have you worked there, Mrs Noble?"

"Three years."

"And before that?"

"Frenchay."

Another local hospital, in Bristol.

"It's a vocation, isn't it?" Diamond rambled on. "Nursing isn't a job, it's a vocation. So is doctoring. Better paid, but still a vocation. I'm less sure about some of the others who work in hospitals. The administrators. It's out of proportion. All those managers."

She didn't take his pause as an invitation to join in.

"They tell me the Health Service managers are the only lot who are on the increase," he said. "Oh, and counsellors. Counselling is the biggest growth industry of all. We need it for everything these days. Child care, education, careers, marriage, divorce, unemployment, alcoholism, bereavement. I don't know how we managed before. If there's a major disaster—a train crash or a flood—the first thing they announce after the number of deaths is that counsellors are with the families. We even have counsellors for the police. Something ugly comes our way, like a serial murder case, or child abuse, and half the murder squad are reckoned to need counselling. Watch out for the counsellors, Mrs Noble. If they haven't found you yet, you may be sure they're about to make a case study of you."

She didn't respond. She was looking out of the window.

"Me, too, probably," said Diamond.

7

"Give me the dope on the Porterfields," Diamond asked as Julie steered the car out of the police station yard and headed for Widcombe Hill. On his instruction, she'd spent the last hour checking.

"They've lived in Bath for the last five years. Moved out of a terraced house in Bear Flat at the end of 1993 and into this mansion by the golf course. There must be good profits in car parts."

He grunted his assent. "You're talking to a man who just had to buy a set of new tyres."

"She drives a Porsche and he has a Mercedes."

"And people like me paid for them."

"Oh, and her name isn't really Serena. It's plain Ann."

"What's wrong with Ann?" he demanded. "I once had a girl-friend called Ann. The last word in sophistication. Stilettos and hot pants. Don't suppose you know what hot pants are."

"Were," murmured Julie.

"Well, we can't arrest her for changing her name." Diamond wrenched his thoughts back from his steamy past.

"Who's your money on, Julie? Do you still think Glenn Noble had a mistress?"

"Yes—and Trish believes it, too."

"So who's the killer—an angry husband?"

"Or boyfriend."

He didn't mention Jack Merlin's bombshell—that Trish might, after all, have struck the fatal blow. "Any idea who? Basil Porterfield?"

She said, "I'll have a better idea when I meet him."

"You can spot a skirt-chaser at fifty paces, can you?"

"If you don't mind me saying," Julie commented, "that's a rather outdated expression."

"Un-hip?"

"Yes."

"Well," he went on, unabashed, "I have to agree with you that it was some visitor to the house."

"But who?"

He spread his hands. "Could be anyone. Could be the Bishop of Bath and Wells for all we know."

"The Porterfields were friends, close friends," Julie pointed out. "How many of your women friends would you hoist on your back for a photo?"

"All at once?"

She said on a note of exasperation, "Mr Diamond, *sir*, I'm trying to make a serious point. We know that Glenn was often out until the small hours. If we could confirm that he was sleeping with Serena . . ."

"Hold on, Julie. That's a large assumption, isn't it? Trish Noble doesn't seem to think he needed to go elsewhere for sex."

"She had her suspicions, believe me. You have to understand a woman's thinking. She may have said the opposite, but he was getting home so late that something was obviously going on. She's too proud or too puritanical to admit it to you and me."

"He could have been up to something entirely different."

"Such as?"

"A poker school. He wouldn't tell her if he was playing cards into the small hours. God and gambling don't mix."

Julie wasn't impressed by that suggestion. "She said he was tired when he got in."

"Well, it *was* late."

"Too tired for anything."

After a pause, he said, "Was that what she meant? This God-fearing woman who keeps a Bible by her bed?"

"That doesn't mean she's under-sexed."

"Fair point," said Diamond after a moment's reflection. "There's more bonking in the Bible than there is in Jilly Cooper and Jackie Collins together. So she interprets his reduced libido as evidence of infidelity? It's speculation, Julie, whether it's her speculation or yours."

She was resolute. "Maybe it is, but if she's right, Serena Porterfield is in real danger—if she isn't already murdered. We can't ignore the possibility, speculation or not."

The Porterfields' mock-Tudor mansion was on the slopes of Bathampton Down, with all of the city as a gleaming backdrop of pale cream stone and blue slate roofs. The house stood among lawns as well trimmed as the greens of the Bath Golf Club nearby. A gardener was on a ladder pruning the Albertine rose that covered much of one side of the house. A white Mercedes was on the drive. The chances of anyone from here being involved in a stabbing in a small terraced house in Twerton seemed remote.

Basil Porterfield opened the front door before they knocked. There was no question that he was the man in the Minehead photo —a sturdy, smiling, sandy-haired embodiment of confidence, even after Diamond told him they were police officers.

"Perhaps you heard that Glenn Noble is dead, sir?"

"Saw it in the paper. Devastating." Porterfield didn't look devastated, but out of respect he shook his head. "It's a long time since I saw Glenn."

"But you were friends?"

"He was the sort you couldn't help liking. Look, why don't you come in?"

The welcome was unstinting. In a room big enough for

the golf club AGM, they were shown to leather armchairs and offered sherry.

Diamond glanced at the teak wall units laden with pottery and art books. "This is a far cry from Bear Flat."

"We worked hard to move up in the world," said Porterfield evenly.

"You're in the motor trade, I understand."

"Curiously enough, we prospered in the recession. I don't sell new cars, I sell parts, and people were doing up their old vehicles rather than replacing them. The business really took off. We have outlets in France and Spain now."

"You visit these countries?"

"Regularly."

"And your business is based in Bath?"

"You must have passed it often enough, down the hill on the Warminster Road."

"Glenn Noble—was he a business contact?"

"Purely social. Through my wife, actually. She took a school project to the printers he worked for. Serena teaches art, print-making, that sort of thing. You can see her influence all around you."

"Is Mrs Porterfield at home today?"

"No. She's, em, out of the country."

Julie's eyes sought Diamond's and held them for a moment.

He remarked to Porterfield, "She must be devastated, too."

"She doesn't know anything about it."

Diamond played a wild card. "You said you haven't seen the Nobles for a long time. Perhaps your wife saw them more recently."

Porterfield asked smoothly, "Why do you say that?"

Julie, equally smoothly, invented an answer. "Someone answering your wife's description was seen recently in the company of Glenn Noble."

"Is that so? Funny she didn't mention it." He was unfazed.

"Just for the record," said Diamond, "would you mind telling me where you were on Monday afternoon between three and five?"

"Monday between three and five." Porterfield frowned, as if he hadn't remotely considered that he might be asked. "I would have been at the office. I'm sure my staff will confirm that, if you care to ask them."

"And your wife?"

"She's in France, like I said, on a school trip." He smiled. "She left last week. Last Friday."

"Where did you say she teaches?"

8

Cavendish College was a girls' public school on Lyncombe Hill. The Head informed Diamond that Mrs Porterfield was indeed on a sixth form trip to the south of France. She frequently led school parties to places of artistic interest in Europe. She was a loyal, talented teacher, and an asset to the school.

Diamond used a mobile phone to get this information. He and Julie were parked in North Road, with a good view of the Porterfield residence.

"Are you relieved?" he asked Julie. "Serena survives, apparently."

"I still say he murdered Glenn Noble."

"And I say you're right."

Her eyes widened. "Am I?"

"But he had the decency to do it while his wife was away. We'll arrest her when she returns."

"Whatever for?"

"Hold on a little and I'll show you, if my theory is right.

Serena's talent may be an asset to the school, but it's a bigger asset to Basil Porterfield. What time is it?"

"Ten past six."

"After our visit he's not stopping here much longer."

Twenty minutes, as it turned out. The Mercedes glided into North Road and down the hill with Julie and Diamond in discreet pursuit. Porterfield turned right at the junction with the busy Warminster Road. Three-quarters of a mile on, he slowed and pulled in to the forecourt of a building with *Porterfield Car Spares* in large letters across the front.

"Drive past and park as near as you can."

Julie found a layby a short walk away.

When they approached on foot the only cover available was the side wall of Porterfield's building. From it they had a view of the empty Mercedes parked on the forecourt. "I should have called for some back-up, but we can handle this, can't we?" said Diamond.

Julie lifted one eyebrow and said nothing.

Diamond issued an order. "When he comes out, you go across and nick him."

She lifted the other eyebrow.

He told her, "I'm the back-up."

Five minutes passed. The traffic on the Warminster Road zoomed by steadily.

"He's coming."

Julie tensed.

Porterfield emerged from the building trundling a hand trolley stacked with white cartons. He set the trolley upright, took some keys from his pocket, opened the boot of the car and leaned in.

Diamond pressed a hand against the small of Julie's back. She started forward.

Sending in Julie first may have looked like cowardice, but it was not. While her sudden arrival on the scene caught Porterfield's attention, Diamond ducked around the other side of the Mercedes. Just in time, because Porterfield produced a knife from the car boot and swung it at Julie.

She swayed out of range and narrowly escaped another lunge. Then Diamond charged in and grabbed Porterfield from behind and thrust him sideways against the car, pinioning his arms. Julie prised the knife from his fist. Diamond produced a set of handcuffs and between them they forced him over the boot and manacled him.

"Want to see what's in the cartons?" Diamond suggested to Julie over the groaning prisoner. "Why don't you use the knife?"

She cut along the adhesive seal of the top carton and parted the flaps. Neatly stacked inside were wads of French one-hundred franc banknotes.

"*Money?*"

"Funny money," said Diamond. "We'll find the offset litho machine and the plates hidden deep inside the building. What with Serena's artwork, Glenn Noble's printing expertise and these premises to work in, making counterfeit notes was a profitable scam. But just like you said, Trish got suspicious of all the late nights. Glenn hadn't dared tell her what he was up to, even though it helped their bank balance no end. She was too high principled to be in on the secret."

"Why French money?" Julie asked.

"Easier to make. No metal strip. I don't know how good these forgeries are, but Glenn would have got his brother in Devon to make the paper with a passable watermark." He picked one up and held it to the light. "Not bad. A portrait of Glenn's favourite painter, Eugene Delacroix. This has a nice feel to it. They coat the printed notes with glycerine. He'll have handpressed the serial numbers."

"And why was he killed?"

"Because of Trish. Unwisely he told Porterfield that she was asking about the late nights. She would have seen it as her moral duty to shop them all, and Porterfield couldn't risk her wheedling the truth out of Glenn." He hauled Porterfield upright. "You thought you could get rid of Glenn and do the printing yourself, didn't you, ratbag? Last Monday afternoon you called unexpectedly at the house. Glenn let you in, offered you a drink, and when his back was turned you drove a knife into him. You escaped through the back garden just as Trish was coming in through the front. Right?"

"How the hell did you get on to me?" Porterfield asked.

"Through something Glenn Noble wrote on a photograph. Someone took a picture of your day out in Minehead in 1993. Glenn wrote 'wayzgoose' on the back."

"What's that?"

"A word for a printers' outing. When I looked at it first, I couldn't understand why he called it that, since he was the only printer in the picture. Then it dawned that you and possibly your wife were involved in some printing activity. When I saw how well you were doing, and how large his bank balance was, I reckoned you were printing money. Julie, would you call headquarters and ask them to send a car?"

Porterfield asked, "What was that word?"

"'Wayzgoose'," said Diamond. "Funny old word. Worth remembering. It'll get you a large score in Scrabble. Where you're going, you may get the odd chance to play. You'll certainly have the time."

MYSTERY NOVELS
AND SHORT STORIES
BY PETER LOVESEY: A CHECKLIST

I. Novels
(In the following list, the publisher of the first British edition is followed by the publisher of the first United States edition.)

Wobble to Death. Macmillan, 1970; Dodd, Mead, 1970. Sergeant Cribb series.

The Detective Wore Silk Drawers. Macmillan, 1971; Dodd, Mead, 1971. Sergeant Cribb series.

Abracadaver. Macmillan, 1972; Dodd, Mead, 1972. Sergeant Cribb series.

Mad Hatter's Holiday: A Novel of Mystery in Victorian Brighton. Macmillan, 1973; Dodd, Mead, 1973. Sergeant Cribb series.

Invitation to a Dynamite Party. Macmillan, 1974; as *The Tick of Death* Dodd, Mead, 1974. Sergeant Cribb series.

A Case of Spirits. Macmillan, 1975; Dodd, Mead, 1975. Sergeant Cribb series.

Swing, Swing Together. Macmillan, 1976; Dodd, Mead, 1976. Sergeant Cribb series.

Waxwork. Macmillan, 1978; Pantheon, 1978. Sergeant Cribb series.

The False Inspector Dew: A Murder Mystery Aboard the SS Mauretania. Macmillan, 1982; Pantheon, 1982.

Keystone. Macmillan, 1983; Pantheon, 1983.

Rough Cider. Bodley Head, 1986; Mysterious Press, 1987.

Bertie and the Tinman: From the Detective Memoirs of King Edward VII. Bodley Head, 1987; Mysterious Press, 1988. Bertie series.

On the Edge. Century Hutchinson, 1989; Mysterious Press, 1989.

Bertie and the Seven Bodies. Century Hutchinson, 1990; Mysterious Press, 1990. Bertie series.

The Last Detective. Scribners, 1991; Doubleday, 1991. Peter Diamond series.

Diamond Solitaire. Little, Brown, 1992; Mysterious Press, 1992. Peter Diamond series.

Bertie and the Crime of Passion. Little, Brown, 1993; Mysterious Press, 1993. Bertie series.

The Summons. Little, Brown, 1995; Mysterious Press, 1995. Peter Diamond series.

Bloodhounds. Little, Brown, 1996; Mysterious Press, 1996. Peter Diamond series.

Upon a Dark Night. Little, Brown, 1997; Mysterious Press, 1998. Peter Diamond series.

II. Novels under the pseudonym Peter Lear

Goldengirl. Cassell, 1977; Doubleday, 1978.

Spider Girl. Cassell, 1980; Viking, 1980.

The Secret of Spandau. Michael Joseph, 1986.

III. Short story collections

Butchers and Other Stories of Crime. Macmillan, 1985; Mysterious Press, 1987.

The Staring Man and Other Stories. Helsinki: Eurographica. 1989. A signed limited edition containing four stories from *Butchers and Other Stories of Crime*.

The Crime of Miss Oyster Brown and Other Stories. Little, Brown, 1994.

Do Not Exceed the Stated Dose. Little, Brown, 1998; Crippen & Landru, 1998.

IV. Collaborations

The Rigby File. Hodder & Stoughton, 1989.
The Perfect Murder. HarperCollins, 1991.

V. Short stories

"The Bathroom." *Winter's Crimes 5*. Macmillan, 1973; *Ellery Queen's Mystery Magazine*, August 21, 1981, as "A Bride in the Bath." Collected in *Butchers and Other Stories of Crime*.

"The Locked Room." *Winter's Crimes 10*. Macmillan, 1978; *Ellery Queen's Mystery Magazine*, March 1979, as "Behind the Locked Door." Collected in *Butchers and Other Stories of Crime*.

"A Slight Case of Scotch." Collaborative story. *The Bell House Book*. Hodder & Stoughton, 1979.

"How Mr Smith Chased His Ancestors." *Mystery Guild Anthology*. Book Club Associates, 1980; *Ellery Queen's Mystery Magazine*, November 3, 1980, as "A Man with a Fortune." Collected in *Butchers and Other Stories of Crime*.

"Butchers." *Winter's Crimes 14*. Macmillan, 1982; *Ellery Queen's Mystery Magazine*, Mid-July 1982, as "The Butchers." Collected in *Butchers and Other Stories of Crime* and in *The Staring Man and Other Stories*.

"Taking Possession." *Ellery Queen's Mystery Magazine*,

November 1982. Collected in *Butchers and Other Stories of Crime* and in *The Staring Man and Other Stories* as "Woman and Home."

"The Virgin and the Bull." *John Creasey's Mystery Crime Collection.* Gollancz, 1983; *Ellery Queen's Mystery Magazine*, July 1983, as "The Virgoan and the Taurean." Collected in *Butchers and Other Stories of Crime.*

"Fall-Out." *Company Magazine*, May 1983; *Ellery Queen's Mystery Magazine*, June 1984. Collected in *Butchers and Other Stories of Crime.*

"Belly Dance." *Winter's Crimes 15.* Macmillan, 1983; *Ellery Queen's Mystery Magazine*, March 1983, as "Keeping Fit." Collected in *Butchers and Other Stories of Crime.*

"Did You Tell Daddy?" *Ellery Queen's Mystery Magazine*, February 1984. Collected in *Butchers and Other Stories of Crime.*

"Arabella's Answer." *Ellery Queen's Mystery Magazine*, April 1984. Collected in *Butchers and Other Stories of Crime.*

"Vandals." *Woman's Own*, December 29, 1984; *Ellery Queen's Mystery Magazine*, December 1985. Collected in *Butchers and Other Stories of Crime.*

"The Secret Lover." *Winter's Crimes 17*, Macmillan, 1985; *Ellery Queen's Mystery Magazine*, March 1988. Collected in *Butchers and Other Stories of Crime.*

"The Corder Figure." *Butchers and Other Stories of Crime.* Macmillan, 1985; *Ellery Queen's Mystery Magazine*, January 1986. Collected in *Butchers and Other Stories of Crime* and in *The Staring Man and Other Stories.*

"Private Gorman's Luck." *Butchers and Other Stories of Crime.* Macmillan, 1985; *Ellery Queen's Mystery Magazine*, July 1985. Collected in *Butchers and Other Stories of Crime.*

"The Staring Man." *Butchers and Other Stories of Crime.* Macmillan, 1985; *Ellery Queen's Mystery Magazine*, October 1985. Collected in *Butchers and Other Stories of Crime* and in *The Staring Man and Other Stories.*

"Trace of Spice." *Butchers and Other Stories of Crime.* Macmillan, 1985. Collected in *Butchers and Other Stories of Crime.*

"Murder in Store." *Woman's Own*, December 21, 1985. Collected in *Do Not Exceed the Stated Dose.*

"Curl Up and Dye." *Ellery Queen's Mystery Magazine*, July 1986. Collected in *The Crime of Miss Oyster Brown and Other Stories.*

"Photographer Slain." Contest story. *The Observer*, November 30, 1986.

"Peer's Grisly Find." Contest story. *The Observer*, December 7, 1986.

"Brighton Line Murder." Contest story. *The Observer*, December 14, 1986.

"The Poisoned Mince Pie." Contest story. *The Observer*, December 21, 1986.

"The Royal Plot." Contest story. *The Observer*, December 28, 1986.

"The Curious Computer." *New Adventures of Sherlock Holmes.* Carroll & Graf, 1987. Collected in *The Crime of Miss Oyster Brown and Other Stories.*

"Friendly Yachtsman, 39." *Woman's Own*, July 18, 1987; *Ellery Queen's Mystery Magazine*, May 1988. Collected in *The Crime of Miss Oyster Brown and Other Stories.*

"The Pomeranian Poisoning." *Winter's Crimes 19.* Macmillan, 1987; *Ellery Queen's Mystery Magazine*, August 1988, as "The Zenobia Hatt Prize." Collected in *The Crime of Miss Oyster Brown and Other Stories.*

"Where is Thy Sting." *Winter's Crimes 20.* Macmillan, 1988; *Ellery Queen's Mystery Magazine*, November 1988, as "The Wasp." Collected in *The Crime of Miss Oyster Brown and Other Stories.*

"Oracle of the Dead." *Ellery Queen's Mystery Magazine*, Mid-December 1988; *Best*, March 3, 1989.

"A Case of Butterflies." *Winter's Crimes 21.* Macmillan, 1989;

Ellery Queen's Mystery Magazine, December 1989. Collected in *The Crime of Miss Oyster Brown and Other Stories*.

"Youdunnit." *New Crimes*. Robinson, 1989; *Ellery Queen's Mystery Magazine*, mid-December 1989. Collected in *The Crime of Miss Oyster Brown and Other Stories*.

"The Haunted Crescent." *Mistletoe Mysteries*. Mysterious Press, 1989. Collected in *The Crime of Miss Oyster Brown and Other Stories*.

"Shock Visit." *Winter's Crimes 22*. Macmillan, 1990; *Ellery Queen's Mystery Magazine*., February 1990, as "The Valuation." Collected in *The Crime of Miss Oyster Brown and Other Stories*.

"The Lady in the Trunk." *A Classic English Crime*. Pavilion, 1990. Collected in *The Crime of Miss Oyster Brown and Other Stories*.

"Ginger's Waterloo." *Cat Crimes*. Donald L. Fine, 1991. Collected in *The Crime of Miss Oyster Brown and Other Stories*.

"Being of Sound Mind." *Winter's Crimes 23*. Macmillan, 1990; *Ellery Queen's Mystery Magazine*, July 1991. Collected in *The Crime of Miss Oyster Brown and Other Stories*.

"The Christmas Present." *Woman's Own*, December 24, 1990; *Ellery Queen's Mystery Magazine*, mid-December 1991, as "Supper with Miss Shivers." Collected in *The Crime of Miss Oyster Brown and Other Stories* as "Supper with Miss Shivers."

"The Crime of Miss Oyster Brown." *Midwinter Mysteries 1*. Scribners, 1991; *Ellery Queen's Mystery Magazine*, May 1991. Collected in *The Crime of Miss Oyster Brown and Other Stories*.

"The Man Who Ate People." *The Man Who . . .* Macmillan, 1992; *Ellery Queen's Mystery Magazine*, October 1992. Collected in *The Crime of Miss Oyster Brown and Other Stories*.

"You May See a Strangler." *Midwinter Mysteries 2*. Little, Brown, 1992. Collected in *The Crime of Miss Oyster Brown and Other Stories*.

"Murder By Christmas Tree." Contest story. *The Observer*, December 20, 1992. Printed as a separate pamphlet to accompany Crippen & Landru's limited edition of *Do Not Exceed the Stated Dose*.

"Pass the Parcel." *Midwinter Mysteries 3*. Little, Brown, 1993; *Ellery Queen's Mystery Magazine*, Mid-December 1994. Collected in *The Crime of Miss Oyster Brown and Other Stories*.

"Murder in the Library." Contest story. *Evening Chronicle*, Bath, October 6, 1993.

"The Model Con." *Woman's Realm Summer Special*, 1994; Collected in *The Crime of Miss Oyster Brown and Other Stories*.

"Bertie and the Fire Brigade." *Royal Crimes*. Signet, 1994. Collected in *Do Not Exceed the Stated Dose*.

"The Odstock Curse." *Murder for Halloween*. Mysterious Press, 1994. Collected in *Do Not Exceed the Stated Dose*.

"Passion Killers." *Ellery Queen's Mystery Magazine*, January 1994. Collected in *Do Not Exceed the Stated Dose*.

"The Case of the Easter Bonnet." *Bath Chronicle*, April 17, 1995; *Ellery Queen's Mystery Magazine*, April 1997. Collected in *Do Not Exceed the Stated Dose*.

"Never a Cross Word." *You, Mail on Sunday*, June 11, 1995; *Ellery Queen's Mystery Magazine*, February 1997. Collected in *Do Not Exceed the Stated Dose*.

"The Mighty Hunter." *Midwinter Mysteries 5*. Little, Brown, 1995; *Ellery Queen's Mystery Magazine*, January 1996. Collected in *Do Not Exceed the Stated Dose*.

"The Proof of the Pudding." *A Classic Christmas Crime*. Pavilion, 1995. Collected in *Do Not Exceed the Stated Dose*.

"The Pushover." *Ellery Queen's Mystery Magazine*, June 1995. Collected in *Do Not Exceed the Stated Dose*.

"Quiet Please—We're Rolling." *No Alibi.* Ringpull, 1995; *Ellery Queen's Mystery Magazine*, December 1996. Collected in *Do Not Exceed the Stated Dose.*

"Wayzgoose." *A Dead Giveaway.* Warner Futura, 1995; *Ellery Queen's Mystery Magazine*, May 1997. Collected in *Do Not Exceed the Stated Dose.*

"Disposing of Mrs Cronk." *Perfectly Criminal.* Severn House, 1996; *Ellery Queen's Mystery Magazine*, December 1997. Collected in *Do Not Exceed the Stated Dose.*

"A Parrot is Forever." *Malice Domestic 5.* Pocket Books, 1996. Collected in *Do Not Exceed the Stated Dose.*

"Bertie and the Boat Race." *Crime Through Time*, Berkley, 1996. Collected in *Do Not Exceed the Stated Dose.*

"The Corbett Correspondence" (with Keith Miles). *Malice Domestic 6.* 1997.

"Because It Was There." *Whydunit? Perfectly Criminal 2.* Severn House, 1997. Collected in *Do Not Exceed the Stated Dose.*